STEPHEN MORRIS

Nevil Shute was born in 1899 and educated at Shrewsbury School and Balliol College, Oxford. Having decided early on an aeronautical career, he went to work for the de Havilland Aircraft Company as an engineer, where he played a large part in the construction of the airship R100. His first novel, *Marazan* (1926), was written at this time. After the disaster to the R101, he turned his attention to aeroplane construction and founded his own firm, Airspeed Ltd, in 1931. In the war, Nevil Shute served in the Navy, doing top-secret work for the Admiralty. He still found time to write, however, and during this time produced several novels including *Pied Piper, Pastoral* and *Most Secret*. These were followed in 1947 by *The Chequer Board* and, in 1948, *No Highway*, which became a great bestseller and an extremely popular film. In 1948 he went to Australia for two months, a trip that inspired his most popular novel, *A Town like Alice*. He returned there for good with his family, and lived there until his death in 1960. His later novels include *In the Wet, Requiem for a Wren, On the Beach* and *Trustee from the Toolroom*.

D1396112

STEPHEN MORRIS

NEVIL SHUTE

PAN BOOKS LTD
LONDON AND SYDNEY

First published 1961 by William Heinemann Ltd
This edition published 1974 by Pan Books Ltd,
Cavaye Place, London SW10 9PG

ISBN 0 330 23985 6

Printed in Great Britain by
Richard Clay (The Chaucer Press), Ltd, Bungay, Suffolk

CONTENTS

PUBLISHER'S NOTE

When he died early in 1960, Nevil Shute left two novels amongst his papers. They were the earliest complete novels he had written; neither had been published.

As his publishers, we would like to explain why, in collaboration with his family, we have decided to offer these novels to Nevil Shute's public. We believe they should be published because they are good stories in themselves, and published in one volume because of the continuity of some of the characters – particularly Stephen Morris – through both. Not only do they provide evidence of Shute's fine narrative gift, but they each contain strongly personal elements which readers will find an interesting supplement to the author's autobiography, *Slide Rule*.

In one thing only was he often adamant in his dealings with his publishers, and that was in the choice of titles for his novels. However much his publishers argued with him for a change, he was usually steadfast in his refusal. Therefore, in keeping with his wishes, we are retaining the original titles of these novels, but for the sake of simplicity and brevity, using only *Stephen Morris* as the title of the composite volume.

BOOK I
STEPHEN MORRIS

Three reputations cling closely to the Radcliffe Camera in Oxford. To the clever people it is the Reading Room of the famous Bodleian Library and, as such, entitled to the utmost veneration. To tourists and sightseers it is a quaint old circular building, from the roof of which a fine view of the colleges can be obtained. But to the young undergraduates it has more unusual associations, for that same circular roof is one of the very few places in the city of Oxford where they can meet in intimate conversation unchaperoned. Nobody else connected with the University ever dreams of going up there.

Stephen Morris was up there early, fully a quarter of an hour before the time that he had stated.

He moved round to the side of the building from which Helen Riley would approach, and as he did so he saw her down below. She rode her bicycle to the foot of the steps, alighted, and entered the building, very delicate and sweet.

Oh, but he must be firm – must, must be final.

Then she was with him.

'Good evening,' she said nervously.

'Good evening,' he said. 'Let's sit down.'

So they sat down together under the shadow of the grey dome.

'What is it, Stephen?' she asked very gently.

He cleared his throat and looked straight ahead of him. 'I suppose we'd better get to business right away,' he said. 'I wrote and asked you to marry me – you know that. I'm afraid I want to back out of it.'

The girl stirred suddenly. 'You made a mistake?'

'I made a mistake,' he said evenly, 'not in what I said to you about . . . myself, but in other things. One gets carried away, I suppose. I can't afford to marry and I never could, really.'

'But, Stephen,' said the girl. 'You didn't ask me to marry you at once. You told me we should have to wait.'

There was a brief silence. A sparrow came and perched in the sunlight upon the stone balustrade, looked at them for a moment and flew away again.

'I know,' he said. 'But when I wrote that, I had an unusually good job in rubber in sight. I've lost it now – they can't take me on, certainly for a year and probably not then, business being very bad. I had the time in sight when we could get married. Now that's gone.'

'But, Stephen,' said the girl, 'isn't there anything else? What are you going to do?'

'I met your cousin Malcolm yesterday, out at the hill climb. He spoke of a possible job for me in his little business, at three pounds a week. It's flying and mechanic's work – manual labour, I suppose one ought to call it. I don't see that I can do any better than that, other than clerical work or schoolmastering. I haven't been able to find anything that gives me the faintest chance of marrying, now or in the future.

'So I want you to be free,' he said, 'and do your best to forget this. One does, you know.'

'It's a pity it ever happened,' said the girl.

'It's a pity it ever happened,' he repeated.

They got up and for a little time leaned against the parapet, looking out over the spires of the town, sick at heart. At last Morris turned to her.

'I don't think we have anything else to settle, have we?' he asked, very gently.

'I suppose not,' said the girl. She turned and faced him.

'Stephen dear,' she said. 'I don't know what to say.'

Stephen turned away, and avoided her eyes. 'I think I do,' he said. 'There's only one thing I want to say about – this. We've had a good time, haven't we? And nobody can ever take that away from us ...'

Then she was gone.

Stephen Morris walked slowly back to college. He wanted someone to talk to – frightfully badly.

The summer ran on its course, through the sunny indolence of Eights Week, as good an Eights Week as before the war. After that there were a couple of pleasant little dinners in the garden of the pub at Bablock Hythe, and then came Schools.

They were a jest, these Schools. Those who had taken the shortened course had done so with the intention of getting a degree of sorts; what sort did not matter very much to them. First of all came Greats, involving the placid Christie and bearing him swiftly to the Nemesis of five terms' complete idleness. Then the Honours School of Jurisprudence, where Lechlane was offering three years' work as the result of five terms' study, and was expected to get a First on it. History came in due course to plunge Wallace into a sort of feverish indignation, and English to sweep in Johnnie, though what he was doing in that galère nobody could quite make out. Last of all, Stephen Morris presented himself to be examined in his shortened course of mathematics.

He had heard from Malcolm Riley. Riley had consulted Stenning, his partner, and had written to offer Morris the post that he had asked for, the pilot of the third Avro. He was to start immediately he got away from Oxford, in time for the summer rush of passengers at the seaside resorts along the coast. He was to get a screw of three pounds a week and a tenth share of any takings that were left after the Company had paid its expenses for the week.

Morris was left at Oxford after the term was over; the mathematical finals were among the last to be taken. One by one his friends had drifted away; some to rest and recuperate, some, like himself, to find a means to keep themselves, and that quickly. Soon he too was free, free to go where he liked, to do what he wanted to, with nobody else to think about. There was a certain relief in this freedom.

In the last day or two that he was at Oxford he collected

and packed his possessions; one box he would store with his uncle, the old rubber merchant. The gladstone he decided to take with him, and packed it with all that he needed for an indefinite period. In the course of turning out five terms' accumulation of rubbish he came upon his old war-time flying-helmet and gloves, and sat for a long time on his bed, fingering the furry, oily relics.

Well, he was getting back into it again. He never ought to have left it; if he had tried hard enough he might have been able to get a permanent commission in it. But he had depended on civil aviation. Now he was going into civil aviation – to cart airsick trippers about the Solent, seven and sixpence for ten minutes in the air. Well, aviation would grow out of that in time.

The train carrying him to Southampton carried a man who grew perceptibly more cheerful with every revolution of the wheels, with each farm that passed the window. He was sick of Oxford and the humanities. They were for clever people, for dons and embryo dons who would spend their lives in thinking of scholarly epigrams to let off at their fellows, in moulding their manner to fit in with the traditions of the place, in travelling to Athens in the vacations. Ineffective people, who would never do anything in the world but tell young men all about the humanities. He was sick of the lot of them. He was a mathematician and a student of realities.

As the train meandered peacefully into Hampshire, he was almost jubilant. He was getting back at last to the work he loved, the thing he should never have dropped. It had been a mistake, all that rubber-merchant business; he should have stuck to aviation. Already in his mind's eye he could see the open spaces of an aerodrome, the dirty, oily grass, the delicate wings, the clean dull gleam of a rotary engine dripping oil, the feathery substance of a cloud.

He crossed to Cowes on the paddle-steamer past the long lines of ships laid up on Southampton Water, mystery ships, ships with bow and stern so much alike that it was practically impossible to tell which was which. Past the Avro works on the

Hamble shore, past the mouth of the Hamble River, marked by a big red buoy, and on down to the seaplane station on Calshot Spit. Here were three big flying-boats at anchor; F.4s, he thought they were, delicate great things lightly swaying to wind and tide, straining gently at their buoys. It would be good sport to fly one of those; he had never flown a flying-boat. He thought you had to be pretty careful on them. Then on to Cowes, past one or two yachts in the Roads, white and gleaming in the sun.

An hour later, he was walking up the hill behind the aerodrome. He had taken the little railway on the Island from Cowes, had left his bag at the station, and had inquired his way to the aerodrome. Presently he came in sight of it on top of the hill and stopped to look.

It was an aerodrome in the grand manner. Evidently one of those white elephants built on the supposition that the war would last for ever, it consisted of four immense concrete and steel hangars with a perfect host of smaller buildings, huts and stores, all beginning to show signs of decay. A flagstaff on one of the hangers floated a long red and white streamer, showing that the huge place was still inhabited by some vestige of aeronautical life. Morris walked on and inquired at a sort of lodge for the Isle of Wight Aviation Company. A slatternly-looking woman with a pleasant, cheerful face directed him to one of the hangars. He walked on up a broad asphalt road, down another, past several more, and entered the hangar.

There was one machine in it, an Avro, dwarfed by the vastness of the hall. Over in one corner a mechanic was working at a bench; he straightened up and watched Morris as he walked towards him.

'Morning,' said Morris. 'Is Mr Riley about, or Mr Stenning?'

The man laid down his tools. 'No, sir,' he said, '–nobody but me in this morning. Mr Riley's flying from Portsmouth today, and Mr Stenning from Newport.' He looked at his watch. 'They should be back in an hour – an hour and a half. Are you Mr Morris, sir?'

Morris nodded.

14

'I was to tell you to get your things into the hut where they lives – Number 11 hut down the road by the gatehouse. They lives in there and the caretaker's wife does for them. Mr Riley says I was to tell you that if you wanted the car you was to have it, only you wasn't to put it in first gear because it won't go in. I'm to see about it when I get a minute.'

'Right,' said Morris. 'I'll get my things in now. Where's the car kept?'

He found it by itself in an immense garage, and drove down to the station for his bag. Coming back, he found the hut and went inside.

They had made themselves fairly comfortable. There were several camp bedsteads, one of which he appropriated, and three deck-chairs. A deal table in front of a cylindrical iron stove, one or two trunks and boxes, pegs for clothes, shelves, a few novels and magazines, a splintered propeller in a corner, shaving-tackle, basins, and general oddments littered about the place. Morris arranged his things and talked a little to a woman who came in, the caretaker's wife, who promised to make up a bed for him. Then he had a wash and walked back to the hangar, wondering at what he had seen. This firm was unlike any other that he had ever come across. He wondered if it was paying at the moment. Anyway, they lived economically enough.

He entered the big hangar, talked to the mechanic, and walked over to have a look at the Avro. The man told him this was to be his machine. It looked in very fair condition, well kept and decently painted. He placed a hand on the lower plane; the fabric drummed taut beneath his fingers. The engine, he was told, was practically new; the whole machine looked smart and efficiently cared for. He was agreeably surprised; he had expected a far more 'commercial' state of affairs. He might have known that any machines of Riley's would be in apple-pie order. Moreover, as he found later, a smart machine did better business than a dirty one.

He examined the machine carefully, feeling queerly light-hearted. He had not flown at all for eighteen months, and it was long before that that he had last flown an Avro. He called the mechanic over, and they lifted the tail of the machine on to a trestle till it was in the flying position. Then the man went back to his work; Morris climbed up on to the lower plane and lowered himself into the pilot's seat.

It was all just as he remembered it. Avros never seemed to change. It was a wonderful design; originated in 1913, it had remained unaltered all through the war as a training machine, and as such it retained the front rank to the present day. The rapidly dying rotary engine still lingered on, chiefly because the Avro had a rotary engine; the machine atoning for the defects inherent in the engine.

Morris slipped his feet into the stirrups on the rudder bar, fingered the stick, and stared ahead of him. He could fly this machine. Here on the ground, trestled up into the position she would be in when flying, she felt just right. The seat was right for him, neither too high nor too low; his legs were not cramped; he had a good view. The wings stretched out on each side of him, solid and friendly and familiar. He was all right in this machine, could fly her all day – as, indeed, he would have to. He sat on in her, daydreaming; he was back in aviation at last, away from the humanities and all that they implied.

Presently he got out of the machine and walked back to the hut. He was hungry; it was after his usual teatime. He found a pot of jam and some bread and made a satisfactory meal. Then he lit a cigarette and walked back along the wide, deserted roads to the hangar. The mechanic was shaping a new tail-skid.

'We always keep one on 'em in reserve,' he said. 'Mr Riley bust one the day before yesterday.'

'Where was that?' asked Morris. 'On this aerodrome?'

'Just out there,' said the man, and walked to the door. 'You see that big bush in the hedge over the far side there? Well, there's a ridge runs right away from there to that corner. You want to be careful of that when you're coming in of an evening, especially with a bit of north in the wind, you know, or you'll land right on it.'

'Mr Riley did that?'

The mechanic nodded, and glanced up at the streamer on

16

the flagstaff. 'North to north-east – nor-nor-east – you want to watch that.' He turned and walked back towards his bench. 'There's worse things happen at sea nor that,' he remarked inconsequently. Morris laughed, and strolled out a little way on to the aerodrome to examine it for himself.

He was back in aviation again.

He made a circuit of the aerodrome and returned to the hangars, seated himself on a pile of lumber, and produced a pipe.

And then, as the evening drew on, came the complement to the scene, the wide aerodrome and the great white hangars. Somewhere far away he caught a faint hum, rising and dying away, and rising again more distinctly. He got up, and looked into the distance between the hangars. Presently he caught sight of the machine, far away, threadlike against the sunset.

He called to the mechanic. 'Who's this coming in from the west?'

'Oh, ay,' said the man, 'that'll be Mr Stenning coming in first then.' He came out and stood by Morris to watch the machine land.

The machine came swiftly to the aerodrome, not very high, the note of the engine rising evenly and true. The pilot made a wide sweep to the south and turned into the wind with a vertical bank and a flash of light from his planes in the sunset, switched off his engine, and came in to land. Morris watched tensely; he would not have believed it possible that the sight could move him so. His hair seemed to bristle with a sense of adventure; he moistened his lips and dug his nails into his palms. His spirits rose like a great crescendo in music; he was back, back in aviation again.

He had not known how much he wanted to be back. He was keen on nothing else.

The machine slipped lightly down over the hedge with two sudden little growls from the engine as the pilot lengthened out his glide. Then she settled to the aerodrome and skimmed lightly over the grass, perhaps two feet up, the pilot holding her off the ground till the last moment. Then he put her down; she touched, undulated gently in a vertical plane, ran along with her tail down, slowed, swayed, and turned towards the hangar. A small figure, the clerk who had been with him to take the money, jumped out and ran to a wing tip to help the machine on the turn; she taxied slowly to the hangar.

'Lands her nicely, don't he?' said the mechanic.

'Yes,' said Morris, 'he lands her well.'

He taxied her up to the hangar. Morris watched for him to stop, but he went on. The great sliding doors were open, and he taxied the machine right inside, managing her cleverly with little bursts of engine at crucial moments. Not till the machine was well inside and berthed alongside the other one with the help of the clerk did he switch off and allow the engine to come to rest. Morris watched, interested, wondering if he could have done that so easily on a rotary-engined machine. Evidently it was a trick that had to be picked up on this work.

'Very pretty,' he said.

'He always does that,' said the man, 'saves a terrible lot of handling. There's none too many of us.'

The pilot jumped down from the machine and came towards Morris; a small, broad-shouldered man with a big chin, in a dirty pair of tweed breeches and gaiters.

'Mr Morris?' he said. 'My name's Stenning.' Morris made the usual greetings; the little man unbuckled his leather helmet. 'Mr Riley told you how things are here?'

Morris nodded.

'Things aren't going so badly as they were,' said Stenning. 'It's no use denying we had a bad winter – worse than we counted on.'

'Have a fag,' suggested Morris.

'Thanks.' He took a long look at the sky. 'It still holds,' he said. 'I didn't think it was going to this morning. Of course,' he added casually, 'this extra machine will make a difference in the profits. Riley said there wasn't enough work for three machines – nor there is. But what I said to him – what I said to him was that we shan't have three machines. One will usually be in dock for overhaul while the other two carry on. I told him, it means we can keep an efficient service with two machines. And not only that – not only that, I said – there are the incidental passengers, the people who come up here and want a ride and we're both away. Those are the important people, too; the people who come and look you up are the people who want a ride, or who want a machine for an hour. That's what I said to him; we want a third man so that one of us can be on the spot most days . . .'

'I see,' said Morris. 'Do you get much special charter work?'

The other glanced at him shrewdly. 'No,' he said. 'Between you and me, we don't. It's been a great disappointment that – a great disappointment to both of us. We've only had one real charter since Easter; a man called Simpson whose wife started dying in Manchester one Sunday morning – I got him there in about three hours. But that's the only one,' he added impressively, '– the only one since Easter.'

'I suppose you depend on that rather in the winter. Try and work it up when joy-riding's slack?'

'Try hard enough,' said Stenning grimly, 'the people just don't come. Cut our prices for long distances to rock bottom – too low I say. The people don't come and we don't make any profit to speak of on the ones that do . . .'

He spat a little fragment of tobacco from his lip. 'It's been a great disappointment, that side of it,' he repeated. 'Riley says it needs more advertising and boom than we can afford. I don't know about that – he does all that side of it. All I know is that we don't get the business. Of course, the joy-riding pays all right in the warm weather.'

He entered on a string of admonitions, mostly concerned with the upkeep of the machines and the method of picking up passengers with the least expenditure of time and petrol. Morris listened respectfully; the little man knew his business from end to end. Riley had chosen his partner well; a plain little man who knew his own limitations and who would work like a horse at the practical running of the business.

He was a great talker; he rambled on from one subject to another. Morris had been to the hut? They had thought it out when they started up in this business, and Riley had said it would be best if at first they lived like on Service, or more so.

It cut the overhead charges. It suited them well enough. It had been a bit of luck getting this place. It had been quite empty when they came; they fixed up to rent it from the farmer on whose ground it stood, who could get nothing out of the Air Ministry for it. It had been put on his land during the war and just left there. They paid a very low rent. The farmer grazed cattle on the aerodrome; one had to watch them when taking off or landing. Riley said they had no legal tenure here at all. Six weeks after they had come, a caretaker had arrived and reported that they were there. There had been a little fuss about it at first, but the Air Ministry had not gone to the length of evicting them. Riley said that so long as they paid rent to the farmer and the Air Ministry didn't, they were all right – unless the Air Ministry took away the buildings. He (Stenning) didn't know much about the Law. He thought the Air Ministry didn't want to bust up a company that was doing good work. Anyway, they had been there just over a year now, and nothing had happened.

Then a low hum from the north announced the other machine. Riley came in low over their heads and waved a hand as he passed, went to the south of the aerodrome, turned into the wind, and put the machine down just outside the hangars. He, too, taxied into the hangar, assisted by Stenning and the mechanic.

They closed the great sliding doors and walked back to the hut. Presently a hot meal made its appearance.

'Didn't do so badly today,' said Riley. 'You've got those Air Ministry licences, have you? The ones I wrote to you about.'

'I got those,' said Morris. 'When do I start work? I'd like half an hour or so on the machine before going out – I never did more than five hours or so on the Avros, and that was years ago.'

'You've seen your machine?' asked Riley. 'Oh well, you'd better stay at home tomorrow. Have an hour or so in the air, brushing up short landings, particularly. It's easy enough work. Then if anyone comes up and wants a flight, you can take them up. They're always doing that, and it's awkward when we're all away.' He paused. 'Did you use the car?'

'Yes,' said Morris. 'That gear's nothing serious. The gate's shifted a bit – it's all loose.'

'Is that all?' said Riley. He yawned sleepily. 'It only happened yesterday – I must see about it some time. Or if you're at home tomorrow you might see if you can do anything, will you? If you find anything bust, get Peters – the chap in the hangar – and put him on to it. He's all right, but he wants watching on any job he hasn't done before. Let's have supper.'

After supper he cleared the table and produced a small typewriter from a case and a bundle of letters. He set up the machine on the table and proceeded to answer the letters in rapid succession. Stenning settled down with a pipe and a novel.

'Can I help at all with those?' asked Morris.

'Don't think so, thanks,' said Riley. 'They don't take long.' He read another. 'Stenning.'

Stenning looked up.

'Town Council of Lymington got an annual fair and horse show on the fifteenth. That's the place I went to alone last year and turned away more than I could take up – you remember. They offer us a field and two policemen.'

'Wish other towns 'd do that.'

'How many machines shall we send?'

'Let's send two, and t'other chap stay at home; then if we want him we can telephone for him, or he can go to Seaview or somewhere for the afternoon. And I say, why not put out a placard like we do for Bournemouth?'

'What's that?' asked Morris.

'Offer the seats in the machines going and coming back at rather reduced rates,' said Riley. 'We often manage to make the cost of sending the machine there and a bit over.' He picked up the letter and read it again. 'I think that's best,' he said, and began to type rapidly.

He looked up again presently. 'Air Ministry want to know why we haven't reported those centre section modifications yet. All the machines have got 'em, haven't they? The front spar fittings, they were – three laminations instead of two to the wiring plate.'

'Mine has,' said Stenning.

There seemed to be nothing for Morris to do; he got up and went to the door of the hut. It was quite dark, and a fine, starry night. It was attractive outside; he put his head back inside the hut.

'Be back in half an hour or so,' he said, and vanished into the darkness.

Stenning took his pipe from his mouth.

'Where's he going?' he inquired, surprised.

'Dunno. He's a queer bird.'

'Well, that's a funny thing, going off like that. It's all dark out there. Anyone would think he had a date.'

Riley smiled. 'He's all right – he's like that. I remember him in the Squadron. What d'you think of him?'

'He's all right,' said Stenning, 'if he can fly. I like him; we might have done a lot worse.'

'Oh, he can fly all right,' said Riley, and bent to his work.

Outside it was cool and fine. A fresh night breeze was blowing down Channel, bringing a tang of salt water with it. It had gone round a bit, Morris thought, and was now easterly, which should be a good sign for this part of the world. He glanced up and tried to see the 'stocking' but it was hidden in the darkness.

He strolled along aimlessly and happily through the derelict air station, along the broad dark roads past towering deserted buildings. Presently he came out on the aerodrome by their own hangar. In there were the machines, his machine. He was back again, back in his own trade, the only thing he could do well.

He paced the roads, speculating, as he walked, upon the future. Aviation was going to be a big thing. It was in a bad way now, and might sink even lower. But one day aviation would be a big business again, a bigger affair than the side-show at a local fair and horse show. Already the air lines were in being, already there were rumours of commercial aeroplanes in the true sense; machines properly designed for the business, with proper cabins and lavatories, just as in a train or any other transport concern. Surely this aviation would be a great thing, would take the place in the world to which it was entitled, and that before so very long.

And he was in it, back in it again, back in this business that he knew. Presently it would develop; he would be there to do his bit in the development of this new industry. More air lines would spring up, more manufacturing companies; he was in it now, in it at the start, when things were bad. There would be big fortunes to be made by men who pinned their faith to it now; one day he might be a rich man. Money meant such a lot – one could do nothing without money. This work that he loved might bring him back in time to that other love that he had lost.

Morris was up early next morning; the sunlight, streaming in on to his bed, coupled with the novelty of his surroundings, made sleep difficult. He got up and went to the door of the hut and stood in the sun, looking out over the Solent towards the twin chequered forts of Spithead and the mist over Portsmouth. It was a brilliant summer morning, with a sort of crisp freshness in the air that was never felt at Oxford. He shivered a little, turned back into the hut, and set to work to start up the Primus to boil some water for a wash.

'There's a bath outside,' said Riley sleepily from his bed, 'a bath-house with a shower. Second building as you go along.' He relapsed again into a comatose condition.

Morris went and looked at it, disliked it, braced himself, and returned with a glow of conscious pride. Breakfast appeared in due course, and the mechanic and two boy clerks arrived on bicycles. After the meal they walked down to the hangar and set about the business of the day.

There was little to be done. Riley and Stenning both seemed to accept entire responsibility for their own machines, and Morris found himself attending in a similar manner to his own. He fussed about it for a little, replaced the plugs in the bottom cylinders and filled the tanks. Then Stenning and Peters came to help him get the machine out into the open.

He ran a final eye over the machine, put on his helmet, and clambered into the pilot's seat. He busied himself for a little, head down in the cockpit, getting quite comfortable, feeling the run of the levers, adjusting them for starting the engine. He strapped the safety belt around him, and was struck by an old feeling, the feeling that the machine was a part of himself. It would be intensified when he got in the air. He only had it on relatively small machines – one never had that sympathy with a Handley Page.

Then he looked up. 'Right,' he said to the mechanic.

'Switch off, sir.'

'Switch is off.'

It was familiar, that formula. The mechanic stepped to the propeller and turned the engine by it over nine compressions. Then he looked at Morris.

'Contact, sir.'

Morris moved his hand a little. 'Contact.'

The mechanic threw his weight on to the propeller and swung clear. The engine gave a half-hearted spit and was silent.

'Switch off, sir.'

'Switch is off.'

The man pulled her over once or twice more. Then he swung her again; she fired with a spit and a rumble, sending a queer, familiar quiver through the structure. Morris let her run for a little, then signalled the man round to the tail. Riley joined him and they held the tail down in a gale of wind as Morris ran the engine up to its full speed.

Satisfied, he shut her down again, settled himself comfortably in his seat, wriggled his shoulders a little, and took the stick in one hand. He nodded to Riley and waved to the mechanic, who pulled the chocks from under the wheels and ran clear. Morris gave her a little burst of power and moved out on to the aerodrome.

As he taxied over to the far side, he was quite clear what he would do. He would take her off gently, let her fly herself off the ground, in fact, and take her up to about fifteen hundred in a slow climb. Perhaps a little higher. He didn't want to go stalling and spinning into Mother Earth just because he'd forgotten how to fly. No, he would take her up carefully to a safe height and then play about on her. When he felt comfortable, he would come in and land her at a safe speed. After that he would try one or two slow landings.

He reached the middle of the aerodrome, turned, and faced her up into the wind. He had a long, clear run for it.

Instinctively he gave a look round at the sky above, as though for other machines. Then he took a light hold on the stick and opened her out. The machine accelerated cleanly and went scudding over the aerodrome.

Almost immediately he pressed the stick forward, got her tail up, and held her balanced on the wheels in flying position as she gathered speed. He stole a quick glance at the air speed indicator – about forty-five. Well, she could have it any time now. Then he knew that if she was to stay on the ground any longer, he would have to hold her there; he eased the stick back a little, delicately, with the pressure of three fingers. The hard vibration of the earth had ceased, and now the grass dropped away beneath the planes. He was clear, and in a moment the hangars were at his side and below him.

The clean rush of air past him was intoxicating.

He let her run on her course, still climbing, till he was over the Solent at about five hundred feet. 'Round we go,' he said, turned her, and headed back to the aerodrome. It struck him, as he climbed higher still, that he had not thought about doing that turn; he had done it naturally, as instinctively as a turn upon a bicycle. He smiled a little.

He passed over the aerodrome at about a thousand feet. Peering forward round the windscreen along the curved nose of the machine he could see the Channel before him on the far side of the Island, blue and corrugated with waves. Then he looked back along the fuselage to the tail and waggled his rudder a little to see it move. He was struck by an old feeling; that he was afloat in a solid medium; that if he were to contrive to fall out of the machine, he would float, like a bottle dropped from a fast motor-boat. It was inconceivable that one could fall.

Then he turned back over the aerodrome again, throttled his engine and put her on the glide, gently pulling her up to stalling point. He pulled her up until the warning came; the sloppiness in the lateral control that meant she was very near a stall. He held her in that critical position for a time, noting the air-speed reading, the feel of the controls, and the position in which he had to sit. Then he let her down into the normal cruising position, switched on his engine, and pulled her level. He would know that stalling feeling again when he met it.

He had thought when he went up that he would find himself out of practice, 'ham-handed'. That was not so; he flew round for a little time essaying various tricks, vertical banks and Immelman turns; his hands seemed as light as ever they had been. Finally he was ready to land.

He brought her down in a wide spiral glide a mile from the aerodrome, faced into the wind at about three hundred feet, eked out the glide with a little engine, came in low over the hedge rather faster than he had meant to, and skimmed the grass. He was going too fast, but there was heaps of room. He held her off till the speed dropped, sailing along a foot above the grass.

Then he put her down, bounced once, and came to a standstill.

He took her off again from where he was and went up to about two hundred feet to try again. This time he brought her in slowly, so slowly that Stenning bit his lip as he watched. But no disaster ensued; the machine dropped slowly over the hedge, touched ground in a very short distance, and pulled up quickly.

A third trial produced a well-judged sideslip landing in a corner of the field. Stenning turned to Riley.

'He's not bad, that fellow,' he said. Riley smiled.

Morris flew over to the hangars a foot above the ground, and finished up close beside them. He faced her up into the light wind, stopped the engine and leaped to the ground.

'Like her?' asked Riley.

'Very nice,' said Morris. 'The stick seems a bit short. I don't know. The undercarriage doesn't sound happy when you land. Thought it was coming off the first time.'

'So did I,' said Stenning dourly. Riley laughed.

26

They poked about the undercarriage for a little and cured the trouble with a dab of grease. Then they stood for a little time chatting in the sun.

'Well,' said Stenning, 'this won't buy baby a new frock.' He called to Peters and the clerks, and they started hauling his machine from the hangar.

'Better take her up as much as you like today,' said Riley, 'till you think you're quite all right on her – landing in small fields particularly. Only remember she costs money, and it all comes out of our screw at the end of the week. I'm going to Portsmouth today and tomorrow, and Stenning to Newport again. After that, Stenning'll have to lay up for a top overhaul, I think – though she isn't running so badly, considering. You'd better come over to Portsmouth some time today and have a look at the field we fly from, so as you can find it again. You can't miss it – I shall be flying from there – it's about half a mile north-east of two factory chimneys close together on the east of the town. And by the way, there are three of the placards for Lymington in the hut, with the names of the Ryde hotels who'll show them for us on the backs. You might take those along if you've got time. And tell the manager of the Esplanade – no, I'll do that myself.'

'Right you are,' said Morris. 'And if anyone comes along here I take them up?'

'Oh, yes,' said Riley. 'Wait a bit, I'll give you one or two cards.' He fumbled in a breast pocket and produced a couple of printed cards of charges. 'There are more of these on the shelf where the typewriter is in the hut. Don't let them beat you down – they sometimes try it on.'

Morris helped in getting his machine out of the hangar, and swung the propeller for Stenning. The clerks embarked and the two machines went off in quick succession, one to the north, the other to the west.

Peters went into the hangar to overhaul a couple of scrap planes that Riley had picked up off some rubbish heap or other. Morris walked along to the garage to have a look at the gear quadrant on the car, leaving his machine on the aerodrome in the hope that some passengers might turn up during the day. He found tools under the seat of the car, took off his coat, and set to work.

An hour later, the expected happened; he was touched upon the shoulder. He looked up; a man and a young woman stood beside him.

'I say, old chap,' said the gentleman confidentially. 'Can you tell us where the offices of the Isle of Wight Aviation Company are?'

Morris stood scraping a mass of black grease off one hand on to the other and thought of the hut. 'I represent the Company,' he said. 'Would you like a flight?'

'That's what we came for,' he said cheerfully. 'How much is it?'

'How long do you want to be up for?'

'Oh, say half an hour – have a little run round.'

'Half an hour – that would be two pounds ten.'

'Oh, Alfred!' said the girl.

Alfred looked shaken, but came up nobly. 'I'll take it,' he said grandly. The girl sniggered and pinched his arm.

Morris wiped his hands on a bit of waste. 'I expect you'd like to have a look at Portsmouth Harbour and the town, wouldn't you?' he inquired gravely. It was always as well to kill two birds with one stone. 'Where are you staying?'

'At Ryde,' said the girl.

'We can come back over Ryde and then, if we've got time, have a look at Cowes and Newport.'

'Can you do all that in the time?'

'I think so. The lady had better remove her hat, if you don't mind; we can lend you both flying-helmets.'

Morris put on his coat, and they walked to the machine. He showed them the way of the helmets, and then went to call Peters while the toilet was effected. Then he helped them into the machine and got in himself.

'Switch off, sir.' – 'Switch is off.'

'Contact, sir.' – 'Contact.'

'What are they saying that for?' asked the girl. The engine fired and drowned the man's reply. Morris taxied out on to the aerodrome; he must take her off carefully with this full load.

28

He gave her a long run and let her fly herself off the ground. Once in the air she climbed better than he thought she would; he made a couple of circuits of the aerodrome to gain height and then pushed off over the twin forts of Spithead to Portsmouth, still climbing steadily. He kept her at two thousand five hundred for the remainder of the crossing, then dropped a little over Haslar to give his passengers every view of the unlovely country.

He could see the two factory chimneys that Riley had mentioned clearly, and flew east over the town till he could see the field with Riley just taking off in it. He marked it by a little shed in one corner, and then turned and flew seawards. He skirted along the coast till he had gained sufficient height for the crossing; then, when he was opposite Ryde, went straight across, losing height all the way, and circled the town at about a thousand feet. Then, with a glance at his watch, along the coast past Osborne by way of Cowes to Newport, where Stenning's machine was plainly visible at the end of a long street of red villas. Then he made for home.

He made a wide circuit of the aerodrome to fill in the last minute of the time, then glided down to land. The machine touched, bumped a little, slowed. Morris turned her, taxied in towards the hangar, jumped out, and helped his passengers to alight.

'That was a bit of all right,' said the man, '– that was.' He seemed confused, and fumbled with a note-case.

'I'm glad you enjoyed it,' said Morris. 'You pay me – that's right, two pounds ten. I hope the lady enjoyed it too?'

'Oh, didn't I just!' said the girl. 'Alf, wasn't it lovely?'

Morris pocketed the money and directed them off the premises, pressing a card of charges on them. Two pounds ten to the good. At least ten shillings of that should be profit, which would mean a shilling for him at the end of the week.

He returned to the car.

He had no more passengers that day. In the afternoon he distributed the placards, returned, and spent the rest of the day with the mechanic, overhauling the new planes extended horizontally on the trestles.

Riley came in about five o'clock; he had had a slack day. Morris heard him coming and walked to meet him; together they inspected the new planes. Morris handed over his earnings and they stood talking for a little, looking out over the aerodrome to where the sea lay blue and sombre in the evening sun.

'It's good to be back,' said Morris unexpectedly. 'There's a cheerful sort of feeling about living on an aerodrome.'

Riley did not reply, but turned back towards the hut, his mind full of the business. 'We could do without that ridge on it,' he said. 'I bust a tail-skid there the other day.'

3

Life at the aerodrome ran evenly on its way. Morris was initiated into the regular routine of the business, and found it very boring. The hours were long; that to him was rather an advantage; it was good to be able to bury oneself in work. At Oxford, he had never been able to do that successfully. There the work was brain work, at which one could not concentrate for more than a comparatively short period of the twenty-four hours. Here it was easier; one could work at this manual labour for just as long as one liked.

The work on the ground, in fact, atoned for the boredom of the ceaseless joy-rides. To Morris the work on the machines never staled; there was a satisfaction in keeping something in good running order, in keeping a good machine in perfect trim. He found the life amusing enough on the whole; the free and easy atmosphere suited him well, unbusinesslike though it was. There was, as somebody in authority remarked, too much of the 'Cheerioh' business about aviation at this time for it to be a really paying proposition. The Isle of Wight Aviation Company was not alone in its business methods; on the regular air lines it was still customary for a ten-passenger machine to wait for one passenger who was late. Air transport was not yet taken seriously even by those who had most to lose in it.

In spite of its questionable business methods, the Isle of Wight Aviation Company made a considerable amount of money during the summer months. Business at the various seaside resorts was brisk; the novelty of aviation had not yet worn off, though it was on the wane. Morris found himself earning at the rate of six or seven pounds a week, while Riley and Stenning were putting money by steadily, gradually replacing their sunk capital. Though they were making more money than ever they had done before in the business, this seemed to be due solely to the increase in the machines; the actual interest of the public was clearly on the wane. Signs were not wanting that next year joy-riding would be far less popular; there were not enough special orders to justify the inauguration of a special air-taxi service. The business seemed to be coming near its end; Riley and Stenning ceased to buy new material, and devoted all their energies to saving money.

It was one Sunday morning that Stenning came back from the telephone with the information that the lord of the Towers, near Cowes, had instructed his butler to telephone to them to inform them that he would visit them during the afternoon with a car-load of his house party.

'That's the stuff,' said Riley meditatively. 'I wonder if they know our usual charges?'

Stenning snorted democratically. 'They'll ruddy well have to take their turn in the queue, if there's a crowd,' he said. It was evident that he was hoping for a crowd.

'Better put up a flag in honour of the event,' said Morris.

'I don't see any point in that,' said Stenning. 'Besides, we haven't got one.'

'Better not risk it,' said Riley regretfully, still meditating the finance of the visit. 'It gives one a bad name, that sort of thing.'

'Well,' said Morris cheerfully. 'I hope you enjoy yourselves.' His machine was laid up for an overhaul.

Riley turned to him sourly. 'You'll look pretty blue if they tip us half a crown apiece, won't you?'

Morris laughed, and strolled off to work on his machine.

In due time the Rolls-Royce arrived, and from a distance Morris watched the preparations round the machines. He chose a grassy spot near the fence and sat down to watch. Presently two passengers embarked in one machine; the engine burst into life, and Riley moved out over the aerodrome. He faced up into the wind, began to move, swept over the ground faster and faster, and went away in a climbing turn with full load.

There was a kind of grunt from behind Morris; a critical approving grunt. He turned to see who had grunted.

The only person within range was an immense man leaning over the fence, watching Stenning preparing to get off. He was a man considerably over six feet in height, massively built, with a great red face that seemed vaguely familiar and a great untidy shock of red hair, bursting out from under a tweed cap a size or two too small for him. He was well turned out in faded plus-fours; he looked a typical country squire or gentleman farmer. Stenning got away in a less spectacular manner and the stranger grunted again, less approvingly. Then he noticed Morris watching him from the inside of the fence, and spoke to him.

'Clerget?' he asked. His voice, so soft as hardly to be audible, contrasted oddly with his appearance.

'Hundred and ten Le Rhones,' said Morris, naming the engine.

'So?' said the big man softly. 'They get off very well with the load – particularly the first one.'

Morris moved a little closer to the fence.

'That's so,' he said. 'They're good machines – and we spend a good deal of time looking after them, of course.' He liked the look of this chap. 'But, of course, the difference in the get off there' – he indicated the aerodrome – 'was more a matter of pilots. That first one was Malcolm Riley, rather a famous man in his way, though one doesn't see much of him in the papers.'

'Oh yes ... I remember him. Test pilot for Pilling-Henries in 1918, wasn't he?'

'You know him?' asked Morris in surprise.

'Not personally. I have met him.'

Morris wondered who this was, who was evidently no stranger to the business.

'You were in the Air Force in the war?' he said.

'Er, no,' said the man, a little nervously. 'I didn't go to the war. My name is Rawdon.'

Morris knew now where he had seen that face and figure before. It had been in an illustration to one of those foolish articles that technical papers occasionally effect – 'Idols of the Industry', or something of the sort.

'Would you care to come inside?' he said deferentially. 'I'm a pilot here – I represent the firm.'

The big man placed one hand on the top rail of the fence and vaulted it as lightly as a boy.

'Ha,' he said softly. 'I didn't know I could do that still.'

Captain (by courtesy) C. G. H. Rawdon had had an undistinguished career before the war. He had merely been one of a number of gentlemen of private means who had been flying and designing aeroplanes obscurely since 1909. There had been nothing very striking about him; he never saw reporters, never walked about London in flying kit, never did anything that got into the daily papers, never made records of any sort. He had merely gone on in a stolid, bovine manner, building rather good machines in a shed at Brooklands and risking his life upon them daily with about as much emotion as he would have devoted to the manufacture of jam. To those of his friends who attempted to dissuade him, rightly seeing no point in risking life without publicity, he had merely stated that he liked it. There seemed to be no means of prolonging the argument. So they left him to it, and shook their heads over him when war broke out.

His first machine reached the Front after a long series of delays early in 1916; the historic Rawdon Rat. As soon as the first experimental Rat made its appearance, he was organized, protesting, into a Limited Company, and bidden to design like fun; the rank of Captain in the RFC was bestowed on him to save him from conscription. But no encouragement was needed. The next production was the Robin, a single-seater scout that was cordially disliked by all pilots but the very expert, who swore by it until it was passed over in the race for increased horse-power. Next came the Ratcatcher, an improved Rat with a more powerful engine, followed by the Reindeer, a light, high-speed bomber. Last of all the machines to be used in the war came the Rabbit, a single-seater of phenomenal performance. This in turn would have been surpassed by the Runt had the war continued for another six months; as it was, the engine for the Runt was never properly developed, and the type was abandoned.

In his post-war policy he had been unusually fortunate. His factory had been divided into two parts during the war; the experimental section which was located on a small aerodrome near Southall, and the production factory a little nearer London. The grave crisis of the termination of the war did not find him unprepared; he early realized that aircraft would be a small business again, exactly as it had been before the war. His business partners had realized this fact also, with the added significance that the manufacturing of aeroplanes would not merely be a trade that would bring in a negligible profit, but one that might require considerable subsidies from other departments of the firm. Rawdon, then, had found his way easy. He had abandoned his firm and left them in the production factory, blindly confident in their ability to make money by the building of motor bodies, and the mass production of antique furniture, and had retired to his experimental aerodrome.

Here, in the rickety buildings at Southall, he sat surrounded by the best of his old staff, and watched his rival firms drift slowly into bankruptcy. He obtained one or two contracts for the reconditioning of Ratcatchers and Rabbits for foreign governments, and presently the Air Ministry gave him a contract to design and build an experimental torpedo carrier.

Most of this Morris knew already. What he had not realized was that the designer was really an ordinary man, who was not too technically minded to despise the operations of a seaside joy-ride company. It was easy to forget the humanity of anyone connected with this trade. To the daily press, a man, once a pilot, remained an 'airman' for the rest of his life, whether he were to be married, divorced, confined in a lunatic asylum, or hanged. There was no escaping the label.

They stood chatting for a little about the business; then the designer harped back to the original subject.

'Who was that second pilot who got off then?'

'Captain Stenning,' said Morris. 'I don't know if you ever met him; he spent most of his time instructing near Gloucester, I believe.'

But Rawdon had never done so, and the conversation drifted to general subjects. With all his knowledge, the big man had a childlike interest in any new thing connected with aviation.

Morris, amused at his persistence, found himself recounting the minutest details of the business. Soon, by what seemed a natural transition, the conversation drifted to personalities, and his whole career in aviation was laid bare. This was a more serious matter, Morris pulled himself up, began to consider what he was saying and to wonder whether it might not be possible to touch this man for a little information and advice upon his own account. It would not do to let such a man get away without sounding him. Presently the designer gave him the opening that he was looking for.

'And so you're sticking to this business?' he inquired, in his gentle even tone.

Morris glanced at him. 'I'm not so sure about that,' he said. 'Think it worth it?'

The other returned the glance quizzically. 'No,' he said. 'I shouldn't think so.'

'That's rather what I thought.'

The designer considered for a little. 'Mind you,' he said, 'there'll be a great shortage of pilots one of these days; not yet, but soon. There aren't any more coming on.'

'I dare say,' said Morris. 'But what kind of pilots? Engine-driver sort?'

'Of course, it'll come to that – in a very few years.'

There was a minute or two of silence.

'Look here,' said Morris. 'I'm not trying to touch you for a job.' The designer smiled. 'But how does one set about getting on to the design side? It's the only stable part of this industry. I did mathematics at Oxford. Would there be anything doing for me in a design office do you suppose?'

'What as?' asked the designer. It was a disconcerting little query.

Morris rubbed his chin. 'I don't know how things go in a firm,' he said. 'But isn't there any opening on the design side for a man like me?'

'I don't think there's a chance of it,' said Rawdon frankly. 'Take my own firm. I had six or seven of your sort in the war, on stress and performance work. I've got two now, and the rest have taken temporary jobs till they can get back into aviation again. And you don't know anything about it – differential equations won't help you much in the design of aeroplanes – not yet, anyhow.'

Morris considered for a minute or two. 'One must do something,' he said, 'and this won't last for ever. Tell me, on the design side you have people who calculate stresses and loads – stress merchants you call them, don't you? How does one set about that work – how does one start in it? My own idea is that it's pretty easily picked up. One might combine it with piloting.'

'That might help, certainly,' said the designer. 'I had a mechanic pilot once, but he wasn't much good – he always had to be leaving his job for someone else to finish while he went flying. That might not be so bad in the office.'

'What does one have to know?'

The designer looked at him thoughtfully. 'I don't suppose it would be so very much for you,' he said. 'You want to get up to about the Civil Engineer's level – eventually. With some aerodynamics. I suppose one could get it up by oneself all right. The difficulty would be to get anyone to take you on and give you a trial.'

'One might get a job as a pilot and work one's way in,' said Morris.

'It might be done that way, I suppose. I can give you the names of one or two books if you're really thinking of it.'

He wrote down three names on a visiting card and handed it

to Morris. 'If you know something about what's in those,' he said, 'you've got a chance. And I don't really see why a mathematician like you shouldn't be able to pick it up, though it's not a job I'd care about myself.'

The two machines came in in company after flying round the Solent. Stenning came in to land first; then when he was out of the way, Riley put down just outside the hangars. Again Rawdon gave his approving little grunt.

Morris got up. 'Come over and have a look at the machines,' he said. 'Riley would like to meet you again. You'll stay and have some tea with us, won't you? We live in one of those huts.'

They walked over the grass to the machines. The party of visitors were packed into their car and rolled away with dignity.

'Got a job after tea,' said Riley. 'One of us is to go and chuck stunts outside an old lady's bedroom window at the Towers. Twenty minutes or so – loops and rolls.'

'I'll go if you like,' said Morris. 'I've not done anything today yet. Riley, this is Captain Rawdon.' But he was not there when he turned, for Captain Rawdon was away examining the detail of a strut-fitting on one of the machines, full of insatiable curiosity. Riley went up to him.

'This an Air Ministry modification?' he asked.

'Yes,' said Riley. 'Pleased to meet you again, sir.'

After a scratch tea they strolled back to the hangar. Rawdon, it appeared, was yachting about the Solent and had put into Ryde with his host, who held that Sunday afternoon should be spent at anchor. Rawdon had come on shore for a walk and had gravitated almost unconsciously to the aerodrome.

'Better take my machine,' said Stenning. They busied themselves for a little time with ballast; Morris climbed in.

'One moment,' said Riley. 'The old lady's room is on the south side. They're hanging a bath-towel out of the window so that you'll know which it is. She particularly wants to see a loop.'

'I remember,' said Stenning, 'when I used to tell pupils that it wasn't safe to get an Avro into a spin, because she wouldn't come out of it. Of course, I'd never tried . . .'

Rawdon chuckled gravely.

'The dear dead days,' said Morris. Stenning swung the propeller and he moved out on to the aerodrome, faced into the wind, and went away in a climbing turn, just as Riley had done before.

'He's a good man, that,' said Riley to Rawdon. 'Picked up this business remarkably well.'

'I know,' said Rawdon. 'But he's had a good bit of experience, hasn't he?'

There was something in his tone that caused Riley to glance keenly at him. 'Mostly on Rats and Robins,' he said. 'Then he crashed and became a ferry pilot, and after that he went to the Handley Pages. One way and another he's flown pretty well everything.' He paused a little, and then added, 'He'll be a useful man on the design side if ever he gets a chance.'

'That's what he's been telling me,' said Rawdon dryly. 'Can we see his show from here?'

'We ought to be able to see something of him from the other side of the hangars,' said Riley. 'He's only about two miles away.'

Morris found the window easily and fancied he could see the dim outline of an old lady in a chair inside. The house faced on to a wide, park-like stretch of pasture land, unencumbered by trees of any size; not at all a bad place for his show. He flew round for a little, displaying the machine on vertical turns close to the house, showing first the belly of the machine and then the back. Then he climbed a little, dived with full engine on, pulled her up and over in the loop, switched off and pulled her out on to a level keel again. He did one or two more loops, then one or two Immelman turns outside the window, called after the great German fighter who invented the manoeuvre. Then, with a glance at his watch, he climbed in a great spiral till he had gained sufficient height for his spin. He switched off, pulled her up to stalling, kicked on full rudder, and in a moment was spinning nose-first to the ground. Clearheaded and cool he counted the revolutions, allowed her to do four turns, then put her into a straight dive, pulled out gently on to an even keel, and flew past the window again. He raised his hand in salute as he passed, then flew back to the aerodrome and made a slow landing just outside the hangar door.

Rawdon watched him to the ground and departed.

Morris paid the final attentions to his machine, closed the sliding doors of the hangar, and walked slowly back to the hut. He was vaguely depressed; the arrival of the designer on the scene had crystallized in his mind a train of ideas which had worried him before. He went into the hut, washed his hands, and then strolled out of the gates and down the lane.

It led to the sea, that lane running past the hangars. It ran down between cool green hedges, muddy and fragrant. Morris wandered down it, whistling very softly beneath his breath. He was not altogether happy in his prospects. It seemed to him extremely probable that the business would not survive the winter.

During the past weeks he had rather let things slide, but now he must consider the subject seriously.

He was not at all sanguine about the prospects of the air lines. If they failed, there would be still less demand for pilots. The statistics published in the papers showed that the machines on the Paris lines were running with an average load of only about one third of their capacity – that could not be a paying proposition. They were running in competition with subsidized French lines, and the subsidy question had just come up in Parliament, when it had been announced that 'Civil aviation must fly by itself'. That might be the sound policy for the ultimate development of the industry, but it would mean precious few jobs for pilots next year.

What if he were to chuck piloting and make for the design side of the business? That was undoubtedly the sound thing to do, if he could get a job, which seemed very unlikely . . . Anyway, it was a good thing to have met Rawdon, and he would see about getting those books. He did not believe that there was very much in aircraft engineering that could not be picked up by a mathematician reading in his spare time.

He came out on to the shore and walked along the beach.

He would have a look at those books; there was a certain amount of spare time in the evenings. He smiled a little to himself; 'the Virtuous Apprentice'. It was the only course open to him at the moment to better things than this.

He walked backwards and forwards along a little beach in a cove between the rocks, immersed in dreams.

He had thought that pain was an evanescent emotion. But it was not that – it worked out differently. Pain did not vanish, but turned to hardness – a great hardness and regret. One did not forget these things ... he had thought that perhaps one might. Perhaps one did, really, only he hadn't been long enough at the game. He had only had three months, or three and a half. That was not very long to decide the permanence of a grand emotion. Still, he should know his own mind if ever he was going to. He was twenty-five years old.

He left the beach and walked slowly back to the aerodrome by the same road through the cool evening.

At the gate of the aerodrome he met Stenning and Riley.

'Your luck's in,' said Stenning. 'The old lady sent a ruddy great basket of peaches by the chauffeur, for the dashing birdman.'

Morris laughed. 'I'd better write a note this evening. We'll have them at supper.'

A week later the books arrived.

The arrival of what Riley termed the 'light literature' precipitated a discussion on the policy of the firm. This had been brewing for some weeks, only nobody had cared to be the first to put into words what he really thought about the future of the joy-riding business. But when Morris one evening blandly produced the *Theory of Structures* and proceeded to study it, Stenning, after a flippant comment or two, abandoned his magazine.

'Look at that chap,' he said, 'Riley, he's going to leave us.'

Riley looked up. 'Strikes me he's the only one of us that's got any sense,' he said.

Things had not gone well the previous week. Already the

weather was showing signs of breaking and numbers were falling off, though there was still a crowd at the week-ends. But in the middle of the week, business was undoubtedly very slack; much of the time was spent sitting in a field wondering if anyone else was going to turn up or whether they had better go home for the day. All these things were the sure signs of the approach of winter, and the winter this year would be an even less lucrative period than last.

Morris laid down his book. 'Look here,' he said, 'what is going to happen? Are you going to carry on this winter, or are you going to sack me, or are you quitting? I'd rather like to know; one wants some time to poke about for something else.'

'I should poke, if I were you,' said Stenning.

There was a short silence.

'I've been thinking about this,' said Riley. 'It seems to me we've got to make up our minds to something drastic this winter. If we stay on here, we'll lose money steadily till next Easter; we shan't earn our keep.'

'That's right,' said Stenning.

'We can go to Croydon,' continued Riley, 'and start an air-taxi business there, with joy-riding thrown in – or we can go and do that somewhere in the Midlands.'

'Very good scheme,' said Morris dryly, 'only there's somebody doing it already in each case – and losing money on it.'

'I know,' said Riley. 'Or we can quit.'

There was a lengthy silence in the hut. Stenning produced a pipe and lit it, borrowing a match from Riley. Morris sat silent, staring at the stove. This was no business of his; he was a paid employee. It was he, however, who first broke the silence.

'How much of *your* capital have you got back?' he asked.

'I've got a little over half mine,' said Stenning.

'Yes,' said Riley. 'If we could realise the machines we shouldn't have done at all badly out of it – in fact we'd have made money. I don't know that we can.'

'I'm damn sure we can't,' muttered Stenning. 'Nobody wants Avros in the autumn.'

'What'll you do if you chuck it up?' asked Morris.

'I should go and see if there's anything doing at Brooklands,' said Riley. 'I was known there before the war. One could look out for test-pilot work, too. You're going for that stuff, are you?' He indicated the *Theory of Structures*.

'If I can,' said Morris. 'Rawdon put it into my head.'

'He'll take you on if you touch him the right way,' said Riley. 'You've got a chance there if you can work it.'

'I wish I had a head for books,' said Stenning. 'He'll be making a fortune while we're driven to the streets.'

'Well, what's it to be?' said Riley. 'Carry on or quit? If it's carry on, we'll have to put back some of the money we've taken out of it, this winter. It'll need subsidies.'

There was another little silence. Then Stenning took the pipe from his mouth.

'I say, quit while the quitting's good,' he said.

Morris sat staring at the stove. Two more little fortunes – very little ones, merely gratuities – had gone into aviation and been lost. That was the way of money that went into this business; nobody ever saw it again. Of course, this would have happened anyway; this business was just a sideshow at the seaside, like a troupe of nigger minstrels, and the visitors were getting tired of it. It was time for the booth to close down. There was no more money in the business.

But perhaps there was more in it than that. That summer they had carried safely and well many thousands of people; nearly ten thousand, Morris thought. Say twenty thousand since the business started. Most of them had been impressed with the safety of aircraft; some of them one day might become passengers of the air lines of the future, enthusiasts for the new transport, supporters of a strong Air Force. Perhaps, after all, these little fortunes had not been wasted. Perhaps they had been given to the country for propaganda, so that England might one day be once more an island by virtue of a healthy Air Force.

'Of course,' said Riley, 'there's no point in quitting till we stop making money. We may go on for another month or more yet. But if we know what's going to happen, we can each look out for other jobs.'

42

'We'll be in good company, anyway,' said Morris. 'Other people will be quitting this winter – it's not done yet.'

'No, by God, it's not,' said Stenning. 'Some of these air lines must be feeling the draught over the subsidy business.'

'Well,' said Riley, 'it's to be quit, is it?'

'I think so,' said Stenning. 'We've not done so badly out of it, considering that it's aviation.' There was no bitterness in his tone.

Riley drew a little stump of pencil from his pocket and took a sheet of paper. 'I'm going to write to my old firm at Brooklands,' he said.

Stenning grinned. 'Tell them you're an ex-officer – that's the thing nowadays.'

'Shut up,' said Riley. He bent over the paper in the throes of composition, his fair brows knitted in a frown.

'God bless my soul,' said Morris, 'he might be writing to a wench.'

The other looked up. 'This is different,' said Riley, 'this is personal. I always have to think a lot over this kind of letter. I usually carry a rough copy about with me two or three days before sending it. That's why I'm doing it now.'

'I was never so sensitive about my literary style as that,' said Morris. 'Mine goes just anyhow.'

'I like to get it just right,' said Riley. 'If I can bear to read it two days afterwards, I know it'll give a reasonably good effect.'

Morris laughed; this was a side of Riley that he had not seen before.

'All very well for you to laugh,' said Stenning, 'you college people. You've got friends to drop you into a fat little job – secretary at the Air Ministry, or something. It's different for us.'

'Have I hell!' said Morris.

He turned to Stenning. 'What are you going to do?'

'Stay in aviation ... look for another pilot's job.' He glanced at Morris. 'My father keeps a big drapery business in Huddersfield – retail. I could go into that,' he said simply. Then he smiled. 'But I don't see it happening.'

43

'You'll be all right,' said Riley. 'You know one or two people at Croydon, don't you?'

'There'll be jobs on the air lines in the spring,' said Stenning hopefully. 'At the worst, I could live on my fat till then.'

'Wish I could.'

'You'd better go and look up your pal Rawdon,' said Stenning. 'Struck me that you were well away there.'

Morris wondered if there were anything in it. He was very much averse to going to sponge on Rawdon for a job, immediately after taking his advice as he had done. Still, what else was there? It seemed to be the only course open to him at all. Otherwise he must take something temporarily, like Stenning's drapery standby, to tide him over the winter till more pilots were needed. But that was admitting himself a pilot and nothing else.

'How much capital have you got?' asked Riley suddenly.

'Eh?' said Morris, awaking from his reverie.

'How long can you keep yourself for?'

Morris made a little calculation. 'About four months, comfortably.'

'The best thing you can do,' said Riley, 'is to go to Rawdon, tell him what's happened, and offer to work in his offices unpaid for a couple of months for experience. Lots of firms take on juniors like that. After that, he'll either give you a job himself, or else a thumping good testimonial which may get you into some other firm. In any case, you'll be in touch with aviation and on the spot if anyone wants a pilot. If you can get Rawdon to use you as a pilot, of course, he'll give you flying money. You might even be able to earn your keep that way, by casual work like that.'

'They'd never take me on,' said Morris. 'I'd be more nuisance than I'm worth.'

'You can have a shot anyway,' said Riley. 'And I don't see why they shouldn't take you on like that, though whether you'd be worth a screw at the end of two months I don't know. You can push a slide rule, can't you?'

Morris nodded.

'There's nothing in performance work,' said Riley. 'I can't

do it myself, but it's only a matter of worrying out long columns of figures and plotting the results in curves and things. I should think they'd be glad to have you as a sort of calculating machine.'

'I dare say it might work,' said Stenning. 'The more unpaid staff they can get to do the dirty work, the more research they can do with their regular staff.'

Morris got up from his chair. 'I think it's worth trying,' he said. 'I'll write him a line.'

'You'll never get an answer to a letter,' said Riley bluntly. 'The best aircraft firms don't answer letters. Think it over for a day or two, and then go and see him yourself.'

'But will he see me – can one just barge in like that?'

'Of course he'll see you.'

So three days afterwards, Morris found himself in a tramcar being borne out to the neighbourhood of Southall from Shepherd's Bush. The more he thought of it, the more unlikely the scheme appeared; proportionately as he approached the place his spirits fell.

The conductor turned him out at a barren corner in country of a sort; a paper-littered country, dotted about with ugly little houses and embellished with great decaying hoardings of peeling and tattered advertisements of unguents for skin diseases. Morris walked on up the lane.

As he got away from the main road, things became a trifle better, and he emerged into clean, though dull, country. After a walk of about half a mile he came upon the aerodrome, surrounded by the wooden buildings and huts that constituted the whole of the establishment. Only one or two motor-cars outside the largest office building, the droning of a buzz-saw, and the stocking floating from a flagstaff on a roof proclaimed that it was inhabited. It was an unkempt, rather desolate little works.

Morris walked on to where the cars were, and into a building of offices. Here he knocked on a door marked 'Inquiries' and opened it, to find a small girl seated by a telephone eating an apple.

'Er, can I see Captain Rawdon?' he said.

'He's down in the shops, sir,' said the child cheerfully.

There was a short pause.

'Do you know when he'll be back?' asked Morris.

The little girl looked surprised. 'No, sir – I'd go down there if I were you.' Then, with a sudden access of patronage, 'I'll take you down, if you like.'

Morris followed her humbly out of the building, down an alley between various sheds and stores, through a penetrating reek of pear drops. Presently his guide swung through a doorway into a big erecting shop, crowded with aeroplanes in every stage of completion. Most of them, Morris saw, were old Rabbits and Ratcatchers brought from store to be overhauled and reconditioned for the Air Force. In the midst was a new fuselage of a different type in the early stages of construction.

This was the new two-seater fighter, designed experimentally for the Air Ministry to take the new Blundell engine, the Stoat. Great things were expected of the Stoat; the lightest engine for its power yet produced. Rawdon had abandoned the unequal competition for nomenclature and had originated a system of ciphers for his machines which, though less exciting, imposed less strain upon the imagination of the designer. This was to be the Rawdon S.F. Mark I.

At present the board of directors was sitting on it, both metaphorically and physically. Whenever Bateman, the business director, came down from London to visit the firm, Rawdon usually took him to the shops where the exact progress of the work could be seen and proposed innovations illustrated more graphically than in the office. Morris saw them from a distance deep in conversation, and instinctively hung back.

His guide, however, had no such scruples as to the sanctity of a directors' meeting. Apple in hand she marched up to Rawdon.

'A gentleman to see you, sir.' Her part played, she gave her attention to a more important matter. The foreman of the engine shop, passing by, stopped and regarded her.

'Hey, Gladys, don't you know any better than that up in the office?' he inquired pleasantly. 'Standin' eating an apple in the middle of the shop! Settin' a bad example to the men. Ought to be ashamed of yourself – I would. I wouldn't have it if this was my shop.'

One of the carpenters laid down his work. 'Don't you pay no attention to him,' he said. 'He'd have apple and all if this was his shop.'

The little girl grinned shyly and strolled away. Rawdon levered himself slowly off the bright wooden fuselage and went to meet Morris, frowning a little. He had no place for this chap; he diagnosed instantly what he wanted. He hated having to turn people away.

As Morris unfolded his tale, however, the frown melted away and was replaced by a childlike look of innocence that usually rested on his features. He heard him to the end with a penetrating question now and then, and volunteered no comment. Morris finished his tale, and stood while Rawdon stroked his chin.

'As I understand it, then, Mr Morris,' he said, 'you want to come and work for us unpaid for a certain time in the hopes that we can take you on when you've got a little experience or, failing that, that we can pass you on to someone who wants staff?'

Morris assented.

Rawdon picked up a splinter of wood and fingered it. 'I'm afraid I can tell you straight off,' he said, 'that we shall not be taking on any more staff just yet – so far as I can judge. One doesn't see very far ahead in this business. But unless anything very startling happens, we shan't be engaging any more technical staff for many months.'

'I expected that,' said Morris. 'At the same time, I want to get experience in these matters. Can you see your way to allow me to come and work unpaid? Of course, I quite see that the presence of a learner rather interferes with the work of the office.'

'Oh, as to that,' said the designer, 'you can come and welcome – it's all clear gain to us. And when you go, I'll give you what help I can – with consideration to what you're worth. But I must tell you clearly that I don't think there's a chance of a job for you in this firm. I'm sorry, but you know the state of the industry.'

Morris laughed. 'I think I know a good bit about that,' he said.

'One thing, Mr Morris. Are you prepared to take any piloting work?'

Morris considered in his turn. 'Piloting is my only asset,' he said. He glanced at the other. 'I should want flying pay for that.'

'Quite so. We might be able to give you odd, isolated jobs in that way – delivery of these Rabbits chiefly. You would be willing to take that on?'

'Most certainly.'

'Well,' said the designer, 'we should be very glad to have you on those conditions, Mr Morris – only, as I say, I'm afraid there's very little hope of a paid job in the office. Things are too bad to take on any more staff at present. When would you think of coming?'

'In about three weeks? I really can't say till I've spoken to Mr Riley; I'm still engaged to him.'

'That would do very well. If you'll give us a couple of days' notice, will you? ... Good morning, Mr Morris; I'm very glad we've been able to come to some arrangement.'

He walked back to his partner, still sitting on the fuselage of the fighter, and recounted the interview.

'And you told him he could come,' said Bateman.

'Yes,' said Rawdon, 'I told him he could come. Fact is, I like the look of him, and there's no denying that a regular resident pilot would be useful.'

'I thought you said there wasn't enough work for a regular pilot.'

'There isn't,' said the designer. 'But a pilot who can do something else as well is another matter.'

'See how he shapes,' suggested the partner.

'Yes,' said Rawdon, 'we must see how he shapes.'

4

Morris made his way back to London on top of the tram. Things had gone well, as well as could be expected; he had got his nose into another and more permanent side of the industry, something in which there were real prospects. At the moment, of course, it was unlikely that he would get a job on the design side; still, if he could continue to work there and make enough by casual piloting to keep himself in a modest way, he might in time be able to insinuate himself into the office of some firm. He had made a satisfactory start, anyway.

Back in the hut that evening, he told them all about it.

'He asked about the piloting himself, did he?' said Riley thoughtfully. 'Play that well; it's evidently your best line at the moment.'

'I think he's done pretty well out of the whole business, if you ask me,' said Stenning. 'Wish I had the luck some people have.'

'It doesn't mean anything but casual work,' said Morris.

'He hasn't got any other pilots there, has he?' asked Stenning.

'Don't think so,' said Morris taking off his boots by the stove.

'Well then, you'll be chief pilot, test pilot if you like, to the Rawdon Aircraft Company Limited.'

Morris glanced at him quickly, one boot on and one off. Then he realized that his leg was being pulled, and made the appropriate comment.

'No, really,' said Riley, 'that's what it may come to if you can work it properly. I don't see at all why it shouldn't. Rawdon gave up flying himself last year, I heard. And he's been getting in casual pilots, you say?'

Morris did not answer the question. 'Don't know if you call delivering Rabbits and Ratcatchers test flying,' he said sourly. 'Nothing to test.'

'No satisfying some people,' said Stenning.

Morris picked up his boots and went to put them in a corner, treading delicately in his stockinged feet. He turned and spoke bitterly over his shoulder to Stenning.

'Never seen such a ragtime show in all my life as that. I told you that the hall porter was a little girl eating an apple, didn't I?'

'Very nice too,' said Riley. 'Symbol of innocence. Besides, it's aviation.'

Morris laughed. 'It's aviation all over,' he said.

That week the receipts dropped sharply, though there was still a slight surplus to divide. Things the week after were better again, and worse the following week, when there was not sufficient to cover the statutory limit for depreciation and spares.

Then the crowning blow fell, with dramatic suddenness. One morning they became aware of strangers in the land, odd people wandering about the aerodrome. The caretaker announced that they were workmen from the Air Ministry, come to see about the buildings. A brief reconnaissance revealed the fact that they had commenced to remove the roof, door, and windowframes from one of the hangars; that they were proposing to treat every building in the place in a similar manner, and that the material was to be re-erected in an Air Force station on the other side of the Solent, where it was needed more urgently.

'We're done,' said Riley when this was reported to him. 'This is the end of us. We've got no legal tenure here – we've only had this place on sufferance.'

They decided not to dispute the edict, but to shut up shop and go. Riley had heard from his firm at Brooklands, who regretted that they had nothing to offer him at the moment, but in the near future they hoped to be making an attempt on some long distance records, when they would be glad to avail themselves of his services if he was still free. This was as good as could be expected. Stenning alone had nothing to go to, but hoped to pick up a piloting job if he hung about the London Terminal Aerodrome at Croydon long enough.

There was little preparation to be done. They sold most of their spares as junk to a speculative garage-keeper in Ryde and made the mechanic a present of what was left. The clerks were dismissed with a week's wages, and a hangar was secured at Croydon for the housing of the machines till they were sold; there was more chance of selling them near London.

So one bleak morning in early October the three machines were pushed out of the hangars for the last time, and luggage loaded into them instead of trippers. The engines were started and one by one they moved out on to the aerodrome, spun over the grass, and circled for height above the hangars. Riley was the last to leave; he taxied out on to the aerodrome and waited a moment before taking off to join the others circling above his head. He sat in the machine idly for a little, and took a long look out over the wide grassy field, the derelict hangars. Once he had had bright visions for this place. He had hoped to make it a base for a sound taxi business about the south of England, to buy up the place bit by bit as he made money, and to run a big fleet of low-powered aeroplanes for hire.

Well, he had failed. He supposed he ought to have known better than to think that aviation would catch on ... just yet. But it would come one day. He had failed and lost a lot of money on it. One day, in two or three years' time, he would try again with more money behind him, when money was a little easier to get and the bank rate had come down.

He opened out his engine and began to move over the grass. The tail came up and he began to spin swiftly across the field; the uneven motion ceased and his castles in the air dropped away beneath him. Soon he was on a level with Stenning and Morris; in company they headed for Croydon.

An hour and a half later they arrived flying in formation of a sort, waited till an incoming Goliath from Paris had moved its unwieldy bulk from the centre of the aerodrome, and landed in quick succession one after another. They taxied to the side of the aerodrome, over the road to their hangar, and stowed the machines.

In an hour's time their attentions to the machines were at an

51

end; they collected their belongings in a little heap at the door of the hangar.

'Nothing more to be done, is there?' asked Morris.

'Come and have lunch,' said Riley. 'There's a Trust House here somewhere.'

In the restaurant Stenning and Riley found one or two acquaintances. There was a tone of optimistic anxiety about all their news and greetings; the advent of a 'broke' joy-riding concern had pointed the lesson to be learned from the diminishing number of passengers on the air lines. Aviation had ceased to attract as a novelty and was not yet accepted as a serious means of transport. The bulk of the passenger traffic was still represented by American tourists; still at the end of every trip the pilot was photographed in front of the machine with Sadie and Momma by his side. This was not the procedure adopted on the railways ... and air transport must become as matter of fact as railway transport before it became a dividend paying business.

They lunched well, getting a little amusement by prophesying the gloomiest future for the regular air lines to the regular pilots. There was just sufficient uneasiness about for some attention to be given to them; they finished the meal and retired to the lounge in a perfect blaze of unpopularity. Riley paused in the door and fired the parting shot.

'Well, of course, it's nothing to do with me. But you can't get away from those facts. I know, if I was on an air line now, I'd be looking out for something else, just in case ... There'll be a glut of pilots on the market pretty soon. Still, it's none of my business.'

They settled up the last financial details in the lounge and drank a round to their next merry meeting. Then they separated, Morris going up to London, Stenning and Riley to get rooms in the neighbourhood and to see if there was any chance of selling the machines. There was none.

Two days later Morris started work in the design office of the Rawdon Aircraft Company (1919) Ltd.

He did not find the work very difficult after the first few

52

days. The whole business of designing an aeroplane he found to run on certain very definite lines. First of all, certain broad considerations governing the design of the machine came to the designer. Thus if it were a passenger machine for an air line, the air line had certain definite ideas as to what they wanted; the carrying capacity, the speed, the landing speed, and the 'ceiling' or maximum height that it was possible for the machine to attain. Such considerations as these would be settled in conference with the designer, who would indicate tactfully where they were asking for technical impossibilities. If the machine were a military one for the Air Force the procedure was, in general, much the same, with the difference that the purchaser had a habit of asking for technical impossibilities and refusing to discuss the matter. This made the design of military machines a very specialized business.

The conditions for the machine being determined, the chief draughtsman would draw a pretty picture of what he thought such a machine ought to look like, neatly indicating on this first layout the really important features of the machine, such as the way the door opened and the system of heating the cabin. This rough layout would be shown to the customer for approval; in the case of a commercial machine it would be passed without much question.

The procedure now depended very much upon the financial position of the firm. In war-time, when the firms were well to do, a model of the machine would be made at this point and tested in a wind channel. That is, it would be mounted on a special balance in a tunnel and air sucked over it at a known speed, the resulting 'lift' and forces on the model being accurately measured. From this data the performance of the machine, the speed and horse-power necessary could be easily determined and any alterations or improvements to the machine tried out.

This was the counsel of perfection, and a very expensive one. For firms that could not run to the expense of a wind channel – and this was the case with very many firms – there was another method, more laborious and less accurate. This consisted in keeping a careful record of every calculation that had ever been made in the firm since the early days of aviation, and digging in this turgid mass for figures and precedents which would assist in the estimation of the performance of the machine in question. In this the greatest help was given by the various government research departments, who had collected and published a vast mass of aerodynamic data.

In the meantime, as soon as the main essentials of the machine had been decided, the span of the wings and the aerofoil section to be used, certain human calculating machines were let loose and proceeded to calculate the stresses and necessary size of every part of the machine in several different ways, from the main spars in the wings to the luggage racks in the cabin. And last of all, the results of their work were handed over to the draughtsmen, the really important people on whose work the detail design of the machine depended, and who got out the drawings upon which the men in the workshops were to act.

And over all brooded the designer, visiting each man's desk once or twice a day, discussing and approving each man's work with a faculty for switching his mind on to new subjects at a moment's notice that gained Morris's earnest respect. This seemed to be the true function of a designer, to criticise and advise his staff.

Time slipped quickly past; Morris found himself fairly competent to deal with the work that he was called upon to do; odd problems in research and experimentation. The design in hand was that of a torpedo carrier for the Air Ministry. A model was built and tested at the National Physical Laboratory at considerable expense, and was found to behave exactly as was expected. This was disappointing and a waste of money. Then came a galaxy of performance calculations, tangled by empirical allowances for imperfectly understood complications. By the time these difficulties were unravelled, the design of the machine was well on the way; they realized – as so often happened – that it was now too late to make any alteration even if they wanted to; there remained only to hope for the best.

In addition to this, Morris found that a certain amount of

piloting work came his way. Each reconditioned machine had to be taken up for a short flight before the Air Force officer who was to fly it away was allowed to risk his neck on it. This precaution was justified on one occasion, in the instance of a Ratcatcher, rigged by a mechanic who was under notice to quit. This gentleman, whether by accident or design, managed to confuse the wires of the lateral control so that the controls worked in opposite sense to normal. The mistake passed unnoticed by the foreman and by Morris. Attempting a gentle turn at a height of a hundred feet the machine, instead of banking over in a normal manner, shot outwards from the turn in a violent sideslip. Morris, with the fear of God in his heart, managed to prevent a stall and to land where he was, in a field about a mile from the aerodrome. How he managed it he could never quite tell, but he got down with no worse damage than a burst tyre and a damaged wing tip, left the machine and walked back to the aerodrome, meeting an ambulance party on the way. He expressed himself feelingly to these.

It seemed to him a good opportunity to discuss his future with Rawdon.

But Rawdon had already made up his mind. 'I can't give you much of a job,' he said. 'I'm told you're worth about four pounds a week in the office. I can give you that, and flying pay as usual – what you've been getting.'

After this Morris led a quiet life for several months, keeping his eyes open to every piece of information in any way connected with his work, reading in the evenings. He did not see his way ahead at all; it was certainly no good attempting to get ahead quickly in that office – it was far too full of experienced men. Still, he trusted that chances of advancement would open out as soon as the industry got on its feet and began to expand a little.

But at this time the industry was far from expanding. As the year drew to a close it became evident that there would be more disasters, this time among the air lines. A good attempt had been made to carry on unsubsidized in the face of competition from the subsidized French lines. The effort was foredoomed to failure. True, every reason of safety and common sense indicated the desirability of travelling by the English lines rather than the French, but financial considerations proved overwhelming; it was not to be expected that the traveller would pay ten pounds instead of six for the privilege of travelling upon an English line. The three English lines, themselves running in competition with one another, assisted the disaster; passengers fell away and the machines began to run practically empty.

Finally one of them, the line that had really proved aviation to be a commercial possibility, closed down, broken.

Morris from his niche watched these events without much concern. He did not believe in the least that aviation was a failure; on the contrary, the more he saw of the commercial side of it the more determined he became to stay in it. Things were bad and, in his opinion, would be worse; still, it was a good thing and worth staying in – the only thing he could get on in. He had decided that months before, and was not inclined by any of these disasters to change his mind once made up.

In actual fact, and happily for the industry and for the country, he was wrong. This was the low water mark; early in the new year a subsidy was granted and things began to improve a little, not much, but a little. One of the two remaining air lines held a special directors' meeting seriously to consider whether they could not now risk capital expenditure upon the purchase of a new eight-passenger machine to cope with the expected rush of summer traffic. The daring project was argued in all its bearings and reluctantly abandoned, whereupon the Air Ministry stepped in in the most fatherly manner possible and announced a scheme whereby the Government would buy the machines and hire them out to such air lines [sic] as were disposed to avail themselves of the scheme. Thus assisted, the lines began to pick up a little and to regain something of the traffic they had lost during the summer of 1921.

And Morris waited and worked. He had mastered the routine side of his work and was now at the stage when he could look about a little and decide in what line he could most usefully employ his spare time. It amazed him to find that there was apparently no method laid down for the exact calculation of the stresses in a three-ply fuselage, and that empirical methods solely were in use. Here seemed to be a field in which he could use his mathematics to some advantage; he began to consider the problems involved, and immediately discovered the magnitude of the task. Still, he would have a cut at it.

He had not altogether neglected the few people he knew in London. Through the agency of one or two distant relations he had got himself elected to a little club with a considerable library; he was usually to be found there over the week-ends. Occasionally on Sundays he used to go and visit his old uncle and aunt; once he had been to Brooklands and had watched Johnnie coax a diminutive motor-cycle round the track at a most incredible speed. Riley he had lost touch with entirely, though he sometimes came upon references to him in the technical and motoring papers. He seemed to be doing what he said he would; a little test piloting and motor racing, though that was slack during the winter season. It was not considered judicious to race a heavy car at a hundred and twenty miles an hour upon a wet and slippery track.

And one afternoon he called on Wallace at his little flat in Knightsbridge. He had often meant to do this and had never done it; this afternoon he was fed up; it was raining; he would go and beg a tea of Wallace – if he was in.

He was in; a burst of shrill girlish laughter announced the fact as Morris climbed the stairs. He smiled and for a moment thought of turning back – it was a long time since he had spoken to a girl. He'd settled all that sort of thing . . . long ago. But it was raining and he wanted his tea – Wallace did himself pretty well. He walked on up the stairs and rang the bell.

Presently he found himself sitting on a sofa before the fire, laboriously making conversation with a damsel who was most evidently his intellectual superior. He had never seen Wallace's women in bulk before, and was secretly amused. He discovered as his head grew clearer that there were really only two of them there, with one other man; Wallace, simple and unaffected in the midst of his exotic beauties, was sitting on the floor toasting a bit of bread on the end of a knife.

'Or will you have a crumpet?' he inquired. 'Nancy, stop badgering him and give him some tea. If he likes you he'll probably take you up.'

'At this point,' said Morris definitely, 'the member for Southall made an energetic protest—'

'Do you fly?' asked the girl.

Morris subsided. 'I'm afraid so,' he said humbly.

There was an expectant pause.

'The Silver Churn,' said Wallace to nobody in particular.

'You see,' said Morris apologetically, 'this is *commercial* aviation.' He brightened a little, and rubbed his hands together. 'We can do you a very nice line in joy-rides over London,' he said, 'at only twenty-five shillings a head. We find these very popular in the summer months.'

'Jimmie,' said the girl, 'I don't think I like your friends. Come and talk to him yourself.' She moved away and Wallace took her place; they began to chat of common interests and acquaintances.

One by one the results of Schools had appeared, but Morris had missed most of them. Christie had ploughed and had vanished into the Argentine with the Christie Steam Plough. Wallace had taken a pass. Johnnie, to everybody's surprise, had come out with a distinction in English Literature; a circumstance which savoured to Morris of gross impertinence, making a mock of the humanities. He knew that Johnnie had no real interest in life other than motor-cycles. Lechlane had got his First in Law as the result of five terms' work after the war, but then that was Lechlane all over.

'And by the way,' said Wallace, 'you heard about Lechlane?'

'What's that?' asked Morris. He had never been much interested in Lechlane.

'Came in for a young fortune the other day – I saw it in the legacy report in *The Times*. Over a thousand a year, it came to. Some people have all the luck – he never spends a penny. No motor, no friends ...' One of his guests flipped a morsel of biscuit at him.

'Oh well,' said Morris cheerfully, 'I dare say he'll go to the dogs now. No, but I'm glad he's got that; he's not a bad man and it'll help him a lot in his profession. One needs money to get on in politics, I believe.'

'Lechlane won't have much difficulty in getting on,' said Wallace reflectively. 'He's not that sort.'

No, Lechlane was not that sort.

It was safe enough to make that sort of statement about Lechlane. Lechlane was a finite quantity; a man whose course through life could be predicted with considerable accuracy. There was never the very slightest doubt as to what Lechlane would do under any given conditions. Lechlane would do the right thing, and there was an end of it.

It was a hereditary gift.

He was connected in a way with the Rileys; a connection not close enough to involve him in any unpleasant intercourse with the disreputable Malcolm. In point of fact his aunt was Helen's stepmother. There had never been very much connection between the Lechlanes and the Rileys; political differences had held them apart as much as the hearty geniality of old Sir James Riley in his younger days. To the Rileys politics were an occupation; to the Lechlanes a profession. The Lechlanes were Liberals to a man; they did not hit it off with the more hearty elements of the Conservative Party.

There was a curious atmosphere about all the Lechlanes that tended further to the divergence of the families. They were at the very heart of that close corporation of Liberal families who have ruled the country for so many years. Integrity was their hall-mark, yet it was undeniable that, while engaging in no other occupation than politics, money somehow found its way to them all; they all prospered together.

When Roger Lechlane had decided to embark upon a political career, it had merely been a question as to who should secure him his first appointment. He would commence, of course, as a private secretary. That could have been arranged with the greatest of ease by apprenticing him to one of his uncles, but that was not the way things were done in that family. No, he must have a wider outlook than that afforded by the family. He should go as a secretary to somebody quite detached, preferably, even, somebody in the Opposition.

Roger Lechlane, then, to the intense surprise of the writers of the chatty little political articles in the evening papers, made a complete break (politically) with his family, and became a Diehard. It was a great shock to all his feminine relations, and something of a surprise to his uncle by marriage, old Sir James Riley, to whom he went for what he euphemistically termed advice. At Oxford, Lechlane had made a bad slip; Sir James had had a daughter up at one of the ladies' colleges; he should have seen more of her than he had. He cursed himself for his lack of foresight; it would have eased his way considerably if the family had been under some slight obligation to him. It did not matter so very much, after all; Sir James would do all that he wanted him to. Still, he must not make that mistake again. He never did.

Sir James Riley had started him in this profession of politics, and Sir James Riley held a good old Conservative reputation. Lechlane dropped into the habit of frequent week-ends to Bevil Crossways; it was an extraordinarily comfortable house, for the hostess had been a Lechlane and knew how things should be done. Moreover, the old man was deeply interesting upon political subjects. Lechlane hit it off very well with the girl, too – the daughter Helen.

The week-ends were always exactly the same. When he reached the house the butler would be standing at the door, black-coated and ready to welcome him with an austere dignity. The ladies were in the drawing-room, Sir James in the library. Mr Lechlane would wish to go to his room first? He would, and as if by magic hot water would appear in two cans of different temperature. In the morning there were three, but then one was a little one intended for shaving.

At five and twenty minutes past four Mr Lechlane would emerge from his room and would make his way to the drawing-room, where his hostess would be standing in front of the fire to welcome him. Exactly five minutes later, tea would appear and with it Sir James, mellow and spruce, if a trifle tottery.

During tea, Lechlane would talk family gossip to his hostess almost exclusively, and afterwards, if fine, they would walk together a little in the garden, perhaps strolling down the chestnut avenue to inspect the daughter's chickens. ('The dear child – so good for her to have the occupation, Roger. We feel that the University was a mistake in many ways – it has proved very unsettling, I am afraid.') Then he would go and talk to Sir James for a little, and almost immediately it would be time for him to change and have his bath before dinner. And this was the manner of many week-ends, till Lechlane came in for a legacy.

Yet one must not suppose that he did anything impetuously, and hence one presumes that he had considered the matter of his marriage before. The thought recurred as he lay in his bath before dinner, shortly after the happy interview with his solicitor. He was always wanting some more satisfactory establishment than his bachelor rooms and club. If he were to take a big flat, or a small house in Mayfair, say ... And that meant a hostess.

That was the point.

It had never occurred to him seriously that he ought to be married. But why not? A wife would be a great help to him – a wife of the right sort, that was.

He got out of the bath and dried himself, meditating deeply. He would do nothing rash, nothing that he might be sorry for later. He was rather young to marry – he was not yet thirty. And Helen was too old to make a perfect wife; they were too nearly of an age. There was barely five years between them.

He dressed carefully and neatly. It would certainly bear consideration; it would be a very satisfactory marriage in many ways. It would help him a lot to be allied so closely to the Rileys, particularly if the Conservatives got the upper hand ... It would help him in other ways, too; people liked young marriages provided the young couple had enough money to start in life where their parents left off. There was a lot of that sort of sentiment about. Helen was cut out for a hostess by tradition; she would not have to be broken in.

It struck him that he might do a lot worse.

It was characteristic that he took her acquiescence for granted. He hardly gave it a thought. He would be an excellent match for her; her people would probably be delighted, and, after all, the girl had been decently brought up.

He was no fool, however. Though he hardly thought about it, he was aware that the affair would need careful handling. It would not be sufficient merely to ask her parents for her. He would have to play his part, to invest the matter with some elements of romance or very likely he wouldn't get her at all. Girls had funny ideas; they thought about nothing but falling in and out of love. He did not think for a moment that she had got any 'ideas' into her head about marriage, but he had occasionally noticed a sort of aloofness about her, a kind of weariness that had puzzled him a little, almost as if she was tiring of being a hostess, was weary of Bevil Crossways. Well, marriage would be the best thing in the world for her; he would take her out of this – it was a bit dull for a girl, he supposed. Up in London she would get to know everyone who mattered. She was a nice little thing; he thought he could get very fond of her. He could certainly give her a very good time.

He slipped his gold hunter into his waistcoat pocket and stood erect before the mirror; a slim, sombre figure in black and white. The more he thought of it, the more he liked the idea. It would be a great help to him. He would go down and have another look at her.

He blew out the candles, and the door closed softly behind him.

5

The summer drew near, gradually awakening the aircraft industry from the long nightmare of the winter. At this time, and for long afterwards, the operations of the air lines were very seasonal, the volume of traffic being reduced to negligible proportions in winter. With the advent of spring the industry seemed to wake up, machines were reconditioned for the summer traffic, more machines were ordered from the manufacturers. On this occasion things were more hopeful than before, for the Government were tied to a definite policy of assisting civil aviation by direct and indirect subsidies. At first this had the usual result of tending to discourage enterprise and efficiency; later on a more cunning method of distributing the money was adopted, to give full benefit to those companies which displayed an ordinary sense of business.

Stenning had got a job in the spring on one of the air lines. This concern, while chiefly occupied with maintaining a regular service to Paris, had been one of the first to see the possibilities of a special charter business in aeroplanes. That is, it bought up a number of old war machines and converted them into fast three-passenger machines. With these, assisted by a suitable campaign of advertisement, they were working up quite a successful little business which – a notable fact in aviation – paid its way from the very start, without being eligible for a subsidy. The work was very varied. A passenger for a transatlantic liner, having missed the boat-train for Southampton, would fly to catch the boat at Cherbourg. A cinema firm, upon some disaster in Central Europe, would fly there and have the films showing in London thirty-six hours after the unhappy event. An American business man, having just three weeks to spend in Europe, would make a little tour to Paris, Brussels, Hamburg, Copenhagen, Berlin, Warsaw, Vienna, Milan, and Marseilles, arriving back with a day or two to spare, having transacted business in each town. By the summer, about half a dozen machines and pilots were employed. The chief pilot was Malcolm Riley; Stenning flew usually on the Paris route.

But British aviation was in low repute abroad at this time. It was admitted by those best competent to judge that the British air lines to the Continent were the safest, the best organized, and the most efficient of any. Such a testimonial was entirely gratuitous, for the British industry was far too much occupied with its struggle for existence to have any concern for what the outside world might think about it, too hard up even to make known its own efficiency. In the war British aircraft were the best in the world. They were so still, but they were never seen outside England.

A British aeronautical exhibition was held in 1920, and was such a fiasco financially that it was unlikely that another one would be held for several years. Each year, the French taxpayer, by means of the subsidy, paid for a wonderful display of imitative French machines in the Paris Salon; a display made the more impressive by the rigid exclusion of certain foreign machines. Little use for the British to advertise themselves in their own technical papers; little more use for those papers patriotically to issue special catalogues of British progress printed in three languages at the time of the Paris Salon. The machines themselves were the only really cogent argument to support the alleged superiority of British design – and there was not the money to send the machines abroad to be exhibited.

This was the position at the time of the Brussels Exhibition in the autumn of 1921. The affair was said to be the idea of the most noble pilot in the history of aviation, and was to be a great thing for aviation all over the world. It was to be primarily a representative display of the world's commercial aeroplanes in a great hall in the centre of the city; coupled with this there was to be a race similar in nature to the famous Gordon Bennett Cup, recently won outright by France. This was a speed contest pure and simple, to be held on Brussels aerodrome in the presence of the Royalty of two nations. As prizes in the contest there were a large gold cup, a considerable sum of money, and the probability of certain foreign army contracts.

It seemed as if this exhibition would be well supported by the manufacturers of the world. The statistics were briefly as follows. Seventeen French machines would be present, six German, five Dutch, five Belgian, three Swiss, two Italian, and two British. For the race the entries were not numerous; they consisted of four French, two Dutch, one Belgian, and one Italian. There was no British entry.

Indeed, there was no British machine capable of competing in such a race with any chance of success, where speeds of two hundred miles an hour were expected to be realized. It was out of the question to build a suitable machine and send it across; there was no firm which, in its then condition, could regard such a procedure as anything but a rash and unjustifiable speculation. True, it seemed a pity that Britain should not be represented. It simply could not be done.

That was the view of the manufacturers. There were, how-ever, people in England who held a different opinion. There was, in fact, a machine in the country which, if it could not fly at two hundred miles an hour, could show a clean pair of heels to any aeroplane hitherto built in England. This was the Jenkinson Laverock, fitted with one of the earliest editions of that phenomenally light and powerful engine, the Blundell Stoat. The Laverock had been the last effort of the Jenkinson Aviation and Manufacturing Company Limited before the crash came, and the machine, with all others built or building, had fallen into the hands of the Official Receiver. This gentle-man, pressed to allow the machine to compete in the annual Aerial Derby for which it had been built, flatly refused to allow it to be flown. As it stood it was worth a thousand pounds or so from some visionary purchaser; in a crashed con-dition it would not be worth that number of pence. The Lave-rock had been flown once or twice in considerable secrecy; nobody seemed to know of what speed it was capable. It had been intended as the basis for a fighting scout, and had been transformed into a racing machine by the simple expedient of removing all exterior projections and cutting down the wing surface drastically. It was known to be very fast.

It is hard to say what it was that brought home so deeply the necessity of entering a machine for this race to the little band of gentlemen who clubbed together to buy the Laverock. Only one, apparently, had been intimately connected with aviation in the war. Of the others, one had made a fortune out of munitions, one or two had had sons in the Flying Corps, and one or two were nobody in particular, business men, Gov-ernment officials, members of the same club as Baynes, their enthusiastic leader. In some remote, inarticulate way all were convinced that if they bought this machine and entered it for the Brussels race, they would have done something worth doing, something that they would look back to in after years with a queer glow of sentimental pleasure. It was a good thing to do; it would help things on a bit. Baynes, even, seemed to have persuaded himself that the reputation of the country was in their hands. Certainly, if they didn't do it, nobody else would.

They harboured no illusions. None of them expected the machine to win, unless by accident. The real reason for sending it over was to display the neatness of its design, the great beauty of its lines. In its detail design and general finish and appearance, it was, perhaps, the prettiest little machine ever built in England. It might not be very fast but ... they'd show these people we could still build an aeroplane.

It was Rawdon whom they first consulted on the subject, before incurring any expenditure. Baynes, who had been a major in the Flying Corps during the war, had come into contact with Rawdon once or twice; it seemed natural for them to turn to him for advice upon their project. He heard them to the end in his little office on the aerodrome, sitting on a table, swinging his legs. Their story finished, he considered for a little.

'You really think of buying it?' he inquired. 'Well, I should think you'd get it for a lot under a thousand if you went about it the right way. It's no earthly good to anybody else.'

'I dare say we should,' said Baynes. 'What we want to do now is to arrive at some estimate of what the whole lot is going to cost us. As far as I can see, the machine would be about the least part.'

They discussed the details for a little.

'Anyway,' said Rawdon at last, 'you needn't consider the cost of getting the machine in order, or garaging it. It's in fair condition, I suppose; we can manage the erecting of it up here. I'd like to look after that part of the business, if you'll let me in on it.'

The deputation was properly embarrassed. 'That's extremely good of you,' said Baynes.

'Only too glad to have the work in the shops,' said Rawdon. 'Now, what about getting it there? That's going to cost some money, you know.'

Baynes explained to his colleagues. 'It would have to be dismantled and crated, shipped to the aerodrome, and re-erected over there. It means we shall have to take over a staff of mechanics with us.'

'Unless, of course, you flew it over from here,' said Rawdon.

Baynes glanced at him doubtfully. 'It's a very fast machine,' he said. 'There'd be a lot of risk in that, surely?'

Rawdon rubbed his chin. 'I don't know what it really does, what speed it lands at. Oh yes, it wouldn't be a very nice job. It's been done before with fast machines, you know.' He paused a little. 'It rather depends on what sort of a pilot you get for it.'

'It seems to me,' said one of the deputation, 'that if we're going to do this at all, we'd better do it properly and stand the extra expense of sending it by land.'

'I think so, too,' said Baynes.

'It's safest, certainly,' agreed Rawdon. 'You'll have to look sharp about it though. How long is it before the race?'

'Seventeen days,' said Baynes. 'There's no time to waste, but we can do it all right. About the pilot – Graham flew it before, I believe. We'd better get him again.'

'He's in Japan,' said Rawdon.

The other mentioned one or two pilots.

'The man I should choose, I think,' said the designer reflectively, 'would be a chap called Riley – Malcolm Riley. You remember him? Test pilot for Pilling-Henries at the end of the war. He did very well on their fast scouts – very well indeed. He's at Croydon now, I think.'

'You think he'd take it on?'

'I don't see why not. Anyway, I'd rather offer it to him than any of those other chaps, with Graham out of the way.'

Baynes got up. 'I'll see this chap Riley,' he said, 'and see if he can take it on. There's nobody better, you think?'

'I don't think so.'

So Riley was summoned to Baynes's club, and listened attentively while the scheme was expounded to him. When it was finished, he considered for a little.

'Well, I should be very glad to take it on,' he said at last. 'As you know, I've never flown in a race before, but I don't think I should let you down that way. By the way, how are you getting it there? Are you proposing to fly it out?'

The other shook his head. 'We discussed that with Captain Rawdon, and decided that the risk of damaging the machine was too great. No, it's going by sea.'

Riley nodded. 'That's the best way, of course. I saw it in the air once – lands at about eighty-five.'

'I believe so,' said Baynes. 'Well, we'll get the purchase through as soon as we can and get it up to Rawdon's place. I'll let you know when it gets there. And now, Captain Riley, we'd better put things on a business footing at once. Can you let me know – in a day or two – what your fee will be? For the test flights and the race combined.'

Riley glanced at him quickly. Then, 'This is an entirely private venture, as I understand it? It's financed by yourself and some other gentlemen?'

'That is so.'

'I should like my expenses,' said Riley, '– hotel bills and that sort of thing. And fifteen per cent of any prize money.'

There was a moment's pause. 'There won't be any prize money,' said Baynes quietly. 'The Laverock hasn't got a chance – unless by accident. You know that as well as I do. We're only putting it in for propaganda.'

'I guessed as much,' said Riley.

'I don't think we can let you do that, really,' said the other uneasily.

'It's a damn good advertisement for me as a pilot,' said Riley simply. 'I'd much rather have it that way. If it were a firm employing me it would be different.'

'Right you are then,' said Baynes. They stood up. 'I'll get the machine up to Rawdon's as soon as I can and let you know when it gets there. And I say, one thing more. I went round to one or two firms this morning to see if it was possible to insure it. They'd none of them touch it.'

Riley smiled. 'I don't suppose they would,' he said.

Morris had finished his paper on the three-ply fuselages working on an adaptation of the Principle of Least Work. It was not a bad paper at all; he had gone into the subject rather deeply mathematically and had arrived at certain definite results. He realized it was quite useless to leave his results in the form of differential equations, and had managed to evolve a set of relatively simple formulae which could be adapted to give the stresses accurately in most of the cases arising in aircraft work. When it was finished, he showed it to Rawdon.

The designer examined it in private; he was no mathematician, and hated to display the fact. Moreover, he knew well enough why Morris had shown it to him; he wanted more pay, and he'd only been in the firm a little over six months. It was absurd. But the paper undoubtedly was a sound one; he fingered it pensively. Most of it he did not fully understand; he knew the method and saw that the general lines upon which Morris had worked were likely to lead to a correct solution. He drew a little blunt stump of pencil from his waistcoat pocket, and pulled a writing-pad towards him. Taking the first bay of the rear fuselage of the FS1, their empirical calculations had given ... he pulled a loose-leaf ledger down from the shelf in front of him. That was it.

Now taking one of these odd-looking formulae of Morris's at the end of his paper – this would be the one. dz – what was dz? Oh yes, the thickness of the ply. That gave ...

He worked a little on the slide-rule. That gave a longeron of ·27 sq inch less sectional area. That would, if the same ratio were carried on throughout the structure, give a fuselage – slide-rule again – something like forty pounds, thirty-eight pounds lighter. That might very well be the case.

He always had had an idea that that fuselage had come out too heavy. It hadn't looked right in the shops. He'd wondered about that before.

He turned to the paper again. He had always thought that

this chap would be worth hanging on to. He wasn't getting enough now for his technical work, though he was drawing a very fair income out of the firm all told, with his piloting. His technical work was certainly worth another two pounds a week; he must have that, he supposed.

This paper ought to be published; it was good work. And when it was published other people would get to know of this man, and he would have to pay him still more if he was going to keep him. The designer sighed a little. He simply couldn't afford to go spending more money on his technical staff – the money wasn't coming into the firm nearly fast enough. They'd have to skip this next dividend – that was already decided. Lucky it was private money. The orders weren't coming in as they should. He had hoped for some sign of a production order for the two-seater – it had been up months ago and was a long way ahead of anything the Air Force had. And then there was the torpedo carrier coming on – no sign of a contract for either. This reconditioning of machines for foreign governments was coming to an end, and the firm couldn't keep going on the negligible profits from experimental machines.

Anyway, Morris must have his two pounds a week more now. He would see him at once. He pressed the bell; the door was opened by the little girl, who stood expectant. She was a good child and made his tea very well, exactly as he liked it.

'Tell Mr Morris to come and see me,' he said, 'and then go and wash your face. You've got jam on your cheek. I'll have my tea at a quarter past four today.'

The girl disappeared; the designer got up ponderously and stretched his immense form. He moved to his window and looked out over the aerodrome. He would ring up Bateman and go and talk to him this evening. Something must be done to raise the wind, to get a decent production order into the shops.

Morris came in.

'This seems to be very sound, from the rough check I've made on it, Mr Morris,' he said. 'You've been working on it for some time?'

'About three months,' said Morris. 'I think it's all right – I had it checked over by a more experienced mathematician than I.'

They discussed it for a little.

'Of course,' said the designer, 'if it comes out satisfactory in practice, we'd better adopt it. We'd better see about getting one or two models made up for test. If it doesn't cost too much. I'll see Mr Adamson about it. After we've verified it, you'd better see about getting it published.'

He turned to his seat. 'Let me have a copy some time, will you?'

Morris moved towards the door.

'One thing more, Mr Morris. You'll be drawing another two pounds a week for the technical work.'

Morris closed the door softly behind him. One or two more steps like that . . .

He crossed the open space in front of the offices. Suddenly Rawdon's window opened and the head of the designer appeared at it.

'Mr Morris! Come back a moment, if you please.'

As he re-entered the room, Rawdon turned to him. 'There's a job coming on that I think you'd better take charge of. Sit down. You remember the Laverock?'

'The Jenkinson Laverock?'

'Yes. Well, that's been bought privately and entered for the Brussels race. It's going to be reconditioned here, and we expect it very soon. Your friend, Captain Riley, is to fly it. I'm going to get on to whoever there is at the Jenkinson place on the phone and try and fix up to get hold of any performance figures that there may be on the machine. You'd better take that on.'

He gazed out of the window at a hawk, hovering above the aerodrome. 'They say he's got a big negative angle of incidence on his tail-plane when he's doing that,' he said at last.

He roused himself. 'It'll probably mean that you'll have to go down to the Jenkinson place and search through their files.'

'Will they let us have that stuff?'

71

'It's been arranged in the purchase that we should have any aerodynamic data about the machine there is. I don't suppose they've got very much; what one particularly wants to discover is the landing speed.'

Two days later, Morris travelled to the Jenkinson works. He explained his business, and was conducted through streets of desolate, empty buildings to the drawing-offices. Here he was introduced to one solitary clerk, who knew nothing about the Laverock and cared rather less.

'There's all the stuff we've got,' he said. 'You'd better have a look yourself.'

Half an hour later, Morris came upon what he was looking for. He found a wind-tunnel test of the model in its original form, before the wings had been cut down, and one or two sheets referring to the alterations. He searched through the mass again to verify that he had overlooked nothing, and made his way back to Southall.

Here he spent half an hour in calculation and took the results of it to Rawdon.

'I can't find out exactly what the wing section is,' he said. 'That makes the adjustment of this wind-channel test rather difficult.'

'RAF 15 modified, I think,' said the designer.

'I took it as that,' said Morris. 'That makes her stall at eighty-one – eighty-one and a half. I got the engine curve out of our own stuff, but it's for the Mark II Stoat – I think she's probably got the Mark I. That gives her a top speed of a hundred and eighty-five.'

'She won't win the Brussels race on that,' muttered Rawdon. Morris was silent.

'And she lands at eighty-one, you say . . .'

Two or three days later the Laverock arrived on a lorry and was deposited in the erecting-shop. She created a mild sensation on arrival; every draughtsman in the works seemed to have business in the erecting-shop that afternoon. Certainly she was a very pretty little piece of work. The months of neglect in storage had passed lightly over her and she still retained the appearance of newness under her dirt, the show finish that the Jenkinson people had been famous for. The engine came in for a certain amount of inspection, too; apparently it only differed in slight detail from the Mark II, and was supposed to give approximately the same power. Only James, the engine draughtsman, shook his head over it.

'They had a lot of trouble with the Mark I Stoat at Farnborough,' he said.

Malcolm Riley arrived next day, and spent the morning in examining the machine in detail as it was being erected. When he could think of nothing else to inspect, he sat down on a pile of lumber and looked at it; it was in this attitude that Morris found him.

'Cheer oh,' said Riley. 'What do you think of that? Think it'll fly?'

'Don't you worry about that,' said Morris cheerfully. 'It'll do all the flying you want it to, and a bit more.'

'Thank you,' said Riley dryly, 'that had already occurred to me. The question seems to be not so much will it fly as will it stop flying – in an ordinary aerodrome. Eighty-one, you say?'

'Eighty-one and a half.'

Riley turned and looked at him. 'I hear you're doing pretty well in this show,' he said. 'Rawdon said something about a paper on fuselages.'

'Nobody seems to have any mathematics in this business.'

'I've never heard that mathematics cut much ice in aircraft before.'

'It doesn't really,' said Morris. 'Only now and again one has a lucky shot like this.'

'I never got any of those lucky shots,' said Riley. 'But perhaps that's because I don't know mathematics. Tell me, is there anywhere I can put up round here? I want to be on the spot for a bit and see this thing through.'

So Riley took a room in the neighbourhood and haunted the shops for a day or two. Presently the machine was ready.

Morris was working in the office when he heard the sudden roar of an unaccustomed engine.

'Who's that?' he asked at large.

73

'Running up the Stoat for Riley, aren't they?' said the engine draughtsman. 'Sounds a bit wobbly.'

Morris slipped from his seat and made his way down to the aerodrome. He must not miss this.

Riley flew the Laverock very steadily off the ground. There was nothing sensational about the performance. The machine accelerated very quickly and he got her tail up within ten yards or so. After a relatively long run she 'unstuck' and went off in a straight line for Uxbridge, climbing steadily but not fast. In a little time he was seen to be turning and came back over the aerodrome at a good speed, a white glimmer against the blue sky. He circled for a little, then throttled down and came in to land. He slipped down over the hedge at the far side of the aerodrome half a mile away, and flattened out close above the ground. The machine floated on over the grass, without touching, in a nasty-looking, unconventional manner for some hundreds of yards at a high speed.

The little group by the hangars stirred uneasily.

Once the tail dropped a little as if to land; the machine had not yet lost way and rose a foot or two from the grass. Finally she sank, touched lightly, rose again, touched again and held the ground this time, ran along, and stopped near the hangars. Riley taxied her in, jumped down, and came to meet them.

'Don't care about that engine,' he said shortly. 'Not giving half the power it ought to.'

Rawdon and he detached themselves from the group and walked up to the office. Rawdon closed the door behind them.

'Well,' said Riley. 'I had her all out at about a thousand feet – she only did a hundred and fifty-nine on the Pitot. I don't think that engine's doing its work; she can certainly do better than that. I didn't care about the feel of it much. It ran very rough, and seemed a bit sluggish on the throttle, you know. It ran pretty regularly, but for the roughness.'

Rawdon pulled down a file of curves and selected one.

'What were the revs?'

'Thirteen-twenty.'

'Only that – full out on the level? That makes it nearly fifty horsepower down – forty-eight point five.'

'I'd say it was fully that,' said Riley feelingly.

They discussed a possible deficiency in the propeller for a little and abandoned it as unlikely. 'It was designed for her as a racing machine, after all,' said Riley.

Rawdon whistled a little tune between his teeth. 'Did you notice the landing speed?'

'Not when she touched. I looked at it as she was doing that ballooning stunt over the aerodrome; it was rather under ninety – say eighty-seven.'

There was a brief silence in the office.

'The worst of it is,' said Rawdon, 'there's not so much time.' He turned up a calendar. 'If she's going to be packed and crated and shipped over we must allow ten days before the race. That means we ought to start dismantling her the day after tomorrow.'

'I'd be inclined,' said Riley, 'to have that engine down for a top overhaul. It's no good sending her over in her present condition. She'd be a laughing-stock. Let's have her down and see if we can get her any better. Get a man down from the Blundell people – a man who knows all about this Stoat. Then after that I can fly her over in time for the race.'

Rawdon was plainly uneasy. 'I'll ring up Baynes,' he said, 'and tell him about it – ask him to come down this afternoon if he can spare the time. I should think myself that that's the only thing to do, unless he decides to send it over as it is and hope for the best.'

But the decision lay with Riley.

So the Laverock was taken to the engine shop and the Stoat extracted with a tackle. On the bench there seemed nothing in particular the matter with the engine. A gentleman came down on a motor-cycle from the makers, took off his coat, and worked on it for three days, assisted by the usual staff. Finally he expressed himself satisfied.

'But they're no class, the Mark I,' he added, wiping his hands on a piece of waste.

Two days later the machine was ready for flying. It was late one evening when Riley took it up again; Morris and one or

75

two others stayed to watch. The promoters of the venture were also present.

The flight was much the same as before. The landing was every bit as unpleasant to watch, though he seemed to be able to do it with certainty, given enough space. The report was better.

'I got her up to about a hundred and seventy-eight,' said Riley afterwards to Morris. 'I think that's about all she's going to do. One might get another mile or two out of her on the day – I rather doubt it. They're putting a fairing on the tail-skid for me now; I'll have her up again tomorrow morning. Come and have supper at my place; we'll come back afterwards and have a look how they've done that skid.'

It was dark when they returned. Riley went on down to the shop, and Morris turned into the offices to fetch some data that he needed for his private work. He stayed for a time in the deserted office, musing over his papers. Then he went down to the erecting-shop, brilliant with arc-lamps.

The men had finished work upon the tail-skid and were brewing tea over a blow-lamp preparatory to knocking off. Morris examined the skid critically. They hadn't made a bad job of it.

'Where's Captain Riley?' he asked one of the men.

The man jerked his thumb over his shoulder. 'Out on the aer'drome, I think, sir.' He moved away down the shop through the shadowy aeroplanes, softly whistling the air from *Samson and Delilah*. Morris walked to a crack between the great sliding doors and stood looking out into the darkness; behind him the song was gathering strength and throbbing plaintively between the long iron walls.

He moved out on to the aerodrome. It was a bright, starlit night, calm and warm. If it stayed like that, Riley ought to have little difficulty in getting that machine across ... though it was not exactly a job that Morris would have cared to tackle himself.

'Riley?' he called quietly.

There was no answer. He walked on a little past the hangars, a little sobered by the quiet and the darkness. This was as quiet as an Oxford night ... His mind went off at a tangent:

Fair Helena, who more engilds the night
Than all yon fiery oes and eyes of light ...
Fair Helena ...

He smiled a little to himself and walked on past the hangars. Beyond them somebody was smoking a cigarette on a pile of lumber under the hedge.

'That you, Morris?' asked Riley.

Morris sat down beside him. 'They've made a pretty little job of your skid,' he said. 'Probably put another hundred yards on her to carry in landing.'

The other grunted sourly. 'All very well for you to talk,' he said. 'They won't let you go near it, let alone fly it.'

'I sometimes lie awake o'nights,' retorted Morris, 'sweating blood for fear they'll come and ask me to.'

There was a brief silence. Morris suddenly wished his last remark unsaid.

'Oh damn it,' said Riley very quietly. 'What does it matter. It's got to go over. I tell you, if I backed out of this thing now, I'd just hate myself.'

'I know,' said Morris.

'No you don't. You see' – he paused, searching for words with which to frame his ideas – 'I've done this sort of thing all my life, motor-bikes and cars and aeroplanes. It's the only thing I know. I don't go in for other things much – amusements. This is the only interest I've got ... I suppose really it's the only thing I live for. I've got nothing else. It works all right – only sometimes one seems to have missed things, somehow.'

'It doesn't fill one's life – this,' said Morris.

The other smiled. 'It's done well enough for me.'

Morris pursued his subject. 'One ought to go about more, meet more people,' he said. 'It's narrowing this life.' He glanced at the other. 'You ought to be married,' he said gently, 'a hearty old man like you.'

Riley did not answer for a little. 'I suppose so,' he said at last. 'But I'm not like you or Stenning. I don't think I've ever been in love – really in love, that is. Somehow, I cut away from all my people and took up this racing and flying. One doesn't regret it. But in this game one doesn't meet the girls that one would want to marry, the girls that one could run a life with as partners. In some ways, it's just as well. I've got no ties, nobody dependent on me, nobody but myself to think for.'

Morris had simply nothing to say. He was amazed at this outburst that he had provoked, delivered so quietly, in so matter-of-fact a manner. Something showed for the moment behind the man's reserve, something of a great loneliness.

'You know when you go to the pictures,' said Riley steadily, 'and you see one of those American films where the heroine is one of the most beautiful young things on God's earth. She's not really. She's been divorced two or three times, she probably dopes – you'd hate her if you met her. Well, it's like that in getting married. I suppose I've funked it – I don't know . . .'

'The materialization of an ideal,' muttered Morris.

The other did not seem to hear, but spat a fragment of tobacco from his lip and went off on another tack.

'It seems to me that one can manage in different ways about this . . . love. One can live one's life to the full, or one can live it wisely. It's like a band of light – sunlight, you know – that contains every colour there is, all mixed up together. You can take it as it comes. It's not specially beautiful, but it's healthy enough – you can have a pretty good time in it. You can get one of those funny things with a crystal – spectroscopes – and split it all up into violet and green and yellow and orange and red. It's still the same life. You can have a great love and great pain – they go together – or you can have it all mixed up together in a sort of steady dullness, indifference.'

'One never gets anything worth having without paying for it,' said Morris. 'It's not possible.'

The other glanced at him, smiling a little.

'That's so,' he said. 'One can take it either way – I took it the dull way. Or, I don't know that I did really . . . it just came like that. Somehow, one way or another, one misses the summer of one's life – it turns out wet and dull. But one gets compensations. One never gets the disappointment of what you thought was going to be a fine day really turning out wet. And sometimes, if you're lucky, you get a little sort of a St Martin's summer, a pleasure that you've really got no right to expect. That's how I've always felt about this business – I couldn't get on without this aviation now. Something to help along, something to work for. Other people get that with their wives, I suppose.'

There was a silence on the wood pile.

Riley glanced at Morris in the dim starlight. 'It doesn't pay,' he said quietly. 'Not in the long run. Don't you forget it. One ought to be married. In a way, one needs it as one gets older. One wants ... I don't know what. Companionship, perhaps.'

Morris cleared his throat. 'I was engaged to be married once,' he said, looking straight ahead of him. 'Or, no. I was very near it – only I broke it off.'

Riley smiled in the darkness. 'It's always like that. Now I suppose you want it on again.'

'It was better off. She was your cousin, Riley. You remember you introduced us – up at Oxford.'

'I did not know,' said Riley quietly. 'You got engaged to Helen?'

'I'd better let you know the whole thing,' said Morris. 'I'd like to.' He paused, searching for words. 'We got to know each other pretty well at Oxford, you know. Going about together. And then I got that job in rubber that looked such a good thing, and I asked her to marry me. It would have meant an engagement of about eighteen months.'

'Did she accept then?'

'She asked for a month to think it over. And in that time the rubber business went wrong, and I hadn't a job or a chance of one. So I saw her and broke it off.'

'Do you know at all what answer you'd have got?' asked Riley gently.

'I know that,' said Morris. 'We were ... pretty far gone. It wasn't an easy job breaking it off like that.' He paused. 'One always hopes,' he said, 'that one'll be in a better position one day. In about two years' time, I think. I think she'll wait for me.'

He did not seem inclined to say any more, and Riley sat on, gazing over the dim aerodrome, desperately puzzled. He knew that Helen Riley was engaged to be married to Roger Lechlane, and was to be married quite soon.

Riley threw away his cigarette and got up off the pile of lumber. It was characteristic of the man that he could not do anything about this affair on the spur of the moment, that he must mentally make his rough copy and keep it for a day or two to see if it were all right. 'Good luck to you,' he said. 'Let me know if ever I'm any use. I'll do what I can when the time comes, if there's any opposition. I don't suppose there'll be much, though. Things have got easier in the last few years . . .'

Morris did not catch his meaning, and they moved towards the gate. 'When are you going over, then?' he asked.

'Thursday, I expect. So long.'

Riley walked slowly back to his rooms. He had funked telling Morris what he knew; he wanted time to think it over. It would be a pretty hard knock for Morris. He was puzzled; there seemed to be no logic in the affair at all, no rhyme or reason. If he really had been working all this time in the expectation of being able to marry Helen . . . He had said that she was waiting. How the devil had he known? Anyhow, he had known wrong, because she wasn't waiting at all. She was going to marry Lechlane, pretty soon. Morris must have been dreaming.

It was a confused business. He had only heard of this engagement a day or two before; it had surprised and worried him. He knew Helen well, and had met Lechlane once or twice; he did not think they had anything in common at all. But did that matter in marriage? He thought it did – he liked to think it did. He had wondered what the dickens the girl was about, and had correctly attributed it to sheer listlessness. Anything to get away from Bevil Crossways.

But why on earth wasn't she waiting for Morris? No, probably Morris hadn't told her that he was coming back; he wasn't the sort of man to do things by halves. But in that case she ought to know.

The more he thought about it the more convinced he became that she ought to know.

He did not think this marriage with Lechlane would be a happy one for Helen. She wasn't his sort at all. Morris was a good deal nearer to her; he imagined that they had a good deal in common. She was probably piqued with Morris for jilting her. If she had ever really cared about him that would disappear with explanation.

But it was a risky thing, this messing about in other people's affairs. He didn't know; he might do the wrong thing. But anyway, she ought to be told, ought to have all the facts before her. And if he did make a fool of himself, what of it? It wouldn't be the first time.

He would write to her.

He began to fumble slowly in his breast pocket for a pencil and a scrap of paper, thinking of phrases that he could put this delicate subject into. He would have to make a rough copy of this letter, probably half a dozen. He was so bad at writing.

Perhaps it would be better if he went and saw her personally. That would be much the best way. There was not much time before this race, though, and he was very clear that she must know at the earliest possible moment before the affair went too far. He would be over in Belgium for a least a week. How much time was there before? He would have to take the machine up tomorrow; then, if all went well, he would fly it over two days later. He might be able to fit in a flying visit to Bevil Crossways. He could go down there tomorrow afternoon and come back the next morning. It was short notice to give them; he could fake up some excuse and telegraph in the morning – they were used to him. He smiled a little. Lechlane didn't do that sort of thing, he'd bet.

That was it. He would go down to Bevil Crossways tomorrow and talk to Helen. He had always been good friends with her; he had been largely instrumental in getting her sent to

Oxford. He could talk to her quietly alone, tell her what Morris had told him, explain things that she might want to know, tell her Morris's prospects. It was always so much better to do these things personally.

He took the Laverock up again next morning and got three more miles out of her, reaching a speed of one hundred and eighty-one miles an hour. This, curiously enough, coincided almost exactly with the estimated speed from wind-channel figures – a coincidence only too infrequent. He managed to steal a glance at the air speed indicator as he landed; it registered eighty-three miles an hour. He thought he could have brought her in a little slower than that.

He had telegraphed to Bevil Crossways announcing his arrival and, with a bit of a scramble, caught the afternoon train down to Gloucestershire. It was good for him to get away for a little before this race, if only for one night. He enjoyed travelling like a gentleman in a train for once in a way. He travelled first-class; it accentuated the pleasurable feeling that he was not responsible for the transport. That responsibility was one that he seldom managed to evade nowadays; whether on the road or in the air he was always controlling the machine. He was tired; it was time he took a decent holiday. He hadn't had a proper holiday since the war. Perhaps after this race . . . he would ask the people at the Crossways if they could have him for a little then.

At the station he found that no car had been sent to meet him. This was very unusual; he wondered if by any chance they had not got his wire. In that case his arrival would be an unexpected pleasure for his hostess. He took one of the station taxis and drove the three miles through the sweet-smelling, stone-walled lanes. He lay back in the old car, very content. Yes, he needed a holiday.

They turned in at the lodge gates and ran up the half-mile of drive, through the rhododendron coppice. There was the house, mellow and grey in the afternoon light, and there on the steps was Helen, waiting for him.

She ran down towards him as the car came to a standstill.

'Oh, Malcolm,' she cried. 'I'm so awfully glad you've come.

I've sent the car for Dr Hastings – Mother's away and I'm all alone.'

It seemed that old Sir James Riley had fallen down two steps out of his bedroom into the passage half an hour before. He was eighty-one years old.

It was immensely unfortunate. Lady Riley had dimly foreseen the possibility of such a disaster and had frequently urged him to move into the south bedroom, used only as a spare room for infrequent visitors. Tenacious of his prestige, the old man had clung to his bedroom approached by the two steps he knew so well. It gave him a feeling of independence to be two steps above the level of the passage; moreover, to give in over this matter of the room would have been a confession of that weakness whose approach he was determined to defer as long as possible. And now the expected had happened. For once the immense foresight of the Lechlanes was at fault, in that the brass carpet-rails on the two steps had not been replaced by oaken ones. Brass rails had to be taken out to be cleaned, and servants seemed to have grown so careless nowadays.

Still, it might have been much worse. No very great damage had been done; the old man had suffered a severe shock and would not be himself for many days. It would be as well, said the doctor, if someone were to sit up with him all night in case of further trouble; Helen took the first watch and Malcolm relieved her at one. As he sat by the side of the peacefully slumbering old gentleman, he turned over the position in his mind. He had had no opportunity to speak to Helen on the subject that he had come for; he saw now that there would be no opportunity forthcoming. Well, it must wait. He must not waste any time over it, though. He would write to Helen immediately after the race, telling her about this business of Morris. He could put it quite simply and briefly, and could suggest that if she wanted any further details, he would come down for a few days – otherwise he would forget all about it. That would be the sort of letter to send; he would post it immediately after the race. That would give him two or three days in which to concoct it.

Back at Southall there was not much to be done. He packed a suitcase and took it up to London, to Baynes, with whom he made the final arrangements. Baynes was going over the evening before he started and was to meet him on Brussels aerodrome when he landed; he was to wait till after lunch before starting.

He spent the evening gossiping with Morris and went to bed early. He was not feeling so awfully fit; it was a pity he had had to be up all last night. He tumbled into bed and slept soundly for ten hours; in the morning he was himself again.

Morris came down to the hangars with Rawdon the next afternoon to see him off. The Laverock had been smartened up a good deal since last she flew; all paintwork had been carefully cleaned and touched up, all woodwork polished over. She was painted a pure white, only relieved by dark-blue registration letters on the wings and fuselage and a dark-blue spinner to the propeller. All her rigging wires were blued, the struts were white, and to the rudder somebody had fixed a little blue silk streamer.

'She's a pretty little machine,' said Morris.

Rawdon nodded. 'Make them sit up with her finish,' he said, 'if not with her speed.'

Riley was taking a last look round the machine, dressed in a tweed suit and a filthy old trench coat, his soiled flying-helmet the only badge of office. Then he got into the machine, levering himself down into the tiny cockpit. He called Rawdon up to him as he was settling into his seat; the designer went and stood beside him.

'I'll send you a wire to let you know I got there all right,' said Riley.

'Right you are. You've got that paper of weights and data? And don't forget what the Blundell people told us – about the Benzole. You'll be able to get it over there – Baynes fixed up all that, I know.'

Riley nodded. 'By the way, you might have my car put under cover, will you? It's in front of the offices. Now we'll get her running.'

'Good luck,' said the designer, and stepped back. The propeller was hauled over and presently the engine burst into life. Riley ran her up slowly, three men clinging to the tail, shut her down again, and waved his hand. The chocks were pulled from under the wheels; he waved again to Rawdon and Morris, and the Laverock moved slowly out over the aerodrome. A hundred yards away he faced into the wind and stopped, remaining stationary with the engine ticking over.

Then the low rumble rose to a higher note, and higher yet. The Laverock seemed to lean forward and began to move. Almost immediately the tail came off the ground; she spun along over the grass and into the air, a wonderful, delicate little thing.

They watched her as she circled the aerodrome on a great climbing turn, as she headed for the south; watched her till she was merely a speck against a cloud, far in the distance. Then she was gone.

'He's coming down at Lympne for Customs,' said Rawdon.

And now the story must be told without embellishment, a plain record of the facts. It ought to have succeeded, this little venture. It was a generous thing – but even generous things may come to failure. It failed, principally through lack of time for the proper preparation of the machine, as so many enterprises in aviation have failed. But the real cause of the disaster lay farther back than that, in the circumstances that led to Britain being represented in a race of such importance by such an entry. If we attempt to follow the cause of this little disaster back still further we quickly get beyond our depth in a morass of arguments hinging on the lack of money to enter a machine properly, the poverty of the British aircraft industry, the defence of the Empire, and the payment of the American debt. The pound goes up in New York – an aeroplane comes down in Kent. There is little connection? Perhaps that is so.

There was only one man, apparently, who actually saw the Laverock come down. He was digging in his cottage garden, which stood beside the biggest meadow for miles around. He was accustomed to aeroplanes. He had never seen one close to, because they never landed anywhere near, though there had been one or two round about in the war. But they passed over his head every day, often as many as a dozen in a day. He had heard they went to Paris and other foreign places. That was what they said at the 'Admiral'.

So when, that afternoon, he heard a rumble in the air, he had not particularly remarked it till it stopped suddenly. True, he thought afterwards on being questioned that it had been a little irregular in its note, but that may only have been the effect of suggestion. What really drew his attention was the stoppage of the noise; he lifted his head and straightened his stiff back to look for the thing.

Sure enough, there it was up there, a pretty little white thing it looked against the sky, going round and round in big circles and coming down with each one. It was coming down somewhere – it was quite close to the ground.

It was coming down in Mr Jameson's meadow.

It seemed very small, and suddenly it seemed to be going very fast, fast as a train, faster. It barely scraped over the hedge into the meadow and flew along just above the grass, in perfect silence. Well, why didn't it stop and settle – flying on like that at such a pace! It couldn't now! it wouldn't have time to stop before it fell into the dike.

There – it had touched lightly and risen a little. It touched again, very close to the dike. It would have to go up again; it should have landed before, right away back.

It was going up; it was hopping the dike to land again on the other side. But it did not seem happy in the air this time. It went up quite steeply and seemed to hang for a moment in the air, some twenty feet up. Then it put its nose down in an odd way and plunged down to the earth on the far side of the dike. It hit with an ugly, crunching noise and seemed to collapse with the impact, tipped forward, stood on its nose for a moment, rolled over on to its back, and lay still.

It was a considerable time before it occurred to him that perhaps there might have been a man in it.

The news came to Morris that afternoon as he was getting out some preliminary figures for the new Commercial Sesquiplane.

The Sesquiplane, built in any size, was rather a new departure in aeroplane design, and introduced some novel features. Rawdon was keen on it; Morris believed he had an order for the machine.

Adamson, the works manager, came swiftly into the office, to Morris's desk.

'Come outside a moment, Mr Morris,' he said incisively.

Morris followed him out into the road.

'Riley's down near Hurstony,' he said, 'crashed. The police have just telephoned through. I'm having the Ratcatcher got out; I want you to go down there.'

Rawdon came out of the offices and joined them.

'I gather from the police that Riley isn't dangerously hurt,' he said. 'They say he's got two ribs broken. He was conscious when they got him out – in a good deal of pain. He was able to give full instuctions about letting us know. They've taken him to the cottage hospital in Hurstony.'

'I'd better go and see him,' said Morris. 'I know him pretty well.'

Adamson nodded. 'I want you to take the Ratcatcher down with a couple of mechanics – I've told them off. Then you must get the wings off the machine and get it loaded on to a lorry and bring it back here. You'd better land there – it's three and a half miles south-east of Hurstony – and leave the men to get the wings off her while you go and find a lorry.'

'Go and see Riley first,' said Rawdon. 'In the cottage hospital. You might ring us up and let us know how he is. And do everything you can for him. I'll be responsible for any expense, a separate room, extra nursing, or anything of that sort. See that he's made really comfortable.'

'You'll want some money probably,' said Adamson. They moved towards his office.

'Damn it, I wish we hadn't let him do it,' muttered Rawdon.

A rumble from beyond the hangars indicated that the engine of the Ratcatcher was running. Morris came out of the office, fetched a helmet and coat from beside his desk in the drawing-office, and went to the machine. He found the mechanics waiting for him.

He taxied the machine out on to the aerodrome, took off, and headed for Hurstony. It was rotten luck. He supposed it had been engine failure – Riley must have turned her over on landing. Well, that wasn't so very serious – but how had he managed to bust a rib if that was it? He'd seen lots of people turn a somersault in the war and come out as right as rain. Anyhow, he'd soon know – already they were well clear of London. It was rotten luck about the machine – Riley had told him how it had come to be entered for the race. Poor old man – he must be feeling sick as muck at having crashed it. It was a wicked little machine for a forced landing.

He was approaching Hurstony. One of the men, seated in the cockpit behind him, stood up against the rush of air and touched Morris on the shoulder. He was pointing forward over the nose of the machine and shouting something in his ear. Morris could not hear what he was saying, but he followed the direction in which he pointed with his eyes.

Right ahead of them in the distance was a large field, crossed near one end by a dark line. On the farther side of this line was a patch of white upon the ground, crumpled and misshapen like a dropped handkerchief, surrounded by a small group of people. That would be the Laverock.

Morris flew on for a little, then throttled his engine and came quite low. He came down to about a hundred feet, flew over the field, and noted the dike running across. It was a good level field; he could land in the larger half of it. That, he supposed, was what Riley had tried for.

He circled round into the wind, slipped in over the hedge, and put her down into the field. She touched lightly, ran along, and came to rest about a hundred yards from the dike; almost before she had stopped the men were out of her and running to the wreck. Morris followed them.

The Laverock lay on her back on the farther side of the dike; from the story of the one spectator and from the evidence of the ground, Morris was able to reconstruct the accident. Riley seemed to have landed on the right side of the dike, and had touched the ground much too close to be able to stop before it. Rather than run straight into it, he seemed to have hoicked her off the ground again to hop it, after she had really lost flying speed. It was a thing that in the hands of such a pilot as Riley might well have come off. Apparently she had risen higher than was necessary, perhaps because he had had to give a violent heave on the stick to get her off the ground at all. Morris was puzzled. It was not like Riley, that; he knew the delicacy of his touch so well. Perhaps he should have taken a holiday before taking on such a job as this – Morris could not say. The machine had stalled hopelessly, put her nose down, and crashed.

The nose of the machine was crushed and shapeless. She must have hit very heavily upon it.

With the help of the spectators, Morris got her turned right way up. In the cockpit one end of the safety belt was broken from its stay; the instrument board in front of the pilot was split in two, and dials crushed and broken. On the seat lay a glove, one of Riley's gauntlets, mutely eloquent. Morris picked it up and put it in his pocket.

He stood for a moment, fingering the broken belt, looking at the crushed instruments. One of the men came up and touched him on the arm. 'Better get the wings off, hadn't we?' he said.

'Oh … yes,' said Morris. 'Carry on. I'm going into the town now – at once. I'll get a lorry there and bring it out. Carry on and get her ready.'

He commandeered the farmer's Ford and was driven into Hurstony. He found the cottage hospital without much difficulty, and was ushered into a bare little waiting-room, a little sunlit place of white paint and green distemper. Morris sat down and waited. Outside in the street a man was walking along selling the local newspaper, clanging a dinner bell to announce his advent; inside there was a quick step dying away along a tiled passage, and a faint odour of iodoform. Morris waited, uneasily. His hands were very dirty from the machine, his hair was rumpled, and he had no hat but the helmet in his hand.

He waited. The dinner bell died into the distance.

A heavier step sounded along the tiled passage; the door opened and Morris rose to his feet. It was a surgeon, a small, dapper little man with a sharp, tanned face, carrying a green pencil in one hand.

'Good afternoon,' said Morris.

'Good afternoon.' The surgeon glanced sharply at the helmet he carried in his hand. 'You have come about the airman, Mr Riley?'

'I've come to take all responsibility for him,' said Morris. 'I represent his firm – the Rawdon Aircraft Company. I want to make all arrangements possible for his comfort – as regards money, if that is of any consequence.'

'I see,' said the other. He did not volunteer any remark, but stood tapping his pencil delicately on one thumb-nail, staring out of the window up the street.

'How is he?'

The other glanced at him. 'You are a personal friend of his? You have been very quick in coming.'

'I know him pretty well,' said Morris.

There was a pause; the surgeon mechanically tapped his pencil on his nail and gazed out of the window at a great cumulus of cloud, beginning to take a faint, rosy colour from the sunset. Somewhere a thrush was calling impudently through the evening; in the bare little room the silence grew pregnant.

'I see,' said Morris quietly. 'He is very bad?'

The surgeon turned from the window and put the pencil in his pocket.

'He is dying,' he said simply. 'You must telephone for his people.'

6

Riley died without regaining consciousness, early the following morning. Morris had telephoned to his invalid brother Benjamin, who arrived with his wife late that evening. But Riley said nothing intelligible. Once, indeed, he seemed to rouse a little and muttered something about bright colours and a spectroscope – it was queer that such an instrument should come into his head. But then, as the nurses told them, nobody could tell what a sick man would say.

His death made a lot of work for his brother. Malcolm had died without leaving any will, and his affairs were in terrible confusion. He had kept very much to himself since the war; nobody had much sympathized with his mode of earning a living and he had not talked about his schemes very much. When Benjamin came to examine his papers, he was amazed at the little he had known about this brother of his, and how much he must now pick up as best he could from old notebooks and receipted bills crushed into forgotten pockets. It was known, for example, that he had had a sort of venture in the Isle of Wight for a time, carrying passengers in aeroplanes. What nobody could discover was where the money had come from, whether there were any outstanding credits or liabilities, who his partners had been – if any. And this had been only one of many such mysteries. His firm at Croydon had written at once to square their account, and had enclosed a handsome cheque which he seemed to have earned by flying to Vienna – of all places. But they added the disquieting information that he had been under contract to race for some firm (unknown) at Brooklands a week or two after his death. It was all very difficult for one who had no idea where or what Brooklands was beyond that it was a place where racing-motors went.

His very death had been something of a mystery. A man called Major Baynes had called and explained the circumstances of the business, and had suggested his willingness to secure some provision for any dependants. As there were no dependants, his financial responsibilities seemed to be entirely at an end. Malcolm had apparently been risking his life for sheer love of the thing. There had never been the least hint of romance about Malcolm, but in the hospital they had found round his neck a thin gold chain with part of a silver and opal pendant attached to it. This, for some reason or other, worried his brother very much; it suggested a whole host of undreamed of complications.

For some days Benjamin struggled with these difficulties from his couch; the sudden journey to Hurstony had knocked up his heart again, never at its best since he was gassed in 1915. He did not see his way in this business, and he was too ill to think much about anything. As a solicitor he was competent enough to deal with all the questions involved; as a man he did not seem to have the strength. Somebody ought to go down to this place Brooklands and find out what Malcolm had been doing down there, and if there was any property of his there. There might be a motor-car, perhaps several motor-cars. And somebody ought to go to this aerodrome at Croydon and see what was there – if anything.

In this extremity, Benjamin bethought him of Roger Lechlane. Roger was a cousin of sorts – anyway, he was one of the family, and could be trusted to make these inquiries delicately and tactfully. It seemed to him that Lechlane would be a very good man to see about the active part of this business – that was, if he would take it on. He did not know very clearly what Lechlane was doing, or whether he would have time to spare for this business. But Lechlane was a secretary, and secretaries could get time off more easily than those who were bound by the routine of an office.

So Lechlane was summoned, and undertook to spend one or two odd days ferreting round these queer places in the suburbs. He returned after his first visit to Brooklands and dined with Benjamin at his flat.

'I found out one or two facts of importance,' he said. 'He had a workshop down there – a sort of shed full of tools. One of those keys you gave me fitted the door; I marked it. I found a man who told me a good deal, too. He hadn't any cars of his own there, only the tools that are in the workshop. He used to drive for the Phillips Company; you'd better send them a letter.'

'I wish to goodness Malcolm had told me something about all this,' said Benjamin fretfully. 'There was a letter from the Phillips Company in that case of his – I forget what that one was about. There's the case over on the sideboard – you might have a look through it and find that letter and read it out.'

Lechlane took the case and opened it. It was a battered old relic, stuffed full of letters and bills. Lechlane spread them out on the table; Benjamin watched him from the couch with half-closed eyes. Thank heavens he had found somebody to do the work of this business, under his direction. There could be no better man for the job; a friend of the family and a man, moreover, who knew something of Law.

'This is it,' said Lechlane. 'It seems to be a bill for eighteen pounds sixteen and threepence – detailed, for repair to a car and general overhaul. That must be his two-seater, I should think.'

'We can pay that out of the Croydon money,' said Benjamin. 'There was another letter about that car, came today. From some friend of his, a man called Morris who wrote from Southall, who wanted to buy the car at a valuation. I think that must be the man who was at the hospital that evening. I put the letter with the case, over on the sideboard.'

'Better let him have it,' said Lechlane. 'You don't want it, do you? It's very shabby – not a car that one would care to go about in.'

Benjamin did not answer. Lechlane turned his attention to the contents of the case, mostly bills and receipts. These disposed of, he felt inside the case for anything that might have been overlooked. There was nothing in evidence. As he put it down, however, it seemed to be stiffer, to have more bulk and backbone than it should have, being empty. He picked it up and examined it more closely. There was a secret pocket in the lining, the sort of thing that might be intended to carry notes. He pulled it out and two pencilled letters fell on to the table, one short and the other long. He opened the short one first; it ran:

Dear Sir,
With reference to the speed attainable by the early models of the Pilling-Henries single-seater fighter in your issue of the 10th inst, I can assure you that you are completely mistaken in your information. I had the pleasure [crossed out and 'privilege' substituted] of testing this machine in all its forms and I can assure you ...

The last words were scored out, and the letter ended in a small sketch of the head and shoulders of a girl, and another of a dropsical-looking pig. Lechlane turned to the other one.

This was a longer letter, written in a crabbed little hand upon two sheets, with many alterations and erasures. It took Lechlane quite a long time to read. When he had finished, he turned it over and read it a second time. Then he stole a glance at Benjamin. Benjamin was apparently in that comatose condition which precedes sleep; he was far from taking any active interest in the things of this world. Lechlane slipped the letter into his pocket.

'Benjamin,' he said distinctly.

The other opened his eyes.

'I've sorted out these and put all the bills on one side. All told, leaving out that one from the motor company, they come to about twenty-two pounds thirteen shillings.'

'Thanks,' murmured Benjamin.

'There was another pocket in this case,' continued Lechlane, 'but it only had a letter to a technical paper in it – a rough copy. It's unfinished.'

'Tear it up,' said Benjamin. 'I found a lot of that sort of stuff. What worries me is this aeroplane business of his; I seem to remember him telling me that he had three aeroplanes somewhere or other. It seems a lot.'

Two days later, Lechlane made a pilgrimage to Croydon aerodrome. He reported that evening to Benjamin.

'It's quite right about those aeroplanes,' he said. 'Only one

94

of them seems to have gone – there are two there now. I saw them. And he had a partner in the business, a man called Stenning, a pilot on an air line to Paris. He'd just gone off when I arrived. I left a note suggesting that he should come here to supper next Sunday – I thought that would be the best thing to do. I expect he'll know a lot, and anyway we can fix up this business of the aeroplanes then.'

So Stenning arrived on Sunday evening. It was a more prosperous Stenning altogether than a year before. He had made good as an air line pilot, having that steadiness and shrewd mechanical sense which apparently enable a man to fly day in and day out without suffering the least ill effect. He took no liberties with himself physically; he had a thoroughly good job and he meant to stick to it. He was making money at the rate of seven hundred a year with plenty of holidays – his firm were careful with their pilots. There seemed no reason why he should not go on flying for another five years or so, and then get a management job on some aerodrome.

Supper over, they got to business.

'There aren't any liabilities,' he said, 'except the rent of the hangar, which we've been dividing. One always hopes to get somebody to buy those machines – we've got rid of one. Riley said we'd better keep them till next spring and then sell them for scrap if we've still got them.'

He told them all he knew of Riley's other ventures.

'Then there was no one else but you two in the Isle of Wight Company?' asked Benjamin finally.

'Only one, a friend of Riley's from Oxford. We paid him regular wages. He had no legal share in it, though he got a percentage of the profits. A chap called Morris.'

'That would be the man who wants the car,' said Benjamin.

Lechlane lit a cigarette. 'Seems to me,' he said indifferently, 'that I must have met him. Do you remember what his college was? The man I mean looked more like a corpse than anything else.'

Stenning stiffened a little. 'He was a very good pilot,' he said, awkwardly defensive. 'I never knew his college. He was Oxford, Riley said. Riley said he knew a lot of mathematics.'

'That's the man,' said Lechlane. 'What's he doing now?'

Benjamin frowned. He was a man with an orderly mind; to him business was business and any insertion of other affairs partook of the nature of adulteration. One could not be too careful in these matters in the Law. He chafed a little; it was not like Roger to go wandering down side tracks when they were discussing business, even if he did happen to have struck the trail of a personal friend. He might just as well have left it till afterwards. It was not – business.

'He went on to the design side when he left us,' said Stenning, 'into the Rawdon Company. Riley told me that he was doing very well there – on design work and test piloting.'

'Test piloting – isn't that very dangerous work?'

'I don't know about that so much – not under ordinary conditions. Riley used to know pretty well exactly what every new machine would be like before he flew it. But anyway, this man isn't counting on remaining a pilot – I know that. He'll get on all right on the technical side.'

Benjamin leaned back in his chair. This was going on for ever, apparently. He wished now that he could have kept the matter in his own hands. It was always like this whenever relations had a hand in business. They were too infernally casual.

'I know him a little,' said Lechlane. 'Tell me, have you any idea what he's making now – or what he's likely to work up to?'

Stenning considered a little. He was by no means sure that Morris would like his affairs discussed in this manner, yet he couldn't very well refuse to say what he knew.

'I don't really know,' he said. 'Riley told me just before – before the accident, that Rawdon thought a lot of him. I suppose he's getting seven pounds a week or so. He's got some money of his own, too. He'll get on pretty well, I should think, and end up in partnership with some designer. Then I expect the flying brings him in a couple of hundred a year or so, in addition. Of course, I don't know at all what terms he's on – it's only guesswork. I haven't seen him since we broke up.'

'He always was pretty bright in his own line,' said Lechlane absently. He roused himself. 'Did you ever hear anything of Malcolm's business with the Phillips Company?'

Benjamin sat up with a sigh of relief.

Early in the summer, the Rawdon two-seater fighter with the Stoat engine had been completed and flown away to Martlesham by an Air Force pilot. She was a good machine, a great advance on anything the Air Force had, both in performance and manoeuvrability. Rawdon had high hopes for her; she had been an expensive machine to build experimentally – in fact he had built her at a loss. That did not matter; there would be a big contract coming along for her in a little time. That was certain.

The torpedo carrier, too, was in the workshops approaching completion. She was a good straightforward design, nothing very startling or original about her, rather like an enlarged edition of the fighter in appearance. Indeed, it was becoming increasingly difficult to design any military machine that had any pretence to novelty or aerodynamic advance. The design of every such machine had to pass stringent, if ill-informed, critics at the Air Ministry; what had not been done before was looked upon with grave suspicion, if not met with an absolute veto. A reliable machine must be produced for the taxpayers' money – that was the one consideration governing all experimental contracts. Hence it came to pass that any innovations in design were applied first to commercial machines as a general rule.

This was the case of the Sesquiplane. During the previous year the French had coined that word and applied it to a racing machine that, they alleged, was neither monoplane nor biplane, but a combination of the two. Unimaginative people would have called it a strutted monoplane with a faired undercarriage axle; the French chose to call it a 'one-and-a-half-plane' and coined a new term for it. The scheme had occurred to Rawdon before as a possibility for a light commercial machine. It was purely experimental, though he had obtained an order for it. It was to be quite small; a three-passenger machine to be used on the air taxi service that Riley had been chief pilot for. Rawdon expected to be able to turn out a stiffer structure altogether than by the usual arrangements of struts and wires.

A model was made and Morris took it down to the National Physical Laboratory to be tested, staying to watch the tests and to assist. In two days he returned, bringing with him the model and a little booklet of ciphers. An examination of these revealed a better state of affairs than Rawdon had even hoped for; by some chance he had evidently hit upon a peculiarly happy combination of body and wing. There were mysterious features about this aerodynamics. Sometimes the air liked a model and flowed smoothly over it at any speed. Make a small alteration in some detail and the whole thing was upset; eddies evidently formed far away from the alteration, where no eddies had been before, and the resistance of the model might be half as much again. That meant less speed for a given horse-power, less load for a given speed. In fact, an inferior machine.

Rawdon leaned over Morris's desk and studied his figures, his great brows knitted in a frown.

'We must go easy with that strut fairing,' he observed, 'or we'll be getting too much dihedral effect.'

'It's rather a pity we didn't have a look at that when it was in the tunnel,' said Morris.

The designer nodded. 'We must manage to get a tunnel of our own,' he said, 'even if it's only a little one. Simply can't get on without it. We ought to have made a dozen comparative tests with this model – different arrangements of wing and body. We don't know enough about it – not nearly enough.'

But there was little chance of finding the money for a wind channel just yet.

Indeed, as the winter drew on, the difficulty of finding money for many things became more acute. The orders for the two-seater fighter, so confidently expected, had not material-ized; instead there came a rumour round the office that another experimental machine was to be designed. But this did not materialize, and work was concentrated on the design of the Sesquiplane. Presently the torpedo carrier was ready, and the question arose as to who was to fly it.

'You'd better take it off,' said Rawdon to Morris one day. 'I'll get that through with the Air Ministry. You were on Handley Pages in the war, weren't you? That will make it all right with them.'

But it did not, for the Air Ministry, for reasons best known to themselves, flatly refused to allow Mr Morris to touch their torpedo carrier, ordered and paid for with the country's money. If Captain Rawdon could produce no better pilot than Mr Morris for this important and delicate work, then they would provide a pilot from the Royal Air Force ... To which Captain Rawdon regretted that he knew of no pilot at present in the country, whether in the Air Force or out of it, to whom he would more readily entrust this work, but would be pleased to give any information about the machine to any pilot they cared to send down. The machine, completed but never flown, lay in the erecting-shop for several months, accumulating a rich coating of dust, till everybody had lost all interest in it, and hated the sight of it. Then the pilot was selected, arrived, and flew the machine away. Six weeks elapsed between its first and second flights. It never made a third, for they crashed it in an ill-advised attempt to land at a slower speed than that for which the machine was designed.

'If only one could design for some country that knew nothing at all about aeroplanes – say the Argentine Republic,' said Rawdon wistfully, 'I believe one could turn out a really good machine.'

The non-technical side of the Air Ministry, however, admirably fulfilled its role of godfather to the industry. Provided with a tiny sum to spend annually on new aeroplanes, it distributed its favours in such a way that while every firm in the industry was on the verge of bankruptcy, the crash was somehow staved off from month to month. At this time it was admitted that if one firm had gone, the rest would have followed suit. But the one firm did not go. Somehow the industry was struggling along through the bad times, plaintively bemoaning the old days when there was a war on, fed with rare commercial orders, constantly saved from extinction by timely orders for military machines and, at all times, bitterly bickering with the Air Ministry. That was, perhaps, the healthiest sign of all.

Apart from that continual sign of life, however, things were not hopeful in the Rawdon Company. As the winter ran on its course, it became a matter of considerable doubt whether the firm would be able to keep going at all. It seemed inconceivable that such a firm should be allowed to break up, in the very interests of the country. Yet the facts were becoming obvious to everyone from Rawdon to the little girl. By Christmas, the design of the Sesquiplane was near its end; already it was beginning to come together in the shops. No more design work appeared, only a monotonous succession of odd jobs. There was a racing motor-car to be fitted with a streamline body, a privately-owned aeroplane to be fitted with a monstrous excrescence of a cabin, two or three Rabbits to be completed for the Dutch Government. In the workshops more than half the men had been sacked; it looked as if they would very shortly start on the office.

By the beginning of January they had already done so. It began with three draughtsmen who, instead of receiving their pay in a little envelope on Friday evening, were told to go and get it at the office. They returned with glum faces and instructions to take a short holiday – unpaid.

There was no more work done in the drawing-office that evening. It did not matter much; the work was of little importance. The men stood about in little groups beside each others' desks, ostensibly in search of data, really in gloomy speculation as to where the blow would fall next.

'Someone said that Pilling-Henries were taking on men,' said James, the engine draughtsman, to one of the discharged men. 'I'd have a shot there, if I were you, old man.'

The other looked a little pinched. He had no illusions about Pilling-Henries, though he would try it, with every other firm that he could think of. He would start tomorrow, walking and omnibusing all over London, calling at various firms, only to be turned away. The evening he would spend talking cheerily about his chances to his wife, and in writing letters to provincial firms. The first three hours of the night he would spend in sleep, and the remaining five in thought. Then the round would start all over again.

Morris was concerned about all this, uneasy as to how it would affect him. He did not think he would be sacked; he thought he would be kept on as the firm's pilot, till the Sesquiplane was flown, anyway. He believed he was to fly it. After that it was difficult to say. If the firm went on, he might go on with it. But if the firm bust?

He did not know what he would do if the firm bust. He had no qualifications, no engineering degree or status whatever. He had saved a good bit during the last fifteen months; latterly he had been making something like six hundred a year, all told. It was on the strength of that that he had bought Riley's car. He could not afford to get married, because the majority of his income came from piloting, and he did not regard that as a certainty. But he could afford to buy Riley's little car.

More draughtsmen were put on that euphemistic holiday, till only a bare skeleton of the staff remained. So far the technical staff, consisting of Nichols, Pocock, and Morris, had been inviolate. Then, one black day, they were sent for one after another.

Morris entered Rawdon's office and found him by himself, if anything a trifle calmer, a trifle more self-possessed than usual.

'Sit down, Mr Morris.' Morris obeyed.

The designer caressed his chin with one hand. 'As you see,' he said, 'this firm is in a serious state. We've had to cut down our staff very much, and we've got to reduce it still further. I hoped to get through without touching any of you technical men. Then I thought that if I'd got to cut any of you, I'd better have you all in and tell you just how things stand.'

'I see,' said Morris.

'We ought to have got a biggish contract for the fighter. It hasn't come, and it won't come for some time now, perhaps with the next budget, perhaps longer. We're going to build another torpedo carrier in place of the one they crashed – there may or may not be a contract for that later. In any case, it won't be for some months, because they crashed the other one before getting any tests done on it, so that nobody knows what its performance is. Then there's the Sesquiplane. I expect that to be out in March, or late in February. If it's a success, we'll probably get an order to build half a dozen for the summer traffic – that will be a rush job if it comes.'

He paused a little.

'So you see the position is that we ought to be all right in three months time – if these things come off. I think we can hang on till then, but only by cutting the staff down to a skeleton. Now I want you to stay on and fly the Sesquiplane – I want that flown by someone who knows it inside out. I don't want another repetition of that torpedo-carrier business.'

Morris smiled.

'Well, Mr Morris,' said the designer, 'it comes to this. Things are pretty bad, but I think we'll get through all right. I don't want you to go off and take another job in a hurry, thinking you're going to be sacked. You're all right till the Sesquiplane has flown. After that, or by that time, I hope we shall be in a stronger position.'

He rose from his desk. 'That's all I wanted to say.'

Morris returned thoughtfully to the drawing-office. There he found that Rawdon had said substantially the same to each of them – with this difference. Pocock and Nichols were to go 'on holiday'.

At the end of an hour's desultory discussion, Pocock looked up with a queer smile.

'I've been in some odd shows in my time,' he said, 'but this is the first time I've ever been on a sinking ship.'

By the end of February the drawing-office, once numbering over twenty, had been reduced to five members. There were Morris, Baker the chief draughtsman, James the engine draughtsman, and two others. Corresponding reductions had been made on the business side. Thus the staff became dispersed, that highly-trained staff that had worked together on the design of aeroplanes since 1916, in the days of the Rat. Pocock had gone north, and was reported to be working in a steel works. Nichols, who had been in aviation for eleven years, had found a safe, well-paid job in a biscuit factory; a permanency which at his age he was unlikely ever to abandon to return to the work in which he was of value to the country. He had children to educate. Of the draughtsmen, some had found other work outside the industry, some had taken to manual labour, and some were simply out of work, pathetically visiting the firm once a week in the hope of finding some improvement in the position, some chance of being taken on again. But no improvement was in sight.

Morris's paper on the fuselages had been published in the February number of the journal. He had searched about for other fields of activity when that was finished, and had determined to investigate the possibility of detecting eddies round an aeroplane by testing a small model in a stream of water tinged with red ink. He had spent a little time in calculation of water speeds and trough dimensions most nearly to approximate to the air-flow; then he fixed up a sort of trough in one corner of the works and paid the model-maker to make him a little model of the Sesquiplane. So far the results were not promising.

As the Sesquiplane approached completion, it became evident that it was going to be a surprisingly neat little machine. It was not easy, even for the initiated, to tell exactly what a machine was going to look like from the drawings. The model had been a pretty little piece of work; the machine itself was the best proportioned aeroplane that Rawdon had ever turned out. He had chosen a high lift section for the wing, which gave it a relatively small span and created the appearance of a small, handy little machine, that would have no difficulty in putting down in any reasonable field. This was important in air taxi work. The landing speed was estimated at forty-six miles an hour.

By the end of February it was ready for flight.

Morris did not anticipate any difficulty in flying it. True, it was of an entirely novel type; a type that neither he nor anyone else in England had had experience of before. That did not seem to matter much. The machinery of design was so perfect, the methods of calculation so accurate and clearly defined, that he knew, could almost say beforehand, what the machine would feel like in the air. He felt that he knew the machine inside out; he had confidence in it; it was a really fine little machine. It would make a big sensation when it appeared at Croydon. So far its existence had been kept a secret from the technical papers.

So when the day came for it to be flown, Morris was very fairly confident in his ability to bring off this, his first real test flight, without untoward incident. The engine had been tested the evening before; it was the middle of the morning when the machine was brought out on to the aerodrome, and Morris climbed up into his seat. In more normal times there would have been a little crowd of draughtsmen slinking about the place, ostensibly on their lawful occasions, actually waiting to see the machine go up. There was none of that now, for the whole staff were on the aerodrome, chatting together as they waited for the flight.

Morris started the engine and ran it up. Satisfied, he waved the chocks away and taxied out on to the aerodrome. Well, she taxied nicely; that was probably due to the new undercarriage, a compression rubber and oleo affair. That, in turn, had been due to an ingenious draughtsman, who was now out of a job, and likely to remain so, unless he took to manual labour.

Morris faced the machine into the wind and stopped, allowing the engine to tick over. He made his final preparations and wondered if the lucky pig, presented to him when he was a child and now reposing in his collarbox, was still valid. With the reflection that this question would shortly be decided, he looked to the pressure in the tanks and the temperature of the radiator water.

Then he settled himself more securely in his seat, one hand on the control stick between his knees, the other on the throttle. Gently he opened the throttle; the machine began to move; he opened it slowly, progressively. Instinctively he lifted her tail off the ground as she ran along, and steadied her in that position. The throttle was nearly full open; now she must fly herself off the ground.

From beside the hangars the little group watched her intently. Much depended on this flight. There was no sign of any Air Force contracts yet, and it was nearly budget time. Perhaps there would be no Air Force contracts this year. In that case, the very existence of the firm depended on the decent performance of this machine.

The Sesquiplane accelerated smoothly and ran lightly over the grass. Light appeared beneath her wheels; she sank again for an instant, then lifted clear and left the aerodrome on a long, slow slant.

At a height of perhaps seventy feet, a curious little incident occurred. The machine, to the watchers on the ground, seemed to sway a little laterally; one wing dropped – and did not come up again. Instead the whole machine side-slipped and seemed to progress sideways for an instant. Then the nose dropped a little and she steadied on to an even keel, with a louder note from the engine than before.

On the ground nobody spoke. They stirred a little when the machine recovered, but never took their eyes off her. They were all experienced men.

She began to turn towards the north, and came round in a wide circle. Apparently he was going to land her at once. Again he hit a bump, and again she sidled out of it in that queer, unconventional manner, losing height terribly.

The machine came in high above the hedge and made a very fast landing a quarter of a mile out on the aerodrome. Morris taxied her in carefully, jumped down, and walked with Rawdon to his office. Rawdon closed the door behind him.

Morris threw his helmet and goggles on the table. 'Well,' he said, 'it was most unpleasant. She's got simply no lateral control at all. One could feel it almost before she left the ground – you know. Then when we hit that first bump – really I didn't think she was going to come out of it. I don't mind telling you, it put the wind right up me. It was only her dihedral that got her out – I hadn't anything to do with it. I could just tip her over enough to make a very wide turn, using full aileron.'

'Very lucky you managed to get her down undamaged,' said Rawdon. He turned absently to a blueprint of the machine. 'I don't quite see it, though . . .'

105

'There was one thing I noticed,' said Morris. 'The lateral control seemed very unstable. At times it was almost as if there was someone out on the wing kicking the aileron, and the force was coming back to one's hand by the control.'

'Oh – ho?' said Rawdon. 'Turbulence?'

'I think so,' said Morris. 'She was too good in the wind tunnel. I was talking to the chaps down there. When the air's running over her so well, the least little thing upsets it, and then you get eddies and things. I don't know . . .'

'It may be that big fairing on the strut,' said Rawdon. 'That's what it's most likely to be. Perhaps if we had that off and simply streamlined it . . .'

The next day Morris took Rawdon down to his water apparatus in the shops.

'Look at that,' he said.

Rawdon looked. He saw in a smooth stream of clear water, submerged beneath the surface, a small model of the Sesquiplane.

'Hullo, where did that come from?'

'Jackson made it for me,' said Morris. 'I've been working on this stuff for some time, you know, and I'd just chucked it as being useless. Then last night I thought I'd have a look at this control business with it – it comes out rather curiously.'

He lifted the model from the water. 'You see this aileron? I've put it down about fifteen degrees; that's extreme, I know, but it doesn't show what I want it to otherwise. And I've got the fairing on that strut in plasticine, you see.'

He put the model into the running water. Then he took a thin glass tube leading to a supply of red ink and, placing this in the water two or three feet upstream from the model, allowed a thin streak of colour to flow down and play about the body and strut. Behind the strut the colour formed itself into a great whorl, which crept outwards from the body and upwards, creeping round up-stream till it formed a complete horizontal oval eddy behind the aileron, extending to half its length.

'What on earth is that thing doing – do you know what it means?' asked the designer.

'I haven't the least idea,' said Morris cheerfully, 'but it

doesn't look very healthy, does it? Funny thing is that it doesn't seem to happen at all with the aileron up normally. And of course, it may not happen in the air. But now, look at this.'

He lifted the model from the water and peeled off the plasticine from the strut. He replaced the model in the water and turned on the colour again. The stream flowed comparatively smoothly over body, wing, and strut, with no sign of the previous eddy.

'No elastic up the sleeve or anything,' said Morris.

'That's what they told you at the National Physical Laboratory, isn't it? That something of the sort might happen?'

'That's about it,' said Morris. He turned off the ink. 'It only really confirms what we always know – that we've hit a case where the body and wing suit each other so well that we've got to be jolly careful what we're doing.'

The designer mused a little. What he had deduced from fifteen years' experience had been definitely proved by Morris with the experience of one. True, it was luck that this effect had happened to show in such a tank.

'Well,' he said at last. 'That's very interesting confirmation of the strut interference, Mr Morris. I was going to have it stripped, anyway. Don't dismantle this apparatus; I'd like to see some more experiments done before we abandon it.'

He moved away towards his office.

Five days later the Sesquiplane was again ready for flight. A small notice on the office door, offering seats in the machine at ten shillings apiece, was eventually attributed to Morris, whose confidence in the machine was not shared by the draughtsmen. He took her off again in much the same manner; there was no longer any sign of aileron weakness, though a nasty draught came into the cockpit and gave him a stiff neck for the rest of the day. He stayed up for half an hour or so, putting her into every position he could think of, short of actual stunts. Finally he brought her in and made a moderately slow landing, and was loud in his grumbles against the windscreen.

Now began a curious period of inactivity, which Morris

found very trying. His purpose in the firm was ended with the flight of this machine; it was unlikely that there would be any more test flying for many months. There was no news of any contract that would enable the firm to keep going; he had not cared to ask Rawdon for details of the firm's position. All the rest of the technical staff had been sacked or put on holiday, and there was very little work for him to do in the office. Indeed, nobody was doing any work; they sat about reading magazines all day and wondered what was going to happen next. The designer sat in his office or went up to London, and gave no sign.

Morris decided that he must go and ask him what his prospects were, what he was to do. It was better to know at once rather than to sit waiting to be sacked. Besides, he was genuinely concerned for the future of the firm; it seemed incredible that it should be allowed to break up. Yet that was what seemed to be happening.

That interview never came off. A week after the successful flight of the Sesquiplane, Morris received an official-looking letter. The notepaper was the office paper of Pilling-Henries, the armament firm, who had dropped aviation at the end of the war. He opened it curiously; it ran:

Dear Sir,
We are reorganizing our aviation department under Mr G. A. Haverton, FRAeS, who has mentioned your name to us. Should you be free, Mr Haverton would be glad to interview you with reference to an appointment any morning during the next week, at eleven o'clock at the above address.

It was signed by somebody he did not know.

Morris sat staring at it for a long time, while his breakfast froze to the dish. So far as he had known, he was a complete nonentity in the industry. He had very seldom visited any of the centres of aviation, such as Croydon; on such occasions as he had, he had merely passed through. So far as he knew, his name had never appeared in any technical paper; he had counted himself as completely unknown. In any case, there it was. It looked as if his financial difficulties were solved.

Presently it occurred to him that there was an unpleasant tone about the letter, slightly disconcerting. The writer evidently knew all about him, and was evidently counting on Rawdon's failure. It was a good deal too much like robbing the body before it was dead. Still, he would go and see them.

Two days later he went. He presented himself at the palatial offices of the armament firm in Westminster. After a brief sojourn in a mahogany-furnished waiting-room, he was shown into a large room. There was one desk in the middle of the office; a pale-faced, corpulent man was sitting at it. At first sight Morris identified him in his mind with the instigator of the letter. So this was Haverton.

'Mr Morris,' said the page. A faint smile spread over the features of the fat man; he got up and shook hands.

'Good morning, Mr Morris. I am very pleased to make your acquaintance. Sit down, will you?'

Morris sat down, a little uneasily.

The other plunged into his business.

'We have heard, Mr Morris, that you may soon be free. I need not comment further on the state of Captain Rawdon's business. We do not know if you are free, or if you are going to be free. We only know that you may be free...'

Morris bowed a little, but did not speak.

'As you know, this firm is starting again in aviation, and we are forming a staff for the design of military and commercial machines. The position at present, briefly, is this. We have no pilot at the moment, and we want men of your stamp – technical men. We can offer you substantially the same appointment as you are filling now. I am right in my facts so far, am I not?'

'That is so,' said Morris.

'I may say that you are not altogether unknown to us,' said the fat man. 'We have read your paper on fuselages, and we have heard of your ability as a pilot – in the matter of the Sesquiplane.'

Morris started, and immediately cursed himself inwardly for a fool. But how the dickens had that got out so soon?

'We propose to build metal machines almost exclusively,' continued the other. 'We can therefore offer you a post in our design office at Sheffield, coupled with some test flying. For that there would be the usual terms. For the office work and pilot's retaining fee combined, we are prepared to offer eleven pounds a week.'

Morris was prepared for this, and flattered himself that he did not move a muscle. It was more than he expected. Still, he did not like it much.

'You have had experience of wind-channel work, have you not, Mr Morris?'

'A little,' said Morris. He did not mention that it had only been two days, and wondered if the other knew. Anyway, there was nothing in it.

'We are setting up a wind channel,' said the other. 'We should probably wish you to make a special study of that.'

There was a pause.

'I can't say anything at all, off hand,' said Morris. 'I should like a day or two to think it over.' He knew that Haverton knew that what he really meant was: 'I'm going back to see if Rawdon will bid any higher.'

'Exactly, Mr Morris,' replied the other. Morris knew that he meant: 'That's our limit, and I think you'd be a fool to refuse it.' Morris was inclined to agree with him there. But he was uneasy; practically every circumstance had disturbed him. He did not care about Haverton or the way he went about his business. The work was to be on metal construction, and Morris had no faith in the future of metal aeroplanes for many years to come. Then again, he was aware that it was unlikely that he would do his best work unless he liked the conditions. Could he rely on working well on these metal machines, under a man that he would probably dislike? He felt rather in the position of the engineer who has been offered a most responsible, interesting, and remunerative job on a sewage farm. Somehow, he did not connect aviation with an industrial area. It was more an affair of wide, open spaces, clean woodwork that did not come off on one's hands, bright shavings in a sunny workshop.

He left the offices and made his way back to Southall after lunch, a little depressed. He would simply hate Sheffield.

He did not go back to the office that day. It suddenly struck him that he was tired, even a little shaky. That was a bad sign in a pilot; he must take things more easily for a bit. Perhaps he had been going too strong lately, with that paper and his water experiments on top of his ordinary work. The flying of the Sesquiplane had been a nervy little job, too, though he had not cared to admit as much. He resolved that he must get about and see more people – get in touch again with Wallace and Johnnie and all that crowd. This living by oneself was unnatural. One ought to be married – Riley had said that.

He had saved a good bit of money, nearly two hundred pounds, in this last year. If only he could have stuck on with Rawdon on the same terms as these other people had offered him! He did not in the least want to go to them. He knew what these big armament firms were. You got a good job in them and stayed there for the rest of your natural life. There was no scope. Approach to the designer was difficult. You were held down by precedent and by the threat of a pension. One could not get to the top of those big firms. One could only get a little higher up. It would be better to stick to Rawdon if he could; he would get on better there, even if it meant a lower salary to start with.

So next morning he went to see Rawdon. But the office was empty; the little girl told him that Captain Rawdon had gone up to London. He did not come back till nearly four o'clock in the afternoon. Morris gave him half an hour to settle down, and then went in to talk about his future.

He found a more genial atmosphere in the office than there had been lately. Rawdon was sitting on his table and swinging his legs, chatting to Adamson, who stood by in his hat and coat, his hands thrust deep into his trouser pockets, a cigar poking jauntily from one corner of his mouth.

'Yes, Mr Morris.'

'Could I speak to you some time, sir?'

Adamson strolled out and closed the door behind him. Morris came to business.

'I got this letter two or three days ago from Pilling-Henries,' he said. He spread it out on the table before Rawdon, who glanced it over.

'Did you go?' he asked.

'I went up there yesterday morning.' Morris briefly recounted what had happened. 'I don't know how they found out about the Sesquiplane,' he remarked.

'They're devils for that,' said Rawdon reflectively. 'There's not much we little chaps do that they don't get to know about. I know them of old.' He turned to Morris. 'Are you going to leave us?'

That was a blunt way of putting it, thought Morris. 'Well,' he said, 'I've got to make up my mind about it. Can you let me know anything of my prospects here? I don't much like the idea of going to them – in fact, I'd very much rather stay here if I'm not going to be sacked.'

'I can tell you this, Mr Morris,' said the designer. 'I'm not considering sacking you just at present, anyway. No, frankly, it's my opinion that you've got just as good a chance of getting on in this firm as with them. Probably better.'

The little girl brought in a cup of China tea and placed it on the table beside Rawdon. Morris waited till the door was shut again.

'I thought so too,' he said. 'But can you hold out any hope of an improvement in my position here? I don't want to press for a rise; I know the firm's in a poor way. But if you could let me know anything about my prospects in the next year or so – it would help me to make a decision about this.'

Rawdon lifted his cup and sipped it delicately. 'I don't know what more you want,' he murmured. 'You're head of our technical department now.'

It had not struck Morris before that the one member of a technical department was head of it; he smiled politely.

'Well, of course, I'm the only person in it.'

Rawdon leaned under the table, brought out a biscuit-box

and opened it, took out a couple of biscuits, and kicked it under the table again.

'I say you're head of it,' he said. 'And you'll get the pay commensurate when we take on more technical staff. They'll be under you. I think we can make your pay equal to this' – he touched the letter – 'when that time comes.'

Morris did not have to consider the matter for long. 'If that's the case then,' he said, 'I'll turn this down. I'd much rather stay here.'

'Right,' said Rawdon, sipping his tea. 'And now, my young man, I've got a bit of news for you. We've got a contract for the fighter.'

'For how many?' asked Morris.

'Forty-two of them,' said the designer quietly.

Morris looked at him. 'That must represent a hundred thousand pounds,' he said.

'There or thereabouts,' said Rawdon. He took a little drink. 'You'll be getting your new screw next month.'

'Then we're over the worst of it?'

'We'll have to go slow for a bit,' said the designer. 'But I think we can see our way now.'

'Well,' said Morris at last, 'it's high time the Air Force had some new machines.' He rose to go.

The other did not move, but looked queerly at him. 'I know,' he said. 'But these are for Denmark.'

Morris did not speak.

'You see,' said the designer, 'we simply can't carry on unless we get a decent production order into the shops. I went and told the Air Ministry so. And they couldn't do anything for us. They haven't got the money.'

'I see,' said Morris.

'So the only thing they could do was to give us permission to sell the fighter abroad. They couldn't risk another firm closing down.'

He paused. 'They were very unwilling to let the fighter go.'

There was an immense silence.

'Well,' said Morris sourly, 'we must hope the government won't risk a war with Denmark. I don't believe any of our machines would stand a dog's chance against the fighter.'

'I know,' said Rawdon.

Morris glanced with sudden sympathy at the other, some-how rather a dejected figure despite the contract.

'It's pretty rotten,' he said.

'One oughtn't let these things count, of course,' said the designer evenly. 'But – oh, it's heartbreaking. I never thought we should come down to this . . .'

7

Rawdon finished sipping his tea and handed the cup to Morris. 'You might stick that on the table,' he said.

Morris took the cup and moved across the room. A faint, irregular tinkling became audible as the spoon rattled a little between the cup and saucer. Rawdon looked up suddenly and glanced sharply at the hand that held the cup. He had for-gotten all about his staff lately – he had so little. Morris placed the cup on the table.

'As for our immediate plans,' said Rawdon on the spur of the moment, 'there won't be much doing in the office for a bit – not till we can get some of the staff back again. I think if I were you I should take a holiday – a real holiday this time, not the sort of holiday we've been offering lately. You'd better take a fortnight off at once, if you care to. I expect we shall have a good bit of work coming along soon – you'd better take it while you can get it.'

Morris smiled. 'Thanks very much sir,' he said gratefully.

'Right you are,' said the designer. 'I'll probably take one myself after a little. You'd better get off as soon as you can – there's nothing for you to do here at present. Tomorrow, if you like. Let's see,' he turned up a calendar, 'you'd better be back by the twenty-second. That do?'

'That'll do me fine,' said Morris.

He worked late that evening, tinkering with his car in one corner of the cavernous erecting-shop, lit at one end by a spluttering arc-lamp. He could not stay in his rooms after dinner; he was restless, too restless for his work. The car would need attention if he was going any distance in it; he thought he would probably go away in it for a little, perhaps down to Cornwall. As he worked at the car he wanted to think out what had happened, and that was just what he could not do. The details eluded him; only a great contentment had come over him. Whatever he had done had been his own work. This happiness was his own making. It was beginning now and it would go on. He need never be lonely any more. He had money now. Money was the most important thing in the world. It brought you the most desirable things of all, love and companionship. He reckoned up his income; with the piloting he would be worth between seven and eight hundred a year, all told.

He could afford to go back to his girl. He could go back to her and ask her to marry him, and this time there would be no parting on the Camera.

He left the car, turned out the arc-light, walked back to his rooms and went quietly to bed.

He was asleep.

Two miles away, Rawdon was telling his wife about that queer, hard-headed pilot of his, one of the clever, unemotional, scientific sort; a man who would probably go far. He would not be surprised if one day he didn't have to take him into partnership. Not yet, of course, but in five or six years' time, perhaps. It would be the only way to keep him in the firm once he got going.

Morris slept well and late next morning. As he shaved he made his plans. He wanted to find someone to talk to about all this, someone who had known what he was up to. He pondered. Of course, he might go to Oxford. That seemed to him the best thing to do. He still knew people there, people who would be glad to see him, who would offer him a glass of beer and a cheerful anecdote or two. He might run down there and spend the night. He could get away this afternoon in Riley's car; he was glad he had bought that car. Riley would have liked him to have it.

That was it; he would run down to Oxford this afternoon. This morning he would go up to town and get himself an overcoat, a thick coat for motoring.

Presently he got his car out and drove up to London. He bought his coat, lunched in town, and returned; packed his Gladstone and filled up the tanks on the car. It was not far to Oxford, forty-five miles perhaps. Starting after tea, he would get there some time before dinner. That would do very well.

He paid a brief visit to the works and made his final arrangements. He would not come back after he had been to Oxford. Perhaps he would stay there a bit. He did not really know what he was going to do, or where he was going. But at Oxford there were people he had met with Helen, mutual friends, dons and people . . .

The evening was beginning to close in when he started. By Beaconsfield he put on his headlights, and by the time he reached High Wycombe it was dark. He knew his road well, though it was nearly two years since he had passed over it; he could remember every corner. He drove quietly through the intricacies of High Wycombe and on towards Dashwood Hill.

It was good to be on the road again.

One was never really clear of London till one was up Dashwood – Wallace had propounded that. There was a radius of thirty miles or so from Charing Cross where the country was still tainted by the town, still defiled with advertisements. The sheep still had dirty coats before High Wycombe; still on the London side of that town the little boys threw stones at passing motor-cars or pelted unfortunate cats with rusty cans. It was not until one got up Dashwood that the country became really unspoilt; on the Henley road the barrier came at Maidenhead.

The hill rose steeply beneath his lamps; he felt himself leaning back in his seat as the nose of the car rose to the ascent. Well, let her take it quietly. Deftly he slipped in second gear and sat back while she ran up the hill steadily at twenty miles an hour. She was a good little car, and Riley had kept her pretty well considering the work she had had to do.

Up over the crest and into top again; on through the woods along the road to Stokenchurch, bordered on one side by woods, on the other side dropping away into fields and pastures; a wide view in the faint moonlight. He wrapped the rug a little closer round him; it was getting very cold.

He passed the cross-roads at the top of the hill, his lamps lighting the arch of the trees before him. He had driven this road before, once when Wallace had lent him his car, and he had driven Helen to the Wittenham Clumps. They had stopped on this hill to see the bluebells – he was passing the very place – he even imagined he could see the scour on the road where the wheels had skidded as he pulled up suddenly ... two years ago. He smiled at himself, and let the car spin down the broad, easy road. At the bottom of this hill was the 'Hornblower'. It was a good pub, the 'Hornblower' – they did you well there. He would like to see the place again, would like to see if, visiting it again, he could not recapture something of the young love that had passed that way, some reminder, some fragrance lingering about the place that would bring him back the image of his girl. He had never visited it with anyone else; it was bound up in his mind with Helen, demurely pouring out tea by a window, open on to a garden, some bright, hot, summer afternoon ...

He would look in there – he could not pass it without visiting it again. Perhaps he would sit a little there – perhaps he would find a comfortable chair and a warm fire where he could rest a little, before going on to Oxford.

The car slid softly to the door; he stopped the engine and got out. He would have gone in at once, but something made him turn as he reached the door, made him pause and stare out over the fields beneath the Chilterns. It was spring, he thought. Perhaps in those fields were the bluebells he had seen and picked ... when he had been there before. Last year they had been there just the same, he supposed, just as beautiful as they had been before. But they had not been there to pick them.

He turned, and laughed at himself a little sourly. 'In the

117

spring . . .' He opened the door and went in.

'Whisky and splash,' he said cheerfully.

'Cold tonight, isn't it?' said the barmaid.

Morris walked towards the fire and stretched out his hands. 'It is that,' he said.

What a good spot this was! One day he would make a list, with the help of Wallace or someone, of pubs that were really worth staying at. The 'Hornblower', the 'Queen Anne' at Chinden, the 'Feathers' at Morting Howell. He took off his coat and settled himself before the fire in an old oak armchair, one of half a dozen around the wide, open fireplace. The fire stood in a brazier, warm and comforting; by his side was an oak table, a great bowl of primroses in the middle.

He sipped his drink and stretched out one hand to the blaze, dreaming.

He looked at his hand, curiously, sleepily. He was not sorry he had done it. It had been the right thing to do . . . and it was over now. Because he had faced it, it had not lasted so long. God, how quickly he had got on! He had had most amazing luck all through his life; luck in getting to know his girl, luck in getting in touch with poor old Malcolm, luck in getting on to Rawdon, luck in sticking with the company over the bad times. He had done in nineteen months what he thought would have taken him four years.

There was a stir behind him, and the door opened and shut. Somebody – two people – had come in and were taking off their coats in silence. Morris did not look round. He was tired, sleepy with the warmth, too tired to stir. He must get on to Oxford for dinner. Or, why not stay and dine here, and go on to Oxford afterwards?

Somebody, a man, was coming up behind him to the fire, rubbing his hands to the blaze. Morris stirred a little in his chair and turned to look at the newcomer.

'Why, Christie,' he said quietly. 'I thought you were in the Argentine.'

'Hullo, Morris,' said Christie in his slow way. 'When on earth did you drop in? I am most awfully glad to see you.'

Morris stirred a little further in his chair, produced a pouch

118

of tobacco, and tossed it on the table towards the other. 'The same stuff,' he said laconically. 'You're quite sure you aren't still in the Argentine?'

Christie chuckled gravely, picked up the pouch, and began to fill his pipe. A slim, fair girl, whose face seemed vaguely familiar to Morris came and stood beside Christie.

'My wife,' said Christie.

Morris got up and shook hands, smiling. 'I had no idea of this,' he said apologetically.

The girl laughed cheerfully. 'It's recent,' said Christie, '– too recent for gossip. Three days, to be exact.' He turned to the girl. 'He lives on gossip, this man.'

'I know where he learned that,' said the girl. She turned to Morris. 'I remember you,' she said. 'I often saw you in the "Cadena" in the mornings – with Robert.'

So Christie was also Robert. Morris remembered the look of the girl; he thought she had been a home student.

Presently she disappeared upstairs. Christie took a chair, and lit his pipe. 'The advantage of regular habits,' he said reflectively. 'One always knows where to go for good tobacco. Where are you making for now? Oxford? Better stop and have dinner with us here.'

'I thought of having dinner here,' said Morris. 'I'm going first to Oxford – I don't know what after that. See what happens in Oxford. Gloucester perhaps.'

There was a pause while Christie filed and docketed this information, then, 'What are you going to Gloucester for?' he asked. 'Got business there?' It was a crude inquiry. Christie knew as well as anyone. The effort to recall the details of a six-months'-old consternation proved detrimental to his tact.

Morris did not answer the question directly. He took up the old, worn poker, and scraped a little white ash from the bars of the brazier. 'One moves on,' he said. 'You've moved on – you've gone and got yourself married. Wallace seems to be falling into the arms of one particular divinity. You know pretty well as much about my affairs as I do. Do you suppose I stand still?'

'And so you're going to Gloucester,' said Christie.

'By heavens, Holmes – this is marvellous!' Morris leaned forward to the fire and began to talk. He told Christie what he had been doing since he left Oxford, what he had done before he left Oxford. He told his tale straight ahead, almost as if he had been telling it to a child at bed-time, making it up as he went along. Christie listened imperturbably to the end.

'She doesn't know you're coming?' he said at last.

Morris shook his head.

Christie routed in his pocket for a match, leaned forward, and lit his pipe again. He blew a long cloud of smoke which, caught by a draught, vanished up the great chimney.

'Morris,' he said, looking into the embers. Morris looked up. 'Morris, I'm afraid she's married.'

The coals fell together with a tiny crash in the brazier.

'Oh,' said Morris softly.

'I'll tell you what I know,' said Christie.

'I'd like to hear that,' murmured Morris, very gently. The blood was slowly returning to his heart.

'I saw it in the *Tatler*, or one of those papers – last autumn. It was a photograph of her as an engaged girl. It was headed – "An autumn wedding" – or something like that; you know the kind of thing. It said she was going to be married next month to Lechlane – you remember Lechlane.'

'He came into money,' said Morris. 'He was a sort of cousin of hers – distant.'

He sat scraping the ash interminably from the brazier. Presently he got up from his chair and stood before the fire, looking down into the coals, one hand on the mantelpiece. Christie, as he watched him, seemed suddenly to see him as he would be in thirty years' time, the same, but different; a little greyer, a little graver. He moved and stood upright; the illusion vanished. 'Thanks for telling me that,' he said. 'It was good of you. Otherwise I might have made a fool of myself.' He turned from the fireplace. 'I must get on. You'll remember me to your wife?'

He took his coat, the new ulster bought only that morning, and put it on.

'You won't stay for dinner?' asked Christie.

'I don't think so, thanks,' said Morris a little pathetically. 'I want to get on.'

Christie did not attempt further to detain him. He walked with him to the door.

'We shall be here for a week longer,' he said. 'We'd be most awfully glad if you'd come in for a night or two – on your way back, if you happen to be passing.'

'That's damn good of you,' said a voice from the darkness, 'but I don't suppose I shall. Cheer oh.'

The headlights flicked on; the engine of the little car purred suddenly, and the car slid away up the road. Christie watched it out of sight; three times there was a crescendo of noise, and then a sudden rumble, gradually increasing in note. The red star of the tail-lamp seemed to fly up the lighted road.

Morris was making that car move.

The barmaid touched Christie on the arm. 'That gentleman hasn't gone, has he? He hasn't paid for his whisky!'

Five miles up the road Morris dropped one hand from the wheel and gathered the rug closer round him. He had not stirred since his hand returned from the gear lever; he had been getting colder and colder. Then it struck him that it was silly to sit there getting cold like that. He had quite enough to worry about without double pneumonia.

He buttoned up the collar of his coat and pulled the rug up round his middle. As he tucked it around him, his foot went down hard upon the accelerator; the car leaped fiercely forward. Well, let it! He had been making a fool of himself ever since he left Oxford; let him now make the final folly and finish up in the ditch! He was no good. All these years he had deluded himself – he had had no shadow of grounds for hope. He saw that clearly now.

But that was no reason for blinding through Tetsworth, scaring all the villagers out of their wits. He slowed a little and passed through the village, cheery with its lighted windows.

He pressed on his way, hurriedly, feverishly. There was no object now in his visit to Oxford, no reason to go there, nothing to do when he got there. But he must go somewhere, somewhere where he could find something to interest him, someone to talk to. He shrank from going back to Christie on his honeymoon, though he was the sort of man he wanted. He wanted to find company ... somebody to talk to and go about with till he could go back to Southall and face his loneliness again.

He pressed on, and began to run down a long hill in the darkness. There was a turn at the bottom, he remembered, where one passed under a railway bridge; one must not come on that too fast. He peered forward, straining his eyes for the first appearance of it. There it was – he was on it, through it, and out the other side.

On past the road to Thame that struck off by the railway bridge, on over the bridge spanning the river. He was nearly at Oxford – it was not far now. He must have moved over this bit of ground. But one must do something, one must keep moving. Because if one did not keep moving, one would not be able to retain one's self-control, and that was all one had left.

Then he was at the fork of the road outside Wheatley, and went spinning up the hill to the right under the overhanging trees. Past the little town in the valley beside him, and on towards Headington. He was tired. He did not want to eat, but he would have dinner somewhere; it would do him good. He must look after himself now, must be very, very careful of himself. It was all he had to do.

He entered the long tunnel of Headington Hill and ran down into Oxford, through the outskirts of the town, out on to Cowley Plain and Magdalen Bridge. He drove quietly on up the High.

He was cold, tired and cold. He must have something to eat somewhere ... he would go to the George Grill. And after that, he did not know. He might go round to college and find out if there were any of his old friends about. It was all so unutterably dreary.

He drew up before the George and sat down in the grill to wait for his solitary meal. Beside him a group of undergraduates were dining not wisely but too well, and reading aloud the snappier passages from *The Pink 'Un*. Morris gathered that there had been a regrettable outbreak of lechery in the university, until the authorities had bestirred themselves, and caught a lecher and sent him down. Morris smiled; a dry humour reasserted itself in him; he felt that he could have made a creditable contribution to such an academic discussion. But presently his neighbours finished their meal and drifted away, and Morris was left to himself in the deserted room.

He finished his dinner and strolled out into the street. He must get on the road again, keep moving, tire himself out, so that when the time came, he could sleep quietly. He started up the car, wrapped himself up warmly again, and moved forward. He would just go straight ahead the way the car was pointing, down George Street and out into the country past the stations and on. That was westwards; he might go on tomorrow down to Cornwall for a little. He might make a night of it – he had plenty of petrol. He might get most of the way to Cornwall before dawn. One must keep moving.

He slipped out under the railway bridge and on down the long dull road to Botley. He did not understand this business, and he had nobody that he could consult. If only Malcolm had lived! But there was nobody. He could not understand about Lechlane; he could not imagine Helen, the Helen that he knew, being happy in that marriage. It all wound itself into his philosophy of life, worrying and rankling. Did things always happen like this? He had always held that the average human being was a pretty good sort – that things mostly worked out all right in the end.

What if he had been wrong – a fool?

He pressed on past the turning to Cumnor and on round by Wytham Woods, the hill looming faintly on his right in the darkness. He did not understand it, and he supposed that now he never would. He drove over the bridge before Eynsham and stopped at the lighted toll-gate, fumbling for coppers.

'Are you coming back tonight?' asked the girl.

Morris shook his head.

On through the main street of the village and out into the country again. He was on the road to Witney; he knew it well. It was a good road this, clear and easy and pleasant enough in daylight, past farm and wood now dimly illumined by his

123

lamps as he passed. He was getting a little cold again, weary and dispirited. Perhaps things always came out this way really, only he had shut his eyes to it. There was an end to everything, to all illusion. Things faded, the bright colours did not last. Riley . . .

He breasted the hill outside Witney and ran down into the little grey town. To the left at the cross-roads and on over the bridge, on through the long main street to the other end of the town. Cheerful lights shone out of the windows; a stream of light, smoke, and laughter came from the door of one little pub. But he must get on.

He took the road to the right at the end of the town and made for Burford.

On out of the town, up the hill, and along the high plateau at the top past the derelict aerodrome, ghostly and desolate and painfully reminiscent of the Isle of Wight. Well, that remained, the work he loved, the designing business that meant so much to him. That was a clean, healthy, unemotional thing; something that lasted, that was permanent. The strength of the wings, the delicate, beautiful strength.

He was very tired; tired, cold and numb; he could not think clearly any longer. But he must go on, must keep his course, all night if necessary. He was numb, but he could not sleep yet; he must go right on wherever this might lead him.

But this was not the road to Cornwall he was on.

He passed by Burford in the valley below him. If he was going to Cornwall he should be farther south . . . there was a road through Newbury or somewhere that he ought to be on. He was twenty, thirty miles too far north. He would have to make a big detour later on – he would have to turn off somewhere.

He was going to Cheltenham, to Gloucester. He would have to turn off in Gloucester and head south for a bit.

He had not cared which way he went when he left Oxford; he had come this way at random. But it was all wrong; he must go on with it now, but it would bring him close, too close, to Bevil Crossways. He must not stop there, or anywhere else in Gloucestershire. He must show them that he could stick a thing like this out without squealing. He would carry on and make for Bristol or somewhere and put up there for the night. There would be all-night hotels in Bristol. And by the time he got there perhaps he would be able to sleep.

He pressed on over the wide, open, treeless country. The moon was bright now; he could see the country almost as well as in daylight. The road wound on over the open fields; one could see it ahead for three or four miles in the daytime, a black line of telegraph poles on the horizon of the next ridge. Morris let the car out and began to run the miles down quickly. He had one narrow shave at an unexpected corner, but did not reduce his speed. It didn't matter – nothing mattered to him now.

Then, before he realized he was so close, he was running down into Northleach, nestling in a hollow. This was typical Gloucestershire country now, the grey stone houses and the stone walls to the fields. He slowed a little through the town, and put the car at the long hill up on the farther side, by the prison. He supposed there were men in there, poor vagrants pinched for stealing a chicken or for sleeping in the road. Yokels who had earned a week's correction for some trivial offence. Poor devils.

He was tired and stiff. Some miles from Northleach he stopped the car and got out, stretching his stiff limbs. He had left the main road to Cheltenham and had taken the little one to Gloucester, hardly more than a lane. He must be somewhere not very far from Bevil Crossways – it didn't matter. He would walk about a little to ease his stiffness and to warm himself, and then he would get on.

It was at the top of a long hill that he had stopped; the country all seemed to be up and down round here. He walked a little way up the lane till he came to a gate in the hedge, where he could look out over the countryside. It was a fine outlook; he could see for miles in the bright moonlight, right away over the valley he had crossed. Down the opposite side, a mile and a half away, he traced the road to Cheltenham on its course, a silver ribbon winding away down the valley.

125

Morris leaned on the gate and stood looking out over the fields. Well, he had made a fool of himself and must start all over again. He had asked a girl to marry him when he couldn't marry her, and had then turned her down. Then he had counted on her waiting and loving nobody else, so that he could come back to her when it suited him to marry. He had been sanguine! And now that he had come to the logical consequence of his folly he must realize that it was his own fault, that it was one of those things that one must accept, that one must learn by. He would not make that mistake again. He was calmer now, and could think about it all quite reasonably and logically.

He was all right now. There would be more pain; it would be a long time before he got over that desolate sense of loneliness. But he could face it now with a quiet mind; he was no longer afraid of his own thoughts. Now he could find somewhere to sleep, and go on his way again in the morning. There was nothing like keeping on the move till you had outdistanced your troubles.

Far away in the valley there appeared a splash of bright light on the road, moving slowly, it seemed, towards him. Some car coming his way. He looked at his watch; it was just after eleven. Well, he would stay here a little longer, and then he would go on into Gloucester and put up for the night. He was all right now, only this news had been a bit sudden.

He could hear the car purring up the road in the distance, perhaps half a mile away. He wondered if it would be able to pass his own in that narrow lane. As it approached he moved out into the road to see how it would negotiate the passage.

It came rapidly towards him and swung round the corner up the hill, its lights flooding the whole road and dazzling his eyes. It was a big landaulette, apparently; a powerful car to have come up that hill so well. It slowed to a walking pace as it edged by his car; Morris stood in the road watching it, bathed in light. It moved clear of the obstruction and accelerated past him. Morris, dazzled, was in darkness again and could see nothing. He walked slowly towards his own car and started it up.

Fifty yards up the hill the landaulette had come to a stand-still. Morris watched it, interested in the black mass of it on the road, the bright red tail-lamp below. The chauffeur had got down and had opened the door, and was talking through the door to the occupants of the car.

Then the chauffeur was walking down the road towards him. Tools, or a repair outfit, he supposed. These chaps never thought about carrying spares on any of these big cars; they left everything lying about the garage and then had to borrow when they got hung up on the road. Careless devils, most of them.

The man came up to him. 'Beg pardon, sir, but are you Mr Morris?'

'My name is Morris,' he replied. Something was sticking in his throat; he could not swallow properly.

'Would you come and speak to Miss Riley?' said the chauffeur.

He looked at Morris curiously in the dim light. Why didn't the gentleman answer? Or make any movement? Perhaps he was deaf or had not understood.

'Miss Helen Riley,' he said in a louder tone. 'Miss Riley would like to speak to you, sir.'

'Right you are,' said Morris mechanically. 'I'll come.'

He moved up the road. The chauffeur was overcome by a horrifying suspicion from the way he walked that this man was drunk, and might insult his mistress. He followed him closely; in his pocket his hand closed upon a tyre lever. He was not a match for this chap physically, but he might be if he was soused.

Morris opened the door of the car. There was only one oc-cupant in the light of the little roof lamp; a girl with deep-brown hair, in evening dress, leaning forward to the door.

'Good evening,' said Morris with a little smile. He had been preparing that.

'Stephen,' said the girl. 'I saw you as we passed, in the light. Why . . . are you staying near here?'

Morris did not answer.

'Stephen,' said the girl again, a little piteously.

'Why, Miss Riley,' said Morris hurriedly, '– I didn't see who it was for the moment – the light . . . I've been wanting to see you to congratulate you.'

It was a poor attempt.

The girl leaned forward in her seat. 'What on, Stephen?' she demanded.

'Why,' said Morris, 'on your – your engagement. I heard . . .' His voice trailed away into silence. 'I only heard this evening,' he added. It seemed to him an extenuating circumstance.

A tender little whimsical smile appeared for a moment and chased the trouble from her face.

'But Stephen,' she said, 'I broke off my engagement years ago. You told Malcolm all about us – don't you remember? And he was going to tell me all about you when – when he was killed. He left the rough draft of a letter to me with all his papers, and Roger got hold of it and sent it on to me. And I broke off my engagement to him.'

A most reliable man, Lechlane; a man who could be trusted always to do the right thing.

Morris stood fingering the tassel of the window. Presently he raised his head and looked at her, a little mistily.

'I see,' he said. 'I suppose you know all about me, then?'

The chauffeur had vanished into the darkness up the road. The girl leaned forward to the door.

'I knew most of it before,' she said.

BOOK II
PILOTAGE

1

Wallace went to the library. He found his father in his usual chair before the fire, a reading-lamp at his elbow, the only lamp alight in the dim room. He crossed to the table, laid a finger against the side of the coffee-pot, and poured himself out a glass of liqueur brandy.

'What d'you think of our guest?' he asked his father.

'Which? Can't say I ever thought much of that boy, Antony.'

'No. Dennison.'

'He seems a pleasant enough young fellow. What is he?'

'Solicitor – just out of his articles.'

'What's he here for?'

Wallace glanced shrewdly at his father. 'He's on an Easter walking tour,' he said. He balanced himself upon his insteps on the fender, his shoulders resting against the mantelpiece.

The old man raised his white head, and glanced keenly up at his son. 'I wouldn't have put him down as the sort of crank that goes walking,' he said.

'No,' said Wallace. He sipped his brandy thoughtfully. 'That's all a put up job of course. It's perfectly obvious what he's here for – the poor, guileless lad. He's come to marry Sheila.'

He laughed suddenly. 'Whoever heard of a man taking a dinner-jacket with him on a walking tour?' he said.

There was silence in the library. The old man sat leaning forward in his chair, stroking his chin. Wallace glanced down at him in some concern. He placed his empty glass upon the mantelpiece. 'He's really not a bad sort,' he said. 'I rather liked him when we met him before, at Aunt Maggie's. He and Sheila were as thick as two thieves then.'

'What's the matter with his leg?' inquired his father abruptly, in a manner reminiscent of the stables.

'Oh, that – that was when we met him. He bust it, you

know, just before the end of the war, and got sent to Aunt Maggie to convalesce.'

He crossed to the table, selected a cigarette with care, and lit it. 'As a matter of fact, it was really rather a creditable story. You know that crack there is between a ship and the quay – where you look down and see the water guggling about? Well, he was getting some liberty men aboard one night – all pretty far gone, I suppose. One of them managed to fall down there – there was a space about three feet wide between the ship and the wall. The man couldn't swim, but instead of chucking him a rope like a Christian, this lad must needs go and jump in after him – Humane Society touch and all that.'

'Down the crack?'

'Down the crack. It was pitch dark and a twenty-foot drop. Some of the chaps in his ship turned up at Falmouth when we were there and came up to ask about him, and told us all the yarn. Seemed to have made no end of an impression on the matloes. Regular cinema thrill – they loved him for it.'

'And he got the fellow out?'

Wallace laughed. 'That's where the fun came in. It was pitch dark; he couldn't see where he was jumping to. You know those great baulks of timber, like railway sleepers, that they let down the side of a ship with ropes to act as fenders? Well, he jumped slap down on to one of those that was floating in the water, and bust his leg in two places. Then they had to haul them both out.

'I can tell you,' he continued, 'it sent up his stock with Sheila. He was quids in after that. I thought he was going to get away with it there and then – and he would have done, too, if he'd had a bean to bless himself with.'

He paused, and went on quietly, 'He just faded away. I'd never seen him till today, and I don't think Sheila had. It's four years.'

His father pondered for a little, the blue smoke from his cigar curling heavily about his head. 'Do you know what he's going to do now?' he said. 'Didn't I hear him say something about Hong Kong?'

Wallace nodded. 'Yes,' he said. 'He's got a chance in his uncle's firm out there – maritime solicitors. I imagine from what he said that he's to go out as a sort of a junior partner.'

'In which case,' said the old man slowly, 'he would probably be in a position to marry.'

'That,' said Wallace, 'had occurred to me.'

His father rose slowly to his feet and threw the stump of his cigar into the fire. 'It's got to come sooner or later,' he said heavily, 'and he seems a decent enough boy.' He turned to his son. 'And anything rather than that Antony. That would be intolerable.'

Wallace laughed. 'I wouldn't worry about that,' he said.

2

For Dennison the week-end passed very quickly. On the afternoon before he left, he went for a walk alone with Sheila.

At the top of a hill a mile and a half from the house, they paused by a low stone wall.

'The leg doesn't seem to bother you much,' she said.

'Not a bit,' said Dennison. He gazed out over the broad expanse of country spread beneath them, chequered with fields. 'It's fine up here.'

The girl did not take her eyes from the scene. 'One sees such a lot of it,' she said. 'I've got an Australian cousin who came over for the war – I brought him up here. He said that English people would talk and get enthusiastic about anything like the Empire or the Navy, but you never heard a word about the beauty of their country. It came quite as a surprise to him to find that England was a pretty country. Afterwards, he told me that he thought England in the summer was just a fairyland.'

'He was a sensible man,' said Dennison.

The girl smiled, and turned to him, 'You ought to know all about that,' she said.

He laughed. 'You mustn't start me off on the sea,' he said, 'or I shall bore you stiff. All England's simply great, of course, but I think the greatest bits of it are the harbours. Coming into a place like Salcombe at dawn, with the mist rising all pearly-like in the river, and a smell of sausages from below ... There's a certain charm in seeing England from the outside.'

'Just like my cousin goes back to Australia, and realizes that he has seen England from the inside.'

'Yes,' said Dennison absently. 'I wonder if he finds Australia as good as England?'

The girl glanced at him curiously. 'Will Hong Kong be as good as England, do you think?'

Dennison started. 'The work will be very interesting,' he said defensively.

'But when you aren't working?' asked the girl, and hated herself for this question.

'Oh, well,' said Dennison. 'There'll be plenty to do, you know. And one will be able to come home fairly often – every three or four years, I think.'

The girl did not speak.

Presently they turned to walk down the hill. 'I shall have to get back to town tomorrow,' said Dennison. 'My walking tour seems to have been a bit of a frost, doesn't it? I meant to do such a lot, too.'

'I don't believe you did,' said the girl. 'And it's been splendid seeing you again.' She walked a little way in silence, and then, 'Don't go and disappear again,' she said. 'You'll – you'll come and stay with us again soon, won't you?'

Dennison glanced at her, smiling gravely. 'I shall be disappearing for good before so very long, you know.'

'Don't look ahead to it. When will you come again? Could you come down for a week-end – the one after next? I expect Antony will be here still.'

'Would you like me to come?' he asked.

She turned to him, a tinge of colour in her cheeks. 'Why,

133

yes,' she said. 'I wouldn't ask you if I didn't want you to come.'

'I'd like to come very much,' he said.

It was that same evening that Antony, who had obviously taken a great liking to Dennison, led him into his bedroom to show him his drawings.

He turned over a sheaf of indifferent attempts and picked out the best for Dennison; the head of a pony, a thin line impression of an old woman with a bundle of sticks, and a small landscape with a smeary look about it. Then from a drawer he took another.

'This is the one I want to give to Sheila,' he said. 'It's one I did quite recently, but I don't know that I care very much for it.'

It was a portrait of Sheila, a head and shoulders in profile. Deficient in technical skill though Antony might be, he had succeeded in catching the likeness remarkably well, the shy, secretive smile, the clustering of the fine brown hair about the neck and ears, the lines of the shoulders. Dennison stood gazing at it; to Antony his silence became embarrassing.

'It's – er – it's rather attractive, isn't it?' he said nervously.

Dennison came to himself. 'It's very attractive,' he said candidly. 'I say, could you . . . I wonder if I might have a print of this?'

Antony flushed with pleasure. 'I'm so glad you like it,' he said, 'but I'm afraid I can't get you a print of it. You see, I spoilt the plate. I wanted to try and intensify it a little, and I did it all wrong and let the mordant get all over it. Perhaps I could let you have this one in a little time, after she's forgotten about it.'

Dennison smiled, and glanced at Antony. 'It's a splendid likeness,' he said.

In person Antony was small and finely built, pale, with smooth black hair and immense black eyes. He spoke rapidly, with a touch of nervousness and with singular charm. The only child of the local rector, he had spent the nineteen years of his life in a perpetual struggle with disease. There was nothing organically wrong with him, yet things that ordinary people never got, Antony had twice. He had been educated at home until he went to Oxford.

3

For the fortnight after Easter Peter Dennison proved an intolerable trial to Lanard with whom he shared rooms in London and a small seven-ton yacht *Irene* on the Solent. He refused to settle down in the evenings, but stood smoking and walking about the sitting-room till Lanard raised a protest. And he was exasperatingly cheerful.

Towards the end of the fortnight he wrote a letter. Lanard watched him dourly from the fireside as he wrote; he knew perfectly well what Dennison was writing about. It was a letter to his uncle in Hong Kong; Lanard suspected that it would be posted after his visit to the Wallaces. Lanard sat watching him, his feet on the fender, a glass of hot water at his elbow. Digestion was a weak point with him.

'They have a sort of thing they call a sampan in China,' he said pleasantly. 'Very good craft, I believe – one can get quite good sport out of them. You have a black boy – or is it a yellow boy? – sitting on the outrigger. And a lateen sail with stiffeners on it like a metre boat. You'll have to have one of those.' He reached out for his hot water.

Dennison put away his letter and came over to the fire. 'I don't think they'd be very much fun,' he said with disarming simplicity. 'You can't work to windward in them.'

'If you ask me,' said Lanard, 'I should think you'd find precious little fun out there at all.'

Dennison did not answer.

'I can't say I've grasped what you're going for at all yet,'

135

continued the other. 'Anyone might think you were simply money-grubbing.' He considered a little, and picked his words carefully. 'You aren't doing so badly here, you know. You're well in with a good firm, and you're making a comfortable little income at work that you're interested in. You've got the *Irene* – or half of her. You've got a pretty good name in the Solent. And you're giving it all up to go on an infernal wild-goose chase like this.'

Dennison finished filling his pipe and dropped into a chair. 'Why?' he asked. 'It's a very good job.'

'You've got a very good job now.'

'Don't be a fool. The Chinese one carries more than double the screw.'

'I see,' said Lanard. 'That's the way it is.' He pondered for a little. 'So that you can marry?'

'So that I can marry.'

Lanard laughed suddenly. 'Pity this job didn't come along in the autumn,' he said cynically.

He rose to his feet and straightened his waistcoat carefully. 'I don't suppose it will do the least good if I say I think you're making a big mistake,' he said. He moved over and stood in the window, a favourite position.

'I shouldn't think so,' said Dennison smiling. 'You think that marriage is a mistake?'

'Good God, no!' said Lanard suddenly. 'That's not the mistake you're making. The mistake you're making is in letting marriage influence your life, or your plans. You're living to suit your marriage – not marrying to suit your life. That's the mistake you're making.'

Dennison glanced at him. 'There's only one thing to say,' he said. 'I've been thinking this over for four years, and I think it's worth it. That's all there is to it.'

'In that case,' said Lanard quietly, 'I suppose there's no more to be said.'

Next day Dennison travelled down to Didcot.

Sheila and Antony were delighted to see him, but the first evening with Antony's added company seemed interminable.

Dennison took his opportunity, when Sheila went out of the room to see about kitchen affairs, to deal with Antony.

'If we're going to do any bird photographs in the morning,' he said to the boy, 'it means getting up very early. I'd go to bed early if I were you.'

Something in his tone checked the indignant comment that sprung to Antony's lips.

'Very early?' he said.

They heard Sheila's footstep in the passage. 'Practically at once, if I were you,' said Dennison gravely.

'All right,' said Antony, 'but I shan't get a wink of sleep before one, you know.'

'I don't care two hoots about that,' said Dennison callously. He said no more, for the girl was in the room.

Presently Antony dutifully put in a plea of fatigue and disappeared. Sheila wrinkled her brows in perplexity. 'He's probably got a novel that he wants to read in bed,' she said. 'I think that must be it. It's hardly ten.'

Dennison threw the end of his cigarette into the fire. He sat down on the edge of the fender. 'It isn't that,' he said. 'I told him that if he was going to get out of bed to photograph birds, he must go to bed early.'

He paused. 'I suppose you know why I told him that,' he said. He glanced up at her, standing beside him, and smiled. 'You see, I wanted to ask you if you'd like to marry me.'

The girl met his eyes with an expression that he could not read. 'Would you like me to go on?' he said. 'Because – I can stop here if you like.'

There was an immense silence.

The girl looked him squarely in the face. 'If I were to tell you to stop,' she said, 'what would you do?'

'Go to bed,' said Dennison, 'and go home by the ten-fifteen tomorrow morning.'

'And if I were to tell you to go on?'

He smiled. 'I should try to tell you how this – how this happened.'

The girl turned, and sat down on the edge of a chair, her chin resting on her hands. 'Please tell me,' she said gravely.

'I see,' said Dennison slowly. There was a long pause, and then he turned to her. 'I don't think it's very much use, is it?'

'I want you to tell me about it.'

'I don't think you do, really,' he said gently.

'But Peter, I do!' she cried.

He moved a little way along the fender towards her, and took her hand in his, turning it over between his own. 'There really isn't very much to say,' he said. 'I love you – you must know that, I think – and I want you to be my wife. I wanted to ask you that four years ago, but it wasn't possible then. I had to wait.'

'You came on a walking tour,' said the girl, 'and you thought I wouldn't see through it.'

'No,' said Dennison. 'You haven't got that quite right. I knew you'd see through it. It didn't matter with you, you see – you were about the only person I wasn't afraid of. It was simply a means of getting in touch with you again. As luck would have it, I happened to meet you on my first day out. I expected to have to hang about the country for a long time.'

'After four years,' said the girl unevenly. 'Oh, Peter!'

'I used to go to your aunt at Falmouth every six months or so,' he said, 'and pay my respects, and usually I'd get a little news of you.' He smiled. 'I used to go down there specially sometimes. And when I was at your aunt's house I could imagine you there again, like it was while my leg was getting well. It's a pity we couldn't have had that time again. I didn't want to tell you this in your own house, and only after two weekends like this. I'm sorry. I didn't see any other way of doing it, and time is rather short. I'm going out to China in September, you see. I want you to come with me.'

'To China?' said the girl.

'Yes,' said Dennison. 'The screw out there puts me in rather a different position. I start as a junior partner, you know.'

There was a long silence. Dennison, watching the girl closely in the firelight, suddenly realized his answer. He knew it quite well. For a moment he sat wondering dully what form it would take, bewildered by his own conviction. Finally the girl broke the silence; her voice was unexpectedly steady.

'Peter dear,' she said quietly. 'I can't. I'm most frightfully sorry – a lot for you, and a little bit for myself. It wouldn't work that way. It isn't you – it's China.'

She paused, and continued, 'Don't think it's because of you. It's not. I've tried to put you out of it, because the thing that really settles it is China. I couldn't live the rest of my life in China.' She paused, tremulous. 'It sounds such a rotten thing to say, in answer to you when you tell me that you love me. When I was a girl I used to think that love was everything worthwhile. But you can't get away from your everyday life. And, Peter dear, I can't change. If it were only for a short time it wouldn't be so bad. One could look forward to coming home, and Daddy could get on quite well for a year or two by himself. I couldn't leave him by himself for always. But I don't want to put the blame on Daddy. Even if he weren't there – I couldn't come, Peter.'

'I know,' said Dennison absently. 'It's – it's a great break.'

The girl leaned forward and laid her hand upon his knee. 'Oh, Peter dear,' she said tremulously – 'I am so frightfully sorry.' Her eyes were full of tears.

Dennison rose to his feet. 'Why, no,' he said gently. 'Don't be sorry. There's nothing to be sorry about, you know. These things happen – they just happen like anything else, and one can't help them. Like a thunderstorm. And one isn't sorry for that.'

And that was all they said.

Before Dennison left to catch the train back to London the next morning, Antony waylaid him in the corridor.

'I say,' the boy murmured confidentially, beckoning Dennison towards his bedroom, 'I've got the etching. I think she's forgotten about it now.'

'Oh,' said Dennison. 'That was awfully good of you.'

Antony produced it from a drawer, wrapped in tissue paper. He handed it to Dennison.

Dennison took it, but did not remove the wrapping. He glanced down at it. 'I don't think I'd better have this,' he said slowly. 'It isn't fair. It was different before.' He handed it back to Antony.

'It was different before?' said Antony keenly.

Dennison nodded.

Antony looked fixedly at him. 'Isn't there any chance of it being different again?' he asked.

Dennison smiled oddly. 'Not much,' he said.

'I'm most awfully sorry,' said the boy simply.

4

Dennison reached London early in the afternoon. Lanard was spending the week-end in Hampshire, and would not be back till late. Dennison drove to his rooms, left his bag, and went to his club. Here he had tea and wrote one or two letters – not because they had to be written, but because it was easier to write them than to sit still. Finally he dined – injudiciously.

Restless, he walked back to his rooms about ten. Lanard was back.

'Matrimony at a considerable discount,' said Dennison, and went to bed without further explanation.

Lanard found this worrying. His was the nature that magnifies disaster; he worried still further when Dennison appeared to breakfast next morning in pyjamas and a dressing-gown.

'What about the daily bread?' he said.

Dennison consigned his office to a future existence for that day, and added a rider embracing the next day and the next. His next query gave his companion a clue.

'Did you leave any food on the *Irene*?'

Lanard considered. 'Two tins of milk, one of bully, about half a pound of coffee, and a little tea. And half a pot of strawberry jam.'

'Marmalade?'

'Ate it.'

Dennison left his breakfast, opened a cupboard, and grovelled in it. He emerged presently, dragging after him a green-stained and battered patent log.

'I wanted that at Easter,' said Lanard. 'If I'd known it was there, I'd have taken it.' He paused. 'Going for long?'

'A week,' said Dennison. 'Where's its line? I brought it up to have it seen to, you know.'

'Line's in the sail store,' said Lanard. 'Saw it when I went to get the light warp for the kedge.'

Dennison continued with his breakfast in a moody silence. 'Pilot's Guide?' he said suddenly.

'On board. And the chart "Weymouth to Owers".'

'Where's "Dodman to Portland"?'

His friend gazed at him keenly. 'You can't get across the West Bay and back in a week,' he said.

Dennison flared suddenly into a temper. 'Damn it,' he said. 'I'll go where I bloody well like. Where's the chart?'

'In the cupboard, I think,' said Lanard gently. He hesitated a moment. 'If you care to wait a day, I'll come with you tomorrow.'

Dennison got up and went into his bedroom. 'No, thanks,' he said wearily. 'There'd be black murder on the high seas.'

'Right you are,' said Lanard. 'Get a new frying-pan if you think of it – it's practically done for. And some prickers for the Primus. Back in a week?'

'Week or ten days,' said Dennison.

Lanard finished his breakfast and departed for his office. Dennison dressed slowly in his sea-going clothes, and packed a bag. For a moment he stood looking round the sitting-room, as if in search of anything that he might have left behind.

'I didn't think it would be like this,' he said aloud.

He turned, picked up his bag, and left the house. He caught a morning train at Waterloo and travelled to Southampton, lunched at a restaurant near the Bar, and caught a bus to Hamble early in the afternoon.

He carried his bag down through the village to the hard, left it there, and went in search of the venerable proprietor of the

141

yard. He found him by the water's edge supervising the finishing touches to a small cutter, brilliant with new paint.

'I'm taking the *Irene* for a week,' said Dennison.

The old man turned and regarded him, his hands thrust deep into the pockets of his overalls. 'Aye,' he said slowly. 'Puttin' out with the last of the ebb, sir? She's no but half an hour to run.'

Dennison glanced down the river; the long green banks of mud and the tall perches bore evidence to his statement. 'She'll run over the flood with the engine,' he said. 'I've got to get some stuff aboard.'

'You'll be staying by the Island?' said the old man.

Dennison shook his head. 'Try and get down west,' he said.

The old man glanced up and regarded the flying southwesterly scud. 'Rain to come,' he said. 'I must get my painting covered. We don't seem to have had no nice weather for drying yet, not as we ought.' He turned to Dennison. 'You'll not do much good this evening,' he said. 'Rain to come, and the tide foul in the channel till after nine.'

'Drop under Calshot for the night,' said Dennison.

They turned and walked up the beach to the sail store. 'Did you hear of Mrs Fleming?' said the old man, 'what kept the baker's shop in the village, died sudden last month.'

He recounted the details of the fatality till they reached the sail store, where he hailed a small boy and directed him to see to the launch of the *Irene*'s dinghy. Dennison fetched his bag, loaded up the little boat with tackle from the store, and rowed out to the yacht.

He opened the hatch and descended into the little saloon. Overhead the dark clouds massed up for rain; the interior of the vessel was damp and smelt unbearably of bilge and the stale fumes of paraffin from the motor under the cockpit. Dennison cast his bag down philosophically upon a settee and opened the skylight. Then he investigated the food that remained mouldering in damp cupboards, collected the cans for the paraffin and methylated spirit, lowered them into the dinghy, and set off again for the shore.

He landed at the hard and walked up the village to the

baker's shop. The baker himself came out of the back premises instead of the florid lady to whom Dennison had been accustomed.

'Afternoon,' he said. 'Two dozen buns and four small loaves, please.'

'Afternoon, Mr Dennison,' said the man. He wrapped the bread in brown paper and wiped his hands upon his apron. ' 'Tis some weeks since we saw you,' he said mechanically.

'Some time,' said Dennison. He paused, and added gently, 'I was most awfully sorry to hear about your loss.'

The remark broke down some barrier of reserve; the baker leaned upon his counter and broke into a flood of simple lamentation. Dennison let him run on. 'And I tell you what I've been doing,' he said. 'I've been gettin' together all the snapshots we took of me and 'er and the kiddies, and binding them up into a little book' – he indicated the size – 'just like that. My sister Em'ly what lives with me now said I didn't ought to do it, an' I ought to think of other things. But I don't see that – do you? I didn't want to let it all go . . . and I wanted them photygraphs.'

Dennison nodded. 'You want to make the most of what you've got,' he said. 'One doesn't get so very much.'

He returned on board with a heavy heart, spread a bun with marmalade and ate it in lieu of tea, and made his bed of blankets. For a time he busied himself setting things in order in the saloon, then he went and stood in the hatchway and took a long look at the weather. It was threatening. He decided not to make sail but to run down to Calshot under the engine and anchor for the night. Under sail it would be a dead beat out against the tide. The rising flood lapped mournfully along the sides of the vessel.

He made the dinghy fast astern, started his engine, slipped his mooring, and stood away down the river, cold and dispirited. Vessel after vessel, perch after perch, passed him with maddening slowness; the thick brown water churned into a loathsome foam at the edge of the mud-flats. Slowly he drew up to the red cage buoy at the mouth of the river, and headed across the water to Calshot. By the time he arrived, it had begun to rain in a misty, undecided fashion; he brought up and dropped anchor in about two fathoms under the lee of the mud-flats, not very far from the castle and the air station. There was nothing to do on deck; he remained in the cockpit till the vessel had found her position and was riding quietly to her anchor; then he went below and trimmed the riding light.

He spent an hour working in his little vessel, an hour of occupation and comparative happiness that carried him on till after dark. He trimmed every lamp in the ship, filled the tanks of the engine, cleaned the Primus stove, set his riding light on the forestay, pumped out the vessel, unpacked his bag and arranged his clothes in the tiny cupboards, put the patent log in a safe place with a bottle of rum and another one of turpentine to keep it company. Then he laid his supper very elaborately, and supped off cocoa, bully beef, and a boiled egg, topping up with bread and jam. He scraped the mildew off the top of the jam and deposited it in the slop-bucket; he was particular about what he ate.

After supper he washed up his plates, emptied the slop-pail over the side, and saw that his riding light was burning properly. Then he went below and tidied up the little forecastle. And then there was nothing else to be done.

He lit a pipe, returned to the saloon, and produced a coil of new wire rope that it was his intention to turn into a new pair of bowsprit shrouds. But it was too dark to go up on deck and measure the length, so that all he could do was to splice one end of it round an eye and serve it, and in half an hour he was again at a loss. In desperation he turned to his charts and sailing directions, and spread them out upon the table. He knew them by heart; every light, every buoy, almost to every sounding upon the sheets. Outside the rain had set in in earnest and dripped monotonously on the deck, pouring in tiny cascades from the puckers of the mainsail at each roll of the vessel. Below, everything was damp and clammy to the touch, with all the grim squalor of a small ship at sea. On deck there was little to be seen through the rain; the air station lay dark and deserted. A couple of seaplanes rocked lightly at their buoys a hundred yards away; in the other direction the water lapped steadily along the mud-banks, gradually vanishing with the rising tide. In the fairway an occasional steamer showed a light.

He was quite alone.

Dennison slept badly, was early awake, got up, and was over the side by six o'clock. It was a threatening morning; a stiff breeze from the south-west with scud flying over the sky. The wind blew bitterly upon him as he scrambled on board again; he swore at it in futile rage. It was the worst possible wind for him, dead in his teeth for going west. When the tide began to run against it there would be a short, wetting little sea in the Solent. For a moment he thought of staying in the shelter of the Island, and abandoned the thought immediately in a miserable spasm of temper. He was damned if he'd change his plans.

He dressed and cooked his breakfast. He did not hurry; it would be useless to attempt to beat down the Solent without the tide under him, and the tide would not begin to run till ten o'clock. He breakfasted moodily, washed his plate, and set to work to cook a piece of steak which he would eat cold later in the day. He put the steak with some cold potatoes and half a loaf of bread in a large pudding-basin, and hid it away in a locker in the cockpit. On such a day as this he would have little time for lunch, sailing single-handed. He thought that he would make for Poole if it proved to be a dead beat all the way. If he got a fair slant of wind at the Needles, he would run for Lulworth or Weymouth. Either course would give him ten or twelve hours' sailing and tire him out. He wanted to be tired.

He got under way about half-past nine with two reefs down, and drew out of the entrance to the Water. From the Castle Point buoy he could lay West Cowes, and crossed the edge of the Brambles in a smother of spray, battened down and huddling in his oilskins. It was his luck to get a wetting at the start. Everything on this infernal day was going to go wrong.

There were few yachts in Cowes; it was too early in the

season for many vessels to be afloat. There was one big white yawl in the Roads, of ninety or a hundred tons, with a spoon bow and a long counter. Dennison strained his eyes at her. There were men working on her deck, and he thought she was getting under way. He had not got his glasses on deck, and was afraid to leave the helm and open up the vessel to get them in so short a sea. He put her down as either the *Laertes* or the *Clematis*, reached in nearly to the beach at West Cowes, and put about on the other tack.

The morning passed wearily away. With the tide under him he made fairly good progress down the Solent in repeated tacks. The big yawl had come out of Cowes and was following him down under her trysail; she had given him three-quarters of an hour start and was drawing up on him steadily. From time to time he turned to look at her, the only other vessel on the waters. She followed him up grandly, carrying her wind well. He was nearly sure she was the *Clematis*; the *Laertes* would not have ridden the seas so cleanly. She had been a racing boat.

By one o'clock he was nearly up to Yarmouth. The deck was wet and glistening with the repeated spray; Dennison was cold and out of temper. He peered ahead into the murk and tried to imagine what sort of sea he would find at the Needles. He wanted to get down to Poole if possible; at the same time he was experienced enough to know the futility of trying to beat his way down against a westerly gale. He determined to run out to the Needles and have a look at it. If he could lay a course for Studland he would carry on; otherwise he would put back to Yarmouth for the night.

Near the entrance to Lymington he put about on to the starboard tack.

The big yawl had practically caught him up, and was crossing to meet him from the other side of the Solent. It was evident now that she was the *Clematis*, owned by a shipping magnate, Sir David Fisher; Dennison wondered vaguely if the owner were on board. She came over from the Island to intercept his course, gently parting the waves with her powerful spoon bow and making nothing of the sea that caused him such

146

discomfort. He watched her admiringly as she drove towards him.

It became evident that she would pass very close across his bows. She approached him on the port tack, only one man visible on deck at the helm. Dennison held on his course; he had the right of way. She would have to bear away a little and pass astern of him; there would be no room for her to cross his bows.

The yawl held on her course. Dennison gazed at her incredulously for a moment; then realized that she was bluffing him. He was cold, hungry, and wet; the discovery sent a sudden flare of anger through him. Damn it, let her put her helm up and bear away! He held resolutely to his course.

As the vessels closed, all the emotions of the last two days burst out in a sudden fit of temper. He was damned if he was going to give way to any *nouveau riche* who cared to barge about the Solent displaying his breeding. There were too many of the swine about. The fellow had only to get one of his men on deck, slip his mainsheet a little, and bear away. He had a full crew aboard; Dennison had seen them. He was damned if he'd give way.

He held on his course.

When she was fifty yards away, he realized that a collision was imminent. He thought rapidly. He might avoid an accident by throwing his little vessel into irons – with the risk of falling on to the *Clematis*, in which case he might be liable for the damages, as not having held his course. He was cold and wet; at the sight of the gleaming paint and winking brass of the yawl, he flamed into a passion. By God, he'd let her have it. She should get what she was asking for. He'd do her as much damage as he bloody well could, and leave her to pay for both. He stood up in the cockpit the better to con his vessel, and held the helm steady.

The sharp white bow crossed his bowsprit; at the last moment the *Clematis* flung up into the wind with a slatting of heavy canvas. It was too late. Dennison held his course, blazing with temper. His bowsprit missed her main shrouds, crossed the bulwarks and stove in the motor-launch that she

147

carried on her deck. The bobstay parted with a sharp twang, and the straight stem of the little cutter crashed home upon the glossy whiteness of the topside, splintering and gouging.

'God,' said Dennison, 'that's marked the swine!' and ran forward to separate the vessels.

The deck of the yawl was suddenly alive with men. A man at the bows shouted something, and somebody was heaving on the end of his bowsprit to push him clear. He ran forward of the mast. At that moment the bow of the Irene dropped into the trough of a sea. Her bowsprit crashed down on to the bulwarks of the *Clematis* as she dropped; then the heel of the spar leaped from the deck and came inboard waist high, straight for Dennison. He jumped backwards by the mast, and brought up against the main halyards. He put out his hand to ward the blow. A wire plucked agonizingly at his thumb, and then the spar was grinding its way along his ribs, slowly, intolerably. Suddenly the vessels freed and lay pitching together for a moment, grinding their sides; the spar jerked and fell heavily at his feet. Dennison caught blindly at the halyards and dropped slowly to his hands and knees beside the little capstan, sweating with pain.

From a great distance voices came to him, and the tag end of a sentence, '– he's hurt, I tell you. Look at him.' Then came a silence; perhaps they were looking at him. Of course he was hurt ... the bloody fools. There was a heavy thump on his deck, and the same voice:

'No, one's enough,' and another thump. Then came silence, an end to the bustle and confusion, and a thin voice in the distance bellowing something about Yarmouth Roads.

Dennison raised his head; immediately the staysail began to beat about him cruelly. Somebody came forward and helped him to his feet.

He looked around him, drawing a deep breath, and winced at a fresh spasm of pain along his ribs. Away up to windward the yawl was lowering her trysail with a six-foot rent in it, laying to under her foresheets and mizzen. There was a man in yachting clothes beside him, and a sailor of the *Clematis* at the helm. His hand throbbed and ached intolerably. He turned aft.

148

'Bear away,' he shouted. 'Slack out some sheet. Let her away – right away. So. All right, keep her at that.' He turned to the man beside him. 'Help me get a line round this spar, or it'll be on top of us.' He fumbled clumsily with his left hand.

The sailor hailed him from the cockpit. 'Cam'ee aft, sir, 'n take her, 'n let me come forrard.'

'Right,' said Dennison. He thrust his injured hand between the buttons of his coat and stumbled aft to the little cockpit. He took the helm and sat down, numb with pain, anxiously watching the sailor moving deftly about the wreckage in the bows. With the help of the gentleman, a lean, cadaverous fellow perhaps twenty-eight or thirty years of age, the sailor got the foresheets off undamaged and passed a line round the spar. Then he turned aft.

'Better start yure motor going, sir, 'n get the sail off her, 'n head up for Yarmouth, I rackon?' His voice ended on the rising note of a question, in true West Country fashion.

'I know about motors.' said the lean man, and jumped down into the cabin, working under Dennison's directions. The sailor came aft.

'Where be tyers tu?' he inquired. He was a genial old man, with a pleasant fatherly air, wearing gold ear-rings. Dennison indicated the locker. 'Be 'ee hurt bad, sir?' He clucked his tongue in sympathy. 'Deary, deary me! Sir David will be turrible upset.'

Dennison smiled faintly. 'Who was in charge of your vessel?' he asked.

The sailor paused. 'Why, skipper had her,' he said. 'We was all below tu dinner, 'n he was tu give us a call when he wanted tu put about.' He continued with his work for a minute, and then, 'Rackon skipper don't take much account o' the little boats,' he said.

'Reckon he don't,' said Dennison grimly.

The motor began to throb, and coughed steadily into the water. The lean man appeared in the hatchway. The sailor called to him and instructed him in the two halyards; Dennison threw her up into the wind and they lowered the sail, wrapping it roughly with the tyers.

149

They came aft. 'I say,' said the lean man, 'I'm extremely sorry about this. We were in the wrong, weren't we? I don't know much about it, I'm afraid – I'm only a passenger.'

The sailor spat into the sea. 'Rackon we was wrong,' he observed.

They settled down to a wearisome run to Yarmouth. Dennison unbuttoned a couple of buttons of his oilskins and gently drew his hand out. The skin was unbroken, but it was swollen and discoloured already, and the thumb stood out in an uncouth attitude. The trouble was evident.

'Can you put that back?' asked Dennison.

The lean man took the hand in his and whistled. 'What bad luck,' he said. 'All right. It'll hurt like hell for a minute, you know.'

He took the wrist in one hand and the thumb firmly in the other, and gave a savage tug at it. Dennison bit his lip, but the thumb had gone back into its normal position and he could move it a little. The stranger glanced at him keenly. 'What about a quick one?' he said. 'All right, I'll get it.'

He disappeared below, and emerged presently with a tumbler half full of rum. 'I nearly as possible poured you out turps,' he said. He watched Dennison as he drank. 'Did that bowsprit hit you when it came back? I thought I saw it.'

'It grazed my ribs,' said Dennison. 'I've got too many clothes on for it to do much damage.'

The *Clematis* was three-quarters of a mile ahead, nearly into Yarmouth. 'Come below and let's have a look,' said the lean man. 'We can get a doctor in Yarmouth.'

Dennison obeyed and relapsed into comparative comfort on his bunk, confident that his vessel was in safe hands. He was accustomed to slight injuries; it was not the first time that he had stretched himself thankfully on his bunk, to watch the lamp gyrating in the gymbals while the vessel hurried for the nearest harbour. The lean man pronounced his ribs intact, made him comfortable, and went on deck. Dennison fell into a doze till he was roused by the bustle of anchoring.

The lean man appeared in the hatchway. 'Look here,' he said. 'Stay where you are for a bit. I'm going to hop off to the

Clematis in your dinghy and tell them about it. I think you ought to have a doctor to look at you. I want to see Sir David. I won't be long – half an hour at the most. The chap will be on board if you want anything; he's tidying up the mess forward.'

'All right,' said Dennison.

The stranger got into the dinghy and rowed off to the *Clematis*. He gave the painter to one of the hands and mounted the ladder; at the top he was met by an immense red-haired man in plus-fours, broad-shouldered and massively built.

'I say, Rawdon,' said the lean man. 'Where's Sir David?'

The red-haired man raised his head and looked at him for a minute in bovine fashion, accentuated by his china blue eyes. Then he broke into a slow smile. 'Having a word with the skipper in the saloon,' he said, in a soft little voice that contrasted oddly with his bulk. 'I wouldn't go down just yet.'

They fell into step and paced together up and down the deck. The lean man gave his companion a brief account of the state of affairs on board the *Irene*. Presently he was interrupted by the owner, who came up from below, followed by a crestfallen young officer, who went about his work without a word.

Sir David walked to meet them. 'Mr Morris,' he said, 'is that young man much hurt?' He was a man well on in life, clean-shaven, with silvery hair and the hard features of the man who knows exactly where his interests lie. 'I can't tell you how sorry I am that this has happened. I've cruised for very nearly thirty years, and I've only once done such a thing before.' His eyes turned expressively towards the young skipper. 'That was under similar circumstances,' he said.

The man that he called Morris gave an account of Dennison's injuries. 'He tells me that this is his first day out of a ten-days' cruise – single-handed,' he said. 'He lives in London.'

The baronet frowned, and fixed the *Irene* with his eye. 'Can he manage by himself?'

'I shouldn't think so – not for a day or two.'

Sir David turned sharply from the *Irene*. 'All right,' he said. 'Then we must manage for him. I'll get a doctor off to see him. Then if it's only rest he wants, we can have him aboard here. I'll have his vessel towed to Cowes for refitting. She'll take about three days. By the time he's fit, she'll be ready for him.'

He glanced at the hole stove in the varnished side of the motor-launch. 'My launch must go ashore,' he said. 'We'll run back to Cowes tomorrow. This young man can go in the companion state-room.' He turned to the lean man. 'I wonder if you would mind getting the doctor?' he said. 'In my name, of course. I'll have you put ashore. Keep the boat and take the doctor off at once if you can get one. I'll go aboard his vessel and see him when you get there. What is his name?'

'I don't know,' said Morris.

'The vessel?'

'The *Irene*.'

Morris went on shore, rowed by a sailor; Rawdon and the baronet turned and went down into the saloon.

The owner gave a few brief instructions to the steward about the preparation of the vacant state-room. Then he turned to Rawdon. 'A most unfortunate business,' he said. He went to the bookcase and picked out *Lloyds Register of Yachts*, laid it on the table, and turned the leaves. 'Here we are. Irene – Irene – Irene. This is the one. I suppose. *Irene* wood cutter, seven ton, twenty-seven foot waterline, paraffin motor, built 1903, Luke. Owner, P. Dennison.'

'That sounds like her,' said Rawdon.

The other did not reply; Rawdon glanced at him. He was frowning and staring absently at the bulkhead. 'P. Dennison,' he said. 'Peter Dennison. It would be odd if this was one of them turned up again.' He left his guest and crossed to one of the settees, dragged the seat cushion from it, and disclosed a locker beneath. He opened it; it was filled with bound volumes of old yachting journals. 'P. Dennison,' he muttered.

He selected one covering August 1911, laid it on the table, and opened it, turning the pages rapidly. He paused at the programme of a long-forgotten race 'Here we are,' he said. 'I thought we should find it. *Runagate*, fifteen ton, helmsman P. Dennison.'

152

He ran his eye rapidly down the letterpress. 'Here we are,' he said. ' "Much interest will be centred on the *Runagate*, whose helmsman, P. Dennison, is only sixteen years of age." '

'That's interesting,' said Rawdon.

Sir David closed the volume and replaced it in the locker. 'I must go off and see him,' he said. 'You won't mind if I leave you?' He moved to the foot of the companion, then paused and came back into the saloon.

'I say, Charles,' he said. 'Do you mind if we have him on board? I take it that if he comes he will be in bed for a day or so.'

His guest knitted his great brows together in a frown.

'I don't mind if you don't,' he said. 'I don't see that it matters very much if he's the right sort. And I suppose another couple of evenings will see us through.'

'I suppose so,' said the baronet. He glanced out through a port over the water to the town, gabled and russet brown. 'I don't quite like to let him go to a hotel, and that seems the only alternative. Anyway, I'll see what he looks like. If he's the Dennison I'm thinking of, he won't be any trouble to us.'

He went on deck. Morris had reached the *Irene* and was helping the doctor on board. Sir David called for the cutter's dinghy, and followed him.

He boarded the *Irene* with some difficulty, and descended into the tiny, crowded saloon. There was no room for more than two to stand; on arrival Morris perforce sat down on the settee opposite Dennison, who wished heartily that the lot of them would clear off and leave him to sort himself out. Sir David stood at the foot of the ladder and apologized in grave, incisive sentences, for the part his vessel had played in the encounter. Dennison responded lamely.

It transpired that he had no plans beyond an idea to 'stay here for the night and clear up the mess in the morning'.

Sir David listened gravely. 'I should like to suggest an alternative scheme,' he said. 'If you would care to come aboard the *Clematis* for a day or two, we have a vacant state-room. In that case, I could tow your vessel to Cowes tomorrow, to refit at Flanagan's. That would take about three days; after that perhaps you would be fit enough to continue your cruise.'

Dennison smiled wryly. 'Flanagan won't have any men to spare,' he said. 'Everybody's fitting out now. He wouldn't look at a little job like this.'

The other did not smile. 'Flanagan will do what I tell him,' he said quietly; at the suggestion of power Dennison opened his eyes. 'I can promise that your vessel will be ready for sea by the time you are able to sail her.'

The doctor broke in with commendations of the scheme. 'You won't be able to do anything with that thumb for several days,' he said. 'And if I were you, I'd stay in bed for a day or so to rest those muscles. You'll be glad enough to lie up once they begin to stiffen.'

The truth of that statement was already painfully evident to Dennison. He made no more demur, but accepted the invitation. The meeting broke up; Sir David went on deck followed by the doctor. Dennison was left with the lean man.

'I say,' he said. 'Was that Sir David Fisher?'

'That's him,' said Morris. He yawned, and rose from the settee. 'Look here, I'd better pack up some things for you. Don't move; tell me what to get.'

'Damn it,' said Dennison. 'I haven't any clothes fit to wear.'

'No ladies,' said Morris. 'There's only four of us on board. Sir David, his secretary, Captain Rawdon, and I. We can fit you up with anything you want.'

So Dennison left the *Irene* and was rowed aboard the *Clematis*. He paused on deck to pass a word or two with the skipper, who thawed a little as they wagged their heads together over the damaged launch. A joyous remark leapt to his mind, 'If I were you, I'd carry your launch on the port side in future', but he refrained from uttering it, and went below with Morris to a little state-room beside the door into the saloon, and was put to bed in a luxurious little berth with soft blankets and, incongruous on a yacht, lavender-smelling sheets. By and by the steward came and rigged a little table that hung on to the side of his berth, and brought him China tea and buttered toast, and several varieties of cake. After that, being warm and replete for the first time that day and moderately comfortable so long as he kept still, he went to sleep. It was dark when he awoke; the lean man came with a supply of novels and an electric reading-lamp that plugged into a socket in the bulkhead. Dennison was accustomed to read in his bunk in a similar manner on board the *Irene* where there was a niche behind his pillow dark with the grease of a hundred candle ends. Presently came dinner.

After dinner he made himself comfortable for the night, turned out his light, rolled painfully on to his uninjured side, and tried to sleep. It was a long time before he succeeded. His side gave him considerable pain, and there was a dull ache in his thumb intensified by the gentle pressure of the bedclothes. Now that he was alone and the events of the day were over, he had time to think; the memory of the last few days came flooding back into his mind, and were the more poignant for having been forgotten. He was in pain, and he was cruelly disappointed; he lay quiet in the darkness, till the darkness seemed to enter and become a part of him; a darkness that, perhaps, would never quite leave him – as it had never quite left Lanard. There would be alleviations, and the sting would go; other friendships would crop up, other ties and interests – but things would never quite be the same again as they had been in the Golden Age, when he had worked four years for Sheila.

Perhaps the gods are merciful. At all events, they relented a little in the case of this young man and gave him a puzzle to occupy his attention, much as a hospital nurse will give a puzzle of cardboard, glass, and silver balls to a child in pain. Dennison's cabin opened on to the companion, close beside the saloon door. From the saloon came a ceaseless murmur of voices from the men inside; they had settled down directly after dinner and had talked incessantly, a rumbling discussion deadened by the bulkhead. About ten o'clock, there was a step on deck, and someone came down the companion jingling a tray of tumblers; the nightcap, thought Dennison. The steward opened the door into the saloon and the conversation became audible. Sir David was the first to speak.

155

'Nine hundred and fifty miles,' he said. 'We will take that as the maximum, then. All right, put it down over there. Now before we fix definitely on that distance, I want you to consider, Mr Morris, whether you are quite satisfied with the margin of safety in taking your departure.'

The lean man spoke. 'I think so,' he said slowly. 'I can't say quite definitely till I've tried it, of course. It looks all right on paper. You see, you give us a kick behind that gives us thirty-eight miles an hour, and then there's a hundred and ten feet clear before—'

The door closed again; the steward passed aft to the other state-rooms, whistling softly as he prepared the beds.

Dennison lay wondering, shaken for the moment from his misery. What on earth had they been talking about? Taking a departure might have reference to navigation – but margin of safety? And who was to deliver the kick behind that would give 'us' thirty-eight miles an hour?

The water lapped quietly along the side of the vessel beside his head; along the timbers came the faint chunking of the rudder, swaying beneath the counter in the tideway. Dennison stirred slightly in his bed, found a comfortable position, and fell fast asleep.

Over the cabin door, upon the glossy whiteness of the bulkhead, was a quaint device; the word 'CLEMATIS' traced in red stones, each circular and set in a little oxidized ring. The morning sun streamed in through the port and lit up the bulkhead, making the red stones glow with sombre fire. Dennison lay sleepily in bed and watched the shifting light upon the deck beams, reflected from the water. Things were beginning to stir about the vessel; there was a sluicing and scrubbing on the deck above his head, voices in the state-rooms aft, and presently somebody passed his door, whistling, went up the companion, and plunged over the side. Dennison lay listening to the silvery tinkle of the bubbles rising against the side of the vessel; he put down the bather as the lean man.

Morris poked his head in at the door as he passed back to his cabin; a tousled figure in a dressing-gown.

156

'How d'you sleep? Oh, that's good. I hope you noted my dive just now – I'll carry the marks to my grave, I shouldn't wonder. It's years since I bathed before breakfast – not since I left Oxford.'

He returned in half an hour or so, dressed and impatient for his breakfast. Dennison was already halfway through his. 'Ours isn't ready yet,' said Morris. 'But I'll have a lump of sugar – thank you. To bridge the chasm.'

He sat down on Dennison's clothes. 'Do you usually sail alone? I should have thought it was taking a bit of a risk.'

'I sail alone a good bit,' said Dennison. He was feeling more himself this morning; he glanced shrewdly at the other. 'One isn't run down every day, you know.'

He was not mistaken in his man; Morris called him by an unparliamentary name and took another lump of sugar. 'In point of fact,' he said, 'it was you who ran us down, from what I saw of it.'

'I say,' said Dennison. 'Are you going to Cowes this morning?'

'I believe so. Going to tow your vessel up to Flanagan's yard.'

Dennison frowned thoughtfully. 'Sir David must be a pretty good man if he can get Flanagan to touch the *Irene* out of her turn,' he said. 'Do you think he has any idea of the rush there is in the yards at this time of year?'

Morris seemed to hesitate for a moment; when he spoke, he picked his words carefully.

'I wouldn't have any anxiety on that score,' he said. 'We've been doing business with Flanagan recently, and Flanagan will certainly do this for us. But as it happens, it won't be necessary for him to make any alteration in his general routine. Sir David is fitting out another yacht at Flanagan's; all that will be necessary is for Flanagan to take one or two men off her for a few days. That is the course Sir David will advise.'

'Another yacht!' said Dennison. 'What is she?'

'A big racing cutter. The *Chrysanthe*.'

Dennison started up in his bunk and propped himself on his elbow with a spasm of pain. '*Chrysanthe!*' he said. 'Lord, I didn't know she was coming out again! Has he bought her, then?'

'I believe so.'

'*Chrysanthe!*' said Dennison, and sank back again into his bunk. He knew the vessel well by repute. She had been built in 1912 and had appeared the following year at the principal regattas in the Big Class. At the outset of her career she had created something of a sensation by beating *Britannia* on *Brittannia*'s day. As fashions went, she had been slightly under-canvassed, and had done little for the remainder of the last season before the war. Since then she had been laid up. Now, it seemed, she was to appear again.

'Another vessel for the Big Class,' said Dennison at last. 'The more the merrier.'

Morris rose to his feet and opened the door. 'I say,' he said, and paused. 'I'd better go aboard your vessel and clear up any valuables, hadn't I? Before we hand her over to Flanagan.'

'I suppose so,' said Dennison thoughtfully. 'There's a pair of glasses in the rack in the cabin, and a sextant in the cupboard on the port side. You might have a look round and bring off anything that strikes you as valuable. Don't bother much – I've never had any trouble in that way.'

Morris made a good breakfast, smoked a pipe, and put off to the *Irene* with a bag. He spent half an hour aboard the little vessel, looked through every cupboard, made a selection of articles of value, and returned on board. He found Rawdon on deck.

Morris walked across the deck and placed the bag on a chair. He beckoned to Rawdon with his head; the red-haired man strolled towards him. 'What is it?' he said.

Morris spoke softly. 'Things I brought off the little cutter,' he said, '– valuables, before she goes in for overhaul.' He opened the bag upon the chair and produced a miscellaneous assortment of objects one by one; a bottle of rum half empty, a pair of Zeiss glasses, a rolling parallel ruler, a few mathematical instruments, a sextant in a case, a prismatic compass, and a chronometer deck watch of navy pattern. The red-haired man stood by in perfect silence while Morris lifted out these articles one by one and replaced them in the bag. 'There were a whole lot of books on navigation there, too,' he said. 'Nautical Almanacks and all sorts of other star tables – specialized things.' He paused; neither of them spoke for a minute. 'You see, it's practically all navigation stuff – all that's of any value.'

He closed the bag and fell into step with Rawdon as he resumed his pacing up and down the deck. 'What's your idea, then?' asked Rawdon.

'I haven't got one,' said Morris. 'Only it's – interesting. I don't mind telling you, I've been thinking a good bit about this matter of the navigator. We've been content to go on the assumption that it will be easy enough to get in an expert at the job when the time comes – and, by the way, we ought to be thinking about that soon. That's a thing we ought to discuss with Sir David while we're here.'

The older man glanced at him keenly. 'It will be easy to get a good man,' he said.

'Easy enough to get a good navigator,' said Morris briefly. 'Not so damned easy to get a good man.' He stopped and faced Rawdon. 'I know nothing about the sea,' he said. 'If we get into any trouble on the way and I only have some pie-faced theorist with me – we might very soon find ourselves in Queer Street. That's what I'm thinking about. The navigation itself is child's play – I could do it myself.'

'I see,' said Rawdon. He stood motionless for a little, meditatively caressing his chin with one great hand. 'Well,' he said at last. 'You know you've got a free hand in that sort of thing. All Sir David cares about is getting the job done. That sort of detail is entirely our affair. Only – don't do anything in a hurry. We shall have to mention it to him before taking any definite steps in that matter.'

They walked aft to the companion; Morris took the bag and went below to Dennison. The latter laid down his book as Morris entered.

'Ha!' he said. 'Feeling twice the man I was. I'm going to get up this afternoon.'

'Much better not,' said Morris. 'Here's your stuff. I brought

159

off all that I thought was likely to get snaffled – glasses, sextant, chronometer, and a lot of odds and ends.' He sat down and lit a cigarette.

Dennison peered into the bag. 'And half a bottle of rum,' he said. 'It was nice of you to think of that.'

Morris blew a long cloud of smoke, and laughed. 'What do you use all those navigating instruments for?' he inquired. 'You never go out of sight of land, do you?'

'Lord, yes,' said Dennison. 'Running down Channel. But you're quite right – one doesn't often need them. Last summer we went to the west of Ireland – we were four days from the Longships to Cape Clear. I took a good many sights then – more for practice than anything else. Give me a fag.'

'Did you make a good landfall?'

Dennison blew a long cloud. 'Oh yes,' he said carelessly. 'There's nothing in it, you know. We hit it off just about as I expected. It's not far, but we took long enough over it. Cat's-paws all the way across.'

Morris gazed at him curiously. 'I suppose you spend all your spare time doing this,' he said. 'Did you cruise at Easter?'

Dennison thrust his cigarette over the side of the bunk and flicked the ash on to the floor with a steady hand. 'No,' he said. 'This Easter was the first I've missed since the war. I was staying with some people in Berkshire – a place called Little Tinney, just under the Downs. Do you know that part at all? Delightful country.'

'I stayed a week-end down in that part of the world once,' said Morris. 'I forget exactly where Little Tinney is, but we weren't very far away. They fetched us from Didcot in a car; a chap who was at Oxford with me. People called Wallace.'

Dennison glanced sharply at the lean man, and smiled queerly. 'I was staying with the Wallaces,' he said.

'No – really? Do you know them well?'

'Not very well,' said Dennison. 'I met them both – Wallace and his sister, about four years ago, but I'd rather lost touch with them till – till this Easter.'

Morris nodded. 'Funny,' he said. 'I knew Jimmie Wallace quite well up at Oxford after the war; I often meet him in

Town. My wife and I went down there one week-end – oh, about eighteen months ago. Charming girl his sister is!'

'Yes,' said Dennison dryly. They chatted for a little, discussing the Wallaces and the house at Little Tinney. Then came a bustle on deck of getting under way under motor power, and of taking the *Irene* in tow. Morris went on deck, and Dennison was left to his own devices, to his newly awakened memories of Little Tinney and all that was there.

But one thing puzzled him, eluding all the efforts of his memory. He was nearly certain that at some time or other he had heard Sheila speak of a man called Morris, and that she had mentioned some peculiar and outstanding fact connected with him. Cudgel his brains as he might, he could not recall the occasion or what it was she had mentioned as peculiar about Morris, what it was that differentiated him from other men. There was something; of that he was quite certain.

The morning was calm and hazy, the tide sweeping down through the roads in placid swirls and eddies. Both vessels weighed anchor and got under way under their engines; then a line was passed to the *Irene* and she was taken in tow, her engine being of little use against the tide. In the *Clematis* there sprang up a subdued, monotonous thudding that drove all coherent thought from the head and jingled the tumblers in the racks. She turned and stemmed the tide, and proceeded up the Solent, towing the *Irene* behind her in the manner of a dinghy.

It was nearly lunch-time when they dropped anchor in Cowes Roads. The *Irene* cast off her tow and motored up the river to Flanagan's, where she berthed temporarily against a quay. From the deck Sir David watched her in, then turned and went below to pay a visit to his guest.

'Your cutter's safely berthed in Flanagan's yard,' he said. 'I'll go ashore this afternoon and see Flanagan about her. How are you feeling?'

'Well enough to get up,' said Dennison. 'Mr Morris tells me you've bought *Chrysanthe*, sir.'

The baronet smiled happily, and sat down on Dennison's clothes. 'We should get some good sport out of her,' he said.

'My brother George always intended to make a bid for her – but he died. And it's only lately that I have had leisure to think about racing. For a man who is still at work, cruising should come first. Don't you find that so?'

'Every time,' said Dennison emphatically.

The baronet glanced round the cabin. 'I've had some good cruises in this vessel,' he said. 'Not very ambitious – but good holidays. I wouldn't like to part with her. As for *Chrysanthe*, I shall sail her under her old rig this season. For one thing, there isn't time to change. But after that, I've been thinking of scrapping her gear and re-rigging her Bermuda fashion. In a similar manner to *Nyria*.'

They plunged into an animated discussion of the technical details of the plan, of the questions of sail area, mast position, and seaworthy qualities of the Bermuda rig. They talked for twenty minutes; then a bell rang for lunch. The baronet rose.

'Of course,' he said, 'we really know very little about her. We shall learn a great deal this season. It's a little early to discuss it before we've had an opportunity to try her paces.'

He passed into the saloon and sat down to lunch in silence. 'He's perfectly right,' he thought. 'She would take more ballast forward. I hadn't thought of that.'

Lunch over, they smoked a pipe in the saloon, then called for a dinghy and went ashore. Morris wandered off to make some purchases in Cowes; Sir David and Rawdon made their way to Flanagan's yard. They passed in at the gates and strolled to the quay where the *Irene* lay, inspected her closely, and turned away. In the background, the *Chrysanthe* lay on a slip, being painted, monstrous and ungainly.

The two men picked their way across the litter to the ramshackle little offices. Sir David entered, knocked at a door, and went in, followed by Rawdon. At a roll-top desk was seated a stout middle-aged man in a suit of sad, plebeian grey, sipping a cup of tea, his feet up on a chair. At the sight of his visitors, he laid down the cup and rose ponderously to his feet.

'Good morning, gentlemen,' he said. 'You'll have come to look over *Chrysanthe*? Getting along with her nicely now. Tell me, did you see the new hollow gaff has come in for her? 'Tis a beautiful gaff, and half again as light as the old one.'

'I'd like to have a look at it,' said the baronet. 'As a matter of fact, I've brought a repair job. I ran down a small cutter in the Solent yesterday, I'm sorry to say, and took the bowsprit out of her.'

'Do you tell me that now!' said Flanagan.

Sir David nodded. 'I want her got ready for sea again at once,' he said. 'At once. You can take men off *Chrysanthe* for her if necessary.'

The stout man clucked his tongue against the roof of his mouth. 'Deary me,' he said. 'Will we go out and see her?' He produced a dishevelled soft felt hat and crammed it on his head. 'But it would be a terrible pity to take the men from *Chrysanthe*!'

They followed him from the office into the yard. He walked to the quay and glanced at the *Irene*. Then he turned to Sir David in obese amazement.

' 'Tis Mr Dennison's little cutter!' he said.

'That's so. Mr Dennison was slightly injured; he's with me in the *Clematis* now. I want his vessel got ready for him by the time he's fit to sail her.'

With surprising agility, the stout man dropped down on to the deck of the *Irene* and made a quick examination. Then he lifted the hatch of the little forecastle and disappeared below. In a minute, he was up on deck again, and on the quay beside them.

' 'Tis no great matter,' he said. 'Will it do, now, if I have her ready for you by the Friday night?'

'That will do excellently.'

'Is Mr Dennison hurt bad?' inquired Flanagan. 'I'd be sorry if anything was to happen to him.'

He was reassured. 'Well, well, well,' he said heavily. 'And now, gentlemen, you'll be wanting to have a look round the *Chrysanthe* and in the big hangar?'

They walked in and out among the smaller vessels to where the *Chrysanthe* lay upon the slip. ' 'Tis here that old Mr Dennison – Mr Peter Dennison's father that was – fitted out before the war,' he said reminiscently. 'He was a fine sailor, he was.

Do you mind the races they won in the *Runagate*, sir?' He laughed to mark the point. 'They was a crew.'

At the thought, the laughter died from his eyes; he walked a little closer to Sir David, and dropped his voice confidentially.

'Did you ever give Mr Dennison the wheel on the *Clematis*?' he said, in a voice that was little more than a whisper.

'No. He's in bed, sick. He's only been on board since yesterday.'

The stout man in the shabby grey suit stopped and caught the baronet by the arm.

'If I was you,' he said earnestly, 'if I was you I'd give him a try-out. Give him a try-out while you've got him aboard, sir. I mind him as a boy, the finest youngster that ever I saw, before or since. The most promising, you might say. I mind him on the *Runagate*.'

He drew the other closer to him. 'Get him for *Chrysanthe*, sir,' he whispered. 'You're after needing a helmsman; give him a chance, and you'll not regret it. Mind what I'm telling you now – you'll not regret it.'

The baronet gazed at him steadily. 'He's really good, is he?'

The stout man released his arm. 'If I was to search from here to Ameriky,' he said emphatically, 'I'd not find you a better man.' He dropped his voice again. 'Give him a try-out round the buoys, sir, and judge for yourself. You'll not regret it.'

They strolled on towards the *Chrysanthe*. 'I'll think it over,' said the baronet. 'Thanks very much, Mr Flanagan, for giving me the tip.'

5

Morris walked up from the slipway through the narrow little main street of West Cowes towards the castle, deep in thought. He was a man of moods and impulses, a man of quick decisions. He walked up to the castle and stood for a time gazing vacantly out to sea, to where the *Clematis* lay in the Roads, then turned about and went to find the post office.

On the steps of the office he hesitated for a moment, then went out again and bought a penny time-table at a stationer's. In the street he consulted this, then returned to the post office and sent off two telegrams. His business finished, he strolled back towards the landing, and met the others in the main street, returning from Flanagan's.

They returned on board for tea; Morris went down to speak to Dennison. Dennison had not got up; in point of fact, he had fallen asleep after a very good lunch, and when he awoke he found that it was so nearly tea-time that he decided to take his medical advice and stay in bed for the day. He greeted Morris cheerfully.

'I'm going to get up tomorrow,' he said. 'I'd have got up this afternoon, only I went to sleep after lunch.'

'As a door upon its hinges,' said Morris sententiously, 'so turneth the sluggard upon his bed.'

'I wish to hell he did,' said Dennison grimly. 'This old side of mine's been giving me gippo whenever I move. Did you hear anything of the *Irene*?'

'They're going to have her ready by Friday evening,' said Morris. 'Though I don't think there's a chance of you being able to sail her by then. Let's have a look at that thumb.'

The thumb was still swollen, though it was rapidly becoming normal again. 'You can't do anything with that yet,' said Morris, 'and you'll have to be jolly careful that you don't go and put it out again, if you go messing about trying to do too much. You don't seem to realize that you've just shaved by what might have been a pretty sticky crash.'

Comprehension came to Dennison in a wave with the words; he remembered now what it was that Sheila had said about Morris. 'In any case,' he said, 'I don't suppose I shall do much more sailing just at present. I only intended to take ten days off, and it will be a week by the time I get on board again, I suppose.'

They chatted for a time, then Morris left him and went to his tea. Dennison was left alone, pondering the information that had come to him. There was a mystery on board the *Clematis*; that was obvious even to him as he lay in his berth. There was something going on that was to be kept dark; Sir David was in it, and Rawdon and Morris, and probably Flanagan, from the way they had spoken of him. His curiosity was piqued; he had little else to interest him in his enforced idleness. He held this clue to the mystery; Morris was a pilot for experimental aeroplanes.

That was what Sheila had said.

Sir David paid him a visit after tea. Very soon, in some manner that he could not afterwards account for, Dennison found himself telling the baronet all about the *Runagate* and the four glorious seasons before the war when they had carried practically everything before them. Sir David fetched his bound volumes from the saloon, and they spent an hour and a half poring over the accounts of old regattas, recalling memories of the crack vessels of ten years before.

After dinner, he was left alone. It is painful to relate that he spent most of the evening endeavouring to interpret the confused murmur from the other side of the bulkhead, with little success. When the steward went in with the whisky, there was a lull in the conversation; Dennison learnt no more. Presently he dropped asleep, and was awakened by voices outside his door and the footsteps of the men as they went to their staterooms. He looked at his watch; it was half-past one in the morning.

Next morning when he awoke, Morris was gone, vanished away in the early hours to catch the paddle-boat from Cowes.

Rawdon came in to Dennison before breakfast, and explained the circumstances in his soft little voice, strangely out of keeping with his red-haired bulk. Morris had had to go up to Town on business, he said, and would be back that evening.

'I think I'll get up after breakfast,' said Dennison.

Morris caught the first boat from Cowes and proceeded to Southampton and London, breakfasting on the train. He reached Waterloo shortly after eleven and walked over Charing Cross bridge. On the Embankment, he paused for a moment before a hoarding on which a brand of face-cream was advertised by the portrait of a girl in evening dress. It reminded him of his wife.

He made his way across Trafalgar Square and up Regent Street, loitering to kill time. Half-past twelve found him in Oxford Circus; he looked at his watch, and took the Tube to the City.

He turned out of the station, walked a hundred yards or so down a side street, and entered a large block of offices. On the first floor he turned in at a door labelled 'Inquiries'. A girl rose from a typewriter.

'Mr Wallace?' said Morris.

The girl led him down a long corridor, knocked timidly at a door, and ushered him into an office in which the Great Man spent his days behind a portentous desk.

'Cheer oh,' said Jimmie. 'I won't keep you a minute. Get a chair. Miss Haynes! Get these sent along to Mr Anderson. Tell him that if he'll endorse them, I'll get them off this afternoon.' He handed her a sheaf of papers.

The door closed behind her. Wallace swept the litter on his desk to one side, and gazed critically at the door. 'She's getting fat,' he said. 'You should have seen her when she came … The sedentary life, I suppose.' He pushed aside his papers, checked, picked out one that had caught his eye, glanced it over, and threw it with the others. 'Heigh-ho,' he said. 'Time for lunch – or near as dammit.' He got up and fetched his hat from behind a screen. 'Come on,' he said. 'There's a sort of eating club just round here that I usually go to. I got your wire yesterday.'

They entered the club and sat down to lunch. Morris broached his subject with the soup.

'I say,' he said. 'You know a man called Dennison, don't you?'

He happened to be watching the other's face, and was vastly surprised to see the effect that his question made upon the other. Wallace laid down his spoon and gazed at him in simple wonder. 'Yes,' he said, 'I know a man called Dennison. Peter Dennison. But I had no idea he was a friend of yours.'

Morris crumbled his bread. 'I only met him recently,' he said. 'Two days ago, in point of fact. But he told me that he knew you and – well, frankly, I came up here because I wanted to find out one or two things about him.'

Wallace wrinkled his brows in perplexity. 'You want me to tell you about him?' he inquired.

'That's it.' Morris paused to consider his words. 'As a matter of fact, it's rather a curious story, and it's all mixed up with – with a business deal that I'm afraid I can't tell you very much about at present. But the main facts are these. I've been yachting in the Solent as a guest on a biggish vessel. The owner and my firm are acting together in this deal, and part of it means that I've got to chuck a stunt.'

'I see,' said Wallace attentively. 'Flying?'

Morris nodded. 'Well, we had the devil of a lot of work to get through, and it was very desirable for us to be near Cowes to do it. So for the last week or so we've been living on board the yacht and working pretty hard in spasms. Well, the day before yesterday, we were cruising down the Solent on a dirty sort of day. While we were at lunch, there was the hell of a row alongside, and when we got on deck, we found we'd run down this chap Dennison in a little cutter, and knocked him about a bit – not badly. He put his thumb out and got a nasty whack on his ribs. His vessel was disabled, so we took him on board while she's being repaired; as soon as he's fit, we're going to push him off again.'

'I see,' said Wallace. 'He's on board now?'

'Yes. I'm going back there this evening. But as soon as I saw him, it struck me that he had certain qualities that – that we

168

could very profitably work into our scheme. In fact, he seems to be just the man for our job. Well, the trouble is that this thing's got to be kept pretty dark for the present, so we don't want to tell more people about it than we can help. Sir David insists on that. I don't mind telling you that the only people in my firm who know anything about it are the directors and myself.'

Wallace nodded slowly.

'Well – you see the difficulty? We want to know rather more about him before we can let him into it so far as to put a proposal to him. That's why I came up today.'

There was a short silence.

'I'm afraid I can't tell you very much about him,' said Wallace at last. 'I first met him four years ago, and I met him again last Easter, when he stayed with us. I think he's a thoroughly sound lad, if that's any good to you.'

'That's exactly what I do want to know,' said Morris. 'That's the main thing. Now, what's his job?'

'Sea lawyer,' said Wallace laconically. Morris raised his eyebrows. 'Maritime solicitor.'

'I see. Is he married?'

Wallace glanced shrewdly at his guest. 'No,' he said. 'He'd like to be, but there seems to have been a hitch about that. A regrettable incident. Is he in very deep mourning?'

'Not that I've noticed,' said Morris. 'Who's he supposed to be in mourning for?'

'Sheila,' said Wallace briefly. He did not seem very much inclined to add to this information.

'I see,' said Morris. 'His matrimonial affairs don't affect our business much, of course. I only wanted to know what ties he has.'

'I don't think he's tied in any way,' said Wallace. 'I think he's quite his own master. He talks of going out to Hong Kong in the autumn.'

'In the autumn? We shall have done with him by then.'

'Probably have done for him, too,' said Wallace, 'if I know anything of you and your schemes. Mad as coots, all the lot of you.'

Morris laughed. 'One more thing,' he said. 'Do you know anything about his Navy record, or what sort of a navigator he is?'

'Not a word. He can navigate his yacht all right. And he broke his leg in the war jumping into the water to pull a chap out. He was reckoned a good officer by his men. That's all I know about his Navy service.'

'I see,' said Morris. 'Well, that's really all I want to know about him.' The conversation drifted to general subjects and reminiscences; at the end of three-quarters of an hour Morris rose to go.

'I'm damn sorry I can't tell you more about this stunt,' he said. 'For the moment it's got to be kept pretty quiet. But look here, come and have dinner with me one night before it comes off, and I'll tell you all about it. It's really rather interesting. I'll let you know later when to come.'

'Right you are,' said Wallace. They moved towards the door. 'I suppose you don't know anyone who wants a thousand sewing-machines, do you? Or we can do you a very nice line in inferior Continental pig iron ... No? Oh well, cheer oh. See you some time.'

Morris left the building, glanced at his watch, and walked up Cheapside. The business that had brought him to London was concluded. He had telegraphed to his wife that he would meet her for tea at her club; he made his way towards the West End.

He noticed his little car outside the club, found his wife, and sat down with her to tea. He had married a girl whom he had met at one of the Oxford women's colleges; Helen, the daughter of Sir James Riley. She was considered by her family to have married badly; a censure that she bore with equanimity. In her life she had only known two men that she respected; one of whom was her cousin and Morris's friend, Malcolm Riley, who had been killed while flying a racing machine a year or two after the war. Morris himself was a pilot of considerable skill, but incidentally to his work. He was a mathematician, and held a position of some importance in the Rawdon Aircraft Company, flying their aeroplanes on test.

He picked a piece of buttered toast from the dish and held it in mid-air between finger and thumb. 'I've found a navigator,' he said. 'At least, I think I have.' Briefly he described Dennison's arrival on the *Clematis*.

'Is he a nice man?' inquired his wife.

Morris munched steadily. 'Not bad,' he said at last. 'Yes, I think you'd like him. Funnily enough he knows the Wallaces; I've just been asking Jimmie Wallace about him. I got quite a good account, so I'll see if he'd like to take it on. Oh yes, and Jimmie told me another thing. This chap's been endeavouring to establish a lien upon Sheila, but there's been a hitch in that.'

His wife smiled. 'He would have to be a very nice man to be good enough for Sheila,' she said.

'That's the funny part of it – he is a very nice man. Sheila will probably go and marry some little squid with a made-up tie and a banjo.' He paused reminiscently.

He accompanied his wife to the door of the club after tea, and watched her get into the car to drive home. He lived in the suburbs on the border of the aerodrome. He stood watching her a little uneasily.

'Go carefully,' he said.

He was one of that great class of Englishmen who love their wives and trust them unquestioningly with their money and their honour, but are apt to hedge a little over their motor-cars. The girl made a grimace at him and laughed, then let in the clutch and moved away. Morris watched her out of sight, a lean cadaverous figure, turned away, took a taxi to Waterloo, and made his way back to Cowes.

Dennison got up stiffly after breakfast and went on deck. From the saloon came a low hum of voices; Sir David was busy with his secretary, a hard-driven bespectacled young man. Dennison spent the morning in the deck-house, smoking and yarning with Captain Rawdon.

He asked no direct question, but he was pretty certain that he could place Rawdon now. During the war he had had several friends in the Flying Corps and, though he had taken little interest himself in aeroplanes, the name Rawdon seemed to recall memories of these men. At one time they had been enthusiastic over a machine called, if he remembered rightly, the Rawdon Rat, and later there was another one, the Rawdon Ratcatcher. It was not a very common name, and, coupled with the fact that Morris was an aeroplane pilot, seemed good evidence to Dennison. It was evident to him that they had some very secret experiment on hand; he guessed that it had to do with aeroplanes and that it was maritime. However, it was certainly no concern of his. It surprised him rather that they had taken him on board.

He went ashore with Rawdon after lunch and walked, a little painfully, to Flanagan's yard to inspect the *Irene*. They met Flanagan and inspected the little vessel. Then, rather to his surprise, Rawdon left him to himself with the intimation that he would meet him at the jetty at four o'clock, and disappeared with Flanagan along the yard, deep in conversation. Dennison finished his examination of his vessel and walked up into the town, a little puzzled at the relations between Flanagan and Rawdon. He had had no idea that Rawdon was interested in yachts. The more he thought about it, the more he became convinced that the relations between them were not those of yacht owner to builder but more intimate, suggesting some closer tie between them. Besides, to the best of his knowledge, Rawdon was not a yachtsman.

He decided to leave the *Clematis* next day and to put up at a hotel till the *Irene* was ready. Now that he was able to get about, it was evident that his presence on the vessel would quickly become an embarrassment to them; they were engaged in some matter that they wished to keep dark. It was clearly his place to leave them as soon as he could. For these reasons, and because his side was hurting him more than a little, he retired to bed after tea, and so did not see Morris on his return, about nine o'clock in the evening.

He heard the dinghy come alongside and bump gently at the ladder, and steps over his head. The door of the saloon opened and he heard Sir David's voice outside his cabin.

'Mr Morris? Have you had dinner?'

Morris came down the companion. 'I had it on the train,' he said. 'A very comfortable journey.'

'Right. Come in and tell us how you got on – after you have taken off your things.'

Dennison heard Morris move into his cabin and presently emerge and pass into the saloon. For a moment the door was left ajar.

'Well,' he said cheerfully. 'I found out quite a lot about him – all that's of any importance, I think. It seems he's quite all right. I asked—' Then the door was closed and the remainder of the sentence lost.

Dennison was immensely disgusted. Though scrupulous, he was a man of keen natural curiosity and he had been eager to hear before he left the vessel exactly what it was that they were engaged upon. He felt that this would be the last chance that he would have, and it had produced nothing that was of any interest whatsoever.

He decided to leave the vessel after breakfast next morning, and dropped off to sleep while the others still sat talking in the saloon, talking away the quiet hours of darkness.

Dennison got up for breakfast and was first into the saloon in the morning. The table was laid and the coffee steaming in the pot, sending a little column of vapour up into a patch of sun. On deck the movements of a couple of men attracted Dennison's attention; he glanced up through the open skylight and saw that they were taking the cover off the mainsail. He was concerned. He had planned to leave the vessel that morning and go ashore in Cowes to wait for the *Irene*. If they were making sail, he would not have an opportunity to leave them.

'It's their funeral,' he thought.

His side began to pain him a little, and he moved to the settee to sit down. It was littered with loose-leaf books full of typescript, a number of loose sheets of pencilled calculations, and one or two great sheets of engineers' blue-print, evidently cleared from the table by the steward when the time came to lay the cloth. Dennison cleared a place to sit down on, and wedged himself into a corner with a cushion, to consider the position. It would be devilish inconvenient if they were to leave Cowes that morning.

His eye fell on one of the blue-prints, open upon the settee beside him. He glanced at it curiously, bewildered by the strangeness of the white lines on the blue paper and by the wealth of minute detail. Gradually, he began to comprehend what he was looking at, and to glean some idea of the outline of the scheme. It was a picture of a flying-boat apparently furnished with wheels outside the hull, perched at one end of a long horizontal structure of steel girders. Close beneath this structure lay a long cylindrical machine, apparently something in the nature of a hydraulic or pneumatic ram.

There was a sound of voices outside the door and Rawdon entered the room, followed by Morris. The latter greeted Dennison, crossed to the settee, and began to tidy up the papers.

'I forgot we left all this stuff out last night,' he said. 'Mr Evans usually tidies it up – Sir David's secretary – but he turned in early last night with a headache.'

'There's no need to put it away on my account,' said Dennison. 'I mean – that sort of thing is a sealed book to me.'

Morris laughed. 'There's nothing here that we mind you seeing,' he said. He turned to Rawdon waving the blue-print in his hand. 'Where do we keep the arrangement of the catapult?'

'In the table drawer, I think,' said Rawdon. Dennison rose to his feet as Sir David entered the room.

'Good morning,' said the baronet incisively. 'A little late, I'm afraid. A good morning for a turn down to the Forts and back. A fine sailing breeze.' He turned to Rawdon. 'You are spending the morning ashore at the yard?'

'I think so,' said Rawdon. 'They're putting the engine in this morning – and Flanagan was worrying about his slipway, too. I'll go ashore after breakfast, before you get under way.'

Here Dennison broke in and diffidently set out his plan to leave the vessel. He proceeded in an embarrassing silence; the suggestion that he had thought would be so welcome to them was evidently received with something approaching consternation. Presently Dennison stopped talking and looked from one to the other, utterly at a loss. Sir David stepped into the breach.

'I shall be very disappointed if you leave us, Mr Dennison,' he said genially. 'As a matter of fact, I was hoping that you would take the helm this morning and wake up my crew for me. These are some of the men that I shall put in the *Chrysanthe*. Of course, we can't do very much till we get her in commission. I thought of having a turn round the buoys, though, to try and rub some of the corners off.'

Dennison flushed with pleasure. 'It would be a great treat to me,' he said. 'But I must tell you, I've never handled a crew before – racing, that is, and I've never happened to sail a vessel with a wheel.'

'The skipper does the hazing,' said the baronet equably, 'you just tell him what you want. As for the wheel, I shouldn't think that ought to worry you very much. Really, I should be very glad if you would take her round a course this morning.'

After breakfast, Rawdon went ashore alone. He paused on the jetty and watched his boat row back to the *Clematis*, watched it hoisted on the davits and secured. Then the mainsail crept to the hounds and took shape, to the accompaniment of a slow rattle of chain from the bows. Finally she broke out a jib and bore away towards the mainland, catting her anchor and crowding on sail as she went, white and majestic in the sunshine. Rawdon turned and made his way to the yard.

Three hours later Flanagan pointed out to Rawdon the *Clematis* returning; he left the large hangar and walked to the jetty. The vessel did not come to an anchor as he had expected, but dropped her topsail and lay to outside the Roads, lowering a dinghy. Presently it arrived at the jetty; he embarked and was rowed out to the vessel.

Morris met him at the gangway. 'Sir David thinks of running down to the Needles this afternoon,' he said. 'It's a great day for sailing.' They dropped into a pair of basket-chairs. 'I say, that chap Dennison's nuts at this game.'

Rawdon glanced round the deck. 'Where is he now?' he asked. 'Have you seen him yet?'

Morris shook his head. 'Not yet. He's in the saloon, talking to Sir David about the *Chrysanthe*. Sir David's all over him – it was an extraordinarily good show, apparently. Even I could see he knew the job all right.' He paused, and laughed suddenly. 'It was the funniest thing out. When he took over, the skipper sort of stood over him to tell him what to do. It took this chap just about five seconds to put him in his place, and then they stood together side by side. I never heard him give any orders, but now and again he'd say something confidentially to the skipper and I tell you – the skipper got those fellows moving all right. Fair made me sweat to watch 'em.'

Rawdon smiled. 'Where did you go?'

'Twice round some buoys, down about as far as Ryde. It was really rather odd to see him standing there sort of whispering shyly to the skipper now and then, and the men sweating blood as a result. There was that spinnaker, for instance ... I couldn't judge the whole nicety of it, of course. I noticed one or two things. Whenever we had to cross the tide between two buoys, he set a course directly we came about that looked as if it would miss the other buoy by half a mile. Well, each time I watched the compass, and I swear he never altered course a degree, but we hit the buoy to within ten yards each time. And another thing I noticed was how smoothly it all went. No fuss, no waste of time, no talking – a clean turn at each buoy and away on the new course like a knife. I'm really very glad to have seen it.'

They lunched, and after lunch got under way again. Morris and Dennison went up on deck; Sir David and Rawdon stayed in the saloon with their cigars.

Rawdon glanced at the other. 'So he did well?' he said.

The baronet blew a long blue cloud. 'Very well,' he said quietly. 'Very well indeed. It's not the first time that Flanagan has put me right.'

Morris and Dennison went up on deck and sat in the basket-chairs, watching the Island slip past them. Dennison was tired and willing enough to rest; the act of standing all morning had made his side ache painfully, though he had not noticed it at the time.

'You must be an authority on this coast,' said Morris. 'I suppose you know pretty well every harbour and inlet in the south.'

Dennison lit a pipe. 'I know a good many,' he said cautiouly.

'Do you know Padstow?'

'Not very well. I've been in there two or three times. But one doesn't cruise up that coast much, you know. Padstow and Bideford are the only two possible inlets, and they're neither of them much fun to get into except in clear weather. Bideford dries out pretty well at low water, and Padstow's got a shocking great sandbank right across the entrance. You have to go carefully into both of them.'

'You know the west coast of Ireland, too, don't you?'

'Lord, no,' said Dennison. 'I spent one summer holiday mucking about between Baltimore and Valentia, but that's all.'

A gull swooped down upon the vessel, made a circuit or two, approached the stern, hovered for a moment, and dropped accurately to perch on top of the mizzen mast. Both watched it intently.

Morris laughed. 'Slow landings,' he said. 'It's having the nerves next to the muscles, I suppose. We'll never get it quite like that.'

The helmsman waved his arm and the gull flew away. Dennison turned to Morris.

'Your business is flying, isn't it?' he said. 'I remember Miss Wallace mentioned you once.'

'That so?' said Morris. 'Yes, my business is flying. Though I work chiefly on design stuff now, under Captain Rawdon. I fly most of the Rawdon machines on test.'

'One sees a lot about commercial aviation in the papers,' said Dennison. 'It doesn't pay, does it?'

'No,' said Morris. 'It doesn't pay to run a regular service – yet. That's why it's called commercial, of course. A pious hope.'

He tilted his chair back. 'I can talk till tea-time on that subject, of course,' he said. 'Probably bore you stiff. But as for civil aviation, it's coming, you know. It's coming faster than you think. One never hears anything in the papers of the steady progress that is made – one only hears of the accidents. But nowadays you can fly fairly reliably twice a day to Paris or Brussels or Rotterdam at any time of year. And that's something.' He paused.

'And of course, the mails . . .' he said. He paused thoughtfully and then continued, picking his words with care.

'Communications . . .' he said. 'It seems to me that communications are the whole keynote of present-day politics. One has means for limited rapid communication already, of course, by wireless and cable. But think what it would mean if one could carry bulky documents rapidly. Or people. Think what it would have meant if in August 1914 we could have had every Dominion Prime Minister in London within a week. By air.'

He leaned back in his chair and ran on. 'Suppose we could expedite the mails to America. Suppose we could start a mail service to America that only took five days instead of seven, and suppose we were able to run that service with, say, eighty per cent regularity. Do you see how we should improve our position with America? Look at the pull that it would give us over every other country in Europe. Suppose we could do that by surprise, and suddenly one day reduce the time from London to New York to five days – and we can save more than two days.'

Dennison glanced at Morris attentively. 'I am no financier, but anyone can see that it would benefit us very greatly – if it could be done,' he said.

Morris gazed over the blue water to the steep bluff of Egypt Point astern. 'It could be done tomorrow,' he said absently, '– it could have been done last year. The Atlantic was flown in eighteen hours, years ago.' He sat up and became animated. 'The real point is this,' he said. 'Can it be done as a commercial proposition? Is it likely to pay? That's the point.'

Dennison considered for a moment. 'I always understood,' he said, 'that a scheme of that sort couldn't pay, because it was all that an aeroplane could do to carry its own petrol across the Atlantic, without any cargo.'

'Seventy years ago they were saying that of steamships,' said Morris. Dennison was silent.

Morris continued after a moment. 'We don't propose to do it by direct flight. It isn't possible at present; we can't hope to make that a paying proposition. The scheme that we intend to try, briefly, is this. We carry a flying-boat on a liner, mounted on a sort of catapult arrangement. The aeroplane is loaded with a small amount of urgent mail which pays a special surcharge. When the liner is in mid-Atlantic, about a thousand miles from her destination, she turns full speed into the wind and catapults the machine off her deck. The machine then flies to land, taking just about ten hours over the thousand miles. In that way we hope to be able to carry five hundred pounds' weight of urgent cargo.'

Dennison gazed at him attentively. 'You say you are going to try this?'

'In about six weeks' time. One of Sir David's vessels is in the Clyde now, being fitted with the catapult. I'm doing it, with another man – a navigator. We do it on the way home – it's really a sort of a full-dress rehearsal. They shoot us off one morning about nine hundred and fifty miles out at sea, and we fly to Padstow. The natural thing would have been to have flown to Ireland, of course, but Sir David won't have that. He doesn't believe in basing any financial calculations on the stability of Ireland just at present.'

Dennison regarded him steadily. 'It sounds to me an uncommonly risky experiment,' he said.

Morris smiled, and picked his words carefully. 'It has its risks,' he said, 'and one would be a fool to deny them. The first is that something may happen to us in the launching and we don't get a clean start from the deck. In that case we flop down into the water under the vessel's bows – and get run over. They won't be able to dodge us, you know. The only other point is that we may have engine failure or run out of petrol, and have to come down. We minimize that by keeping directly on the track of the liner so that she comes along and picks us up – if we float so long.' He blew a heavy cloud of smoke.

'What made you choose Padstow?' asked Dennison.

179

'Because it's the nearest harbour, and because it's usually quite empty of ships. Falmouth was out of the question – too crowded and too public for this rehearsal. As a matter of fact, all this is being kept very dark at present. It may be convenient to publish the fact that we shall land at Falmouth later, if there's much stir about it all. But it will really be Padstow.'

Dennison nodded in silence.

Morris tossed his cigarette over the rail and turned to him. 'I don't know if you are wondering why I've told you all this,' he said evenly. 'As it happens, there's one point still incomplete. We're still without a navigator. I've been wondering if you would care to take it on.'

'I see,' said Dennison slowly. 'Are you the pilot?'

Morris nodded. 'I ought to tell you one thing,' he said. 'This is a serious matter for us, and we didn't want to let a complete stranger in on it. I went up to Town yesterday and got a sort of a reference of you from Jimmie Wallace. I hope you don't mind. It was more a matter of form than anything else – to satisfy Sir David.'

'How do you know I can navigate?' asked Dennison suddenly.

'For one thing, you told me you could. But as for that, the navigation will be very simple. What I really want is someone to work out courses for me in the air, look after the petrol pressure, and the food, and all that sort of thing. And, if we get a chance, to get a sight or two to check our position. The navigation is very simple – I could do it myself, only I shall be flying.'

'I should be all right for that,' said Dennison absently.

Morris rose to his feet. 'Anyway,' he said, 'think it over. After dinner this evening we'll talk about it again, if you like. There's a lot that you ought to know before you decide. Sir David will be able to put the points of the scheme before you much better than I can and he'll go into everything with you – money, for one thing. There's a pretty good fee attached to it. But I told him I'd tell you about it first.'

Dennison rose and walked aft with him. 'Thanks very

180

much,' he said. 'I'll think about it.' He mused a little. 'I've never seen a flying-boat close to.'

Morris laughed. 'Soon put that right,' he said. 'We've got her in Flanagan's yard.'

They cruised on down the Solent till tea-time, then came about and returned to Cowes in the dusk. They came to an anchor in their old place in the Roads just before dinner, and, after dinner, sat down to the usual round-table conference. This time, however, Dennison was of the party.

He had already made up his mind. He was tired of working, willing enough to go wandering for a little. He was willing enough to take some months' leave from his office and come in on this experiment. He listened absently while Sir David laid the matter before him. It was dangerous – he knew that. That was beside the point. This was a thing that would amuse him. It was different. He was free to turn his interests where he liked; there was nobody that had a better claim on him than himself. If he had been engaged, or married, it would have been different. But now he was free, and this would be good fun and would give him something to think about.

He roused himself. 'The real object of this experiment,' Sir David was saying in his level, incisive tones, 'is to demonstrate that the flight is a commercial proposition. This journey hasn't merely got to be completed somehow or other – that's no good at all. We know that it can be done. We know that it is possible to launch a machine from a ship and to fly a thousand miles on it. What we want to find out is if that can be done under the ordinary, normal conditions of service. That is, the flight has got to be done to a time-table. The aeroplane has to arrive at a stated place at a stated time, carrying a stated load. It has to do that under any weather conditions that happen to be prevailing – except a hurricane. If these conditions cannot be fulfilled, then the experiment is a failure.'

Rawdon broke in. 'The weather conditions aren't of any great importance at this time of year,' he said in his soft little voice. 'The flight will take place at the end of May and – as you know – the prevailing wind in the Atlantic is westerly. That, of course, will be a help in this flight – not a hindrance.

A moderate westerly breeze would be the best thing possible for you.'

'That's practically a certainty at the end of May,' said Dennison absently.

He offered evidence of his navigating ability, and they discussed the details of the scheme for a little. Finally Sir David stated the fee that they were prepared to give for a navigator.

Dennison opened his eyes. It seemed a very large sum for a very little work.

'It's like a recruiting poster,' said Morris flippantly. 'See the world for nothing. It's a joy-ride. A first-class trip to America – and half-way back.'

There was a pause. Dennison felt called upon to say something.

'It should be pretty good sport,' he said.

6

It took a good deal to destroy the serenity of Jimmie Wallace's outlook upon the world, but undoubtedly something had happened seriously to impair it. He sat idle at his desk in the palatial little office, chewing his penholder, about a month after Morris had visited him to inquire about Dennison. He was worried. He had dined with Morris the previous evening, when Morris had pledged him to secrecy and had broken to him the news of the wildcat scheme upon which he and Dennison were engaged. It had not altogether been news to Jimmie. Already rumours were beginning to circulate about the City of the great benefits that might accrue if such a scheme were suddenly to come into operation as a regular service; already there were guarded expressions of these rumours in the Press. He had not been long in connecting these tales with

Morris's visit to him. Here was confirmation of the whole thing.

He sat in his chair and chewed his penholder morosely. He did not know how this would affect his family – if at all. He did not know exactly what had passed between Dennison and his sister, though he was capable of making a tolerably good guess. He did not know to what extent his sister was responsible for what Dennison had done. In these first days he had got a very clear idea of the danger of the enterprise. He was a keen motorist, and knew sufficient about aeroplanes to appreciate the position. The success of the flight depended upon an ordinary petrol engine running steadily at full power for ten hours, without attention, under indifferent conditions. Well, it might. It was about a fifty per cent chance. And then there was the launching . . .

He did not know what he should say to his sister – if anything at all, seeing that he was bound under a pledge of secrecy to Morris. So far he had told her nothing of Dennison's connection with Morris; he had thought it wiser to leave the whole subject alone. The more he thought of it, the more clearly he perceived that there was only one thing that could have sent Dennison flying off the deep end in this manner, and that one thing was Sheila. This was a very disturbing conclusion.

What would happen, for example, if the flight were to fail and Dennison were to be killed? He knew that his sister was very much attached to Dennison. On the other hand, what could he do about it? He could not very well go to his sister and tell her what Dennison was up to and make her pull him back by the coat-tails. For one thing, she wouldn't be able to do it. Nobody could pull Dennison back when he had set his mind on a thing, and he was evidently far too deeply involved in this matter to withdraw.

Perhaps it would be better to wait and hope that Dennison would not be killed.

'Oh, damn it all,' said Wallace irritably.

It was in an irritable mood that he travelled down to Berkshire. On the way it struck him to wonder whether by any chance Sheila knew of what Dennison was doing. It was just possible that he was wrong all along the line and that she was in touch with Dennison. He did not think that was the case; Dennison had departed too suddenly. Moreover, Morris had reported him taciturn on the subject of the Wallaces. In any case, he would see if he could not find out more how the land lay during this week-end. If he got an opportunity he would sound his sister on the subject.

Sheila met him with the car and drove him home to tea. Antony had departed three weeks previously for the Engadine, and had written her a rambling, incoherent letter, enclosing a little wooden bear. She had written back to him at needless length, a letter almost equally diverse in which she mentioned everything but Dennison. With the exception of this correspondence she had been quite alone since Antony's departure; her father ranking as somebody to talk to but not company. Wallace, as they drove home, found her far more subdued than usual, and mentally raised his eyebrows. Clearly, it would pay him to go carefully.

It struck him that she looked tired. It would be a good thing if he could get her away for a holiday; it was absurd for her to spend all her life at Little Tinney.

They had tea in the library. After the meal was cleared away they sat gossiping for a little before the fire; Wallace decided to seize his opportunity. He leaned back in his chair and commenced to bore her to distraction with a long account of the family investments in China. He gave her full details of each stock in turn with the history of each company, and the date the stock had come into their possession, the price at purchase and at the present time, the yield, and the prospects of improvement or otherwise. From that he passed to an appreciation of the political situation in China, with especial reference to its effect on certain companies. He noticed that she was growing restive, and smiled covertly to see her smothering a yawn. Finally he passed to the (fictitious) desirability of having an independent observer on the spot.

'I've been wondering lately whether Dennison would care to do anything for us in that way,' he said thoughtfully, and smiled again to see her suddenly stiffen to attention. 'He might be able to send us a weekly cable with certain information. It would be very much to his own advantage.' He was watching her closely, but found time to reflect, 'What utter rot I'm talking.' Still, she knew very little of business methods.

'It sounds a very good idea,' she said. 'Why don't you write to him?'

'One might do that,' said Wallace. 'Where does he live?'

'He's in rooms,' she said. 'I've got his address upstairs. It might be nicer if you went and saw him one evening.'

'Have him to dinner one night,' said Wallace. 'When's he going out?'

She did not answer. He glanced at her and saw that she was not looking his way, but staring into the fire. Presently she turned and met his eyes, a little wistfully. 'I don't know,' she said. 'I don't think he ought to – a bit.' She glanced at him again, and this time he noticed a slight quivering of her lips.

'Lord bless me,' he thought in alarm. 'I believe she's going to cry.'

'Please, Jimmie,' she said. 'I want to tell you about it.'

He sat up in his chair. 'Why, of course,' he said kindly.

The girl slipped from her seat on to the floor beside his feet, and sat with her back against his chair, facing the fire so that he could only see the back of her head.

'I don't think he ought to go out to China,' she said rapidly, 'and he wanted me to marry him and I wouldn't.' Though he could not see her face, Jimmie knew that tears were very near.

'I guessed as much,' he said equably. He ran his fingers down through her soft hair and pulled her ear. 'What are you going to do about it now? Seems to me that you've got your-self into a mess and you don't know how to get out of it. Want me to assist, I suppose.'

There was a pause, but when she spoke again he knew that the danger was over.

'It's not a mess at all,' she explained. 'Only sometimes – one gets worried over it all. It's having nobody to talk to. It was all right while Antony was here, but now ... You see, I knew as soon as Peter came back that he wanted to ask me to marry

185

him. You remember when he came; that first evening? I knew quite well – I think he wanted me to know. And then he told me all about going out to Hong Kong, and I knew that the only reason he was going out there was because it – it gave him a chance to get married, and he wanted that so badly. And then he went away, and I had time to think it all over.'

She turned from the fire and glanced up at him. 'Jimmie,' she said earnestly, 'he wouldn't be happy in Hong Kong. It wouldn't do. He's not that sort. He'd be miserable out there – I know he would. I found out that – he doesn't really want to go a bit. It was only – only for me that he was taking it.' She turned back to the fire and resumed her old position. 'And directly I knew that I – I sort of knew that it was up to me, you see, and if he spoilt his life and gave up all that he cared for, it would be my fault.'

She paused, and played a little with his shoe-lace. When she spoke again it was so softly that Wallace had to listen intently for her words. 'A man isn't like a girl, you know,' she said, almost to herself. 'A girl when she marries is quite happy with her home, and her children, and she doesn't want much else. But a man is different. He's like a little boy that has to have his toys ... a man has to have his toys, and if you take them away from him you – you just kill him. The round of golf, or the club, or – or yachting. Once he gets really fond of a toy ... if his wife takes it away from him she can never make it up to him, however much she loves him. It's just gone, and you can't replace it with anything else.' She paused, and repeated piteously, 'She can never make it up to him.'

'I suppose that's so,' said Wallace.

The girl nodded. 'I know that's true,' she said simply. 'And then, it was pretty obvious that it was up to me to get him out of his mess. Because he really was going to make a frightful mess of things and I sort of felt – I felt that it was up to me to get him out of it all. You see, if he'd gone out to China as a junior partner in that firm, he couldn't have chucked it after a year or two if he didn't like it. He'd have been there for keeps. And so, when he asked me, I told him I was afraid of going to China and I couldn't marry him if he was going out there. I

186

was pretty sure he wouldn't go out there without me. And I think he'll rout about now and find a job in England that we can marry on, and then he'll come back again.' She paused, and then, 'I just couldn't let him give it all up for me, Jimmie. I had to have a shot at – at piloting him out.'

'I see,' said Wallace gently. 'How did he take it?'

For a while the girl did not answer. 'He was so sweet about it,' she said at last, very softly. Then, 'Oh, Jimmie,' she said piteously, 'it was four years since I'd seen him, and he remembered all that time and came back just the same. I – I didn't know men ever did that sort of thing, except in books.'

For a moment Jimmie Wallace had an eccentric impulse to lean down and kiss his sister – an action that he had not performed since he was four years old. Manfully he beat it down, but fell to stroking her short, fine hair as they sat together in the firelight wondering ... wondering ...

What on earth was he to do about it all? And what if Dennison were killed?

That evening Dennison returned to his rooms in Chelsea. He had paid a flying visit to London previously, had told Lanard briefly what he had taken on, and had visited his firm of solicitors. He had had a long interview with the head of the firm and had managed to interest him sufficiently in the scheme to obtain the necessary leave. They were maritime solicitors.

Then he had returned to Cowes, and had lived for the month as the guest of Sir David on board the *Clematis*, watching and taking his part in the arrangements for the flight. During that time the flying-boat had been completed in Flanagan's great hangar, and had made several flights. Morris had flown her off the water alone on the first flight. Then he and Dennison had paid a flying visit to Farnborough, where they had had a lengthy consultation with two or three authorities on aerial navigation. They had then returned to Cowes and proceeded to practise what they had learned by taking observations in the air. During this month the catapult had been completed and fitted to a fast cargo vessel of the Fisher Line, the

Iberian. She was now on her way from the Clyde to the Solent. On arrival she was to take the flying-boat on board for two trial launchings, after which she would pick up a cargo at Southampton and sail for New York. Dennison had returned to London for a couple of days.

'To make my testamentary dispositions, for one thing,' he informed Lanard.

Lanard smiled sourly; the jest was not to his taste. He had seen nothing of Dennison for three weeks, when he had burst in one evening, informed Lanard of his part in the projected flight, and returned to the Solent. Lanard was dismayed; that Dennison of all people should go rushing off upon a mad scheme of this nature struck him as a very bad business. He summed the position up to himself in a trenchant phrase, clarified, perhaps, by the light of his own experience. Dennison was 'on the run'.

He blamed himself most bitterly that he had not gone with Dennison on the *Irene*. Then, if ever, Dennison had needed his friends about him most of all; Lanard had allowed himself to be put off. If he had been there, he thought, this would never have happened.

Dennison began to talk about the *Chrysanthe* and her prospects in the coming summer. It was settled that he was to sail her in her races throughout the season; after the Eastern regattas and Cowes they were to go on down the coast with the object of getting in as much racing as possible to gain experience on the vessel. It would mean a good two months of it, said Dennison cheerfully.

'But look here,' said Lanard. 'What about your work? You're having six weeks' holiday now over this infernal American trip. You aren't going to get leave for the *Chrysanthe* as well? If you aren't pretty careful, you'll find yourself upon the cold, hard world.'

Dennison kicked the coals down into the fire. 'The Lord will provide,' he said calmly.

Lanard gazed hard at him. 'Do you mean Sir David Fisher?' he said at last.

'Perhaps,' said Dennison. 'The sparrows and the crumbs –

and the rich man's table, and all that, you know.' Lanard had to make what he could of that, for he could get no more out of Dennison. He was in a queer temper.

Lanard picked up *The Times*, and Dennison lit a pipe; for a full twenty minutes neither of them spoke a word. Then Lanard dropped the paper into a rustling heap beside his chair.

'What about Hong Kong?' he said.

'What about it?'

'Are you going out there?'

'Shouldn't think so,' said Dennison curtly. 'It was a damn silly scheme at the best of times. I turned it down.'

'Exactly,' said Lanard dryly. 'But it brings us back to the immediate question – what do you propose to live on when your firm sacks you?'

Dennison grinned. 'Probably on a yacht,' he said.

Lanard knew very well that at times his friend was capable of displaying the rudiments of a subtle sense of humour; he considered this reply with some care. 'Do you mean that Sir David's going to keep you all the year round simply to sail the *Chrysanthe* in the summer?' he said. 'It seems an optimistic view of the situation.'

'Lord, no,' said Dennison. 'Whatever put that idea into your head?'

He was silent for a little, and knocked out his pipe against the heel of his boot. Presently he spoke again. 'You're barking up the wrong tree,' he said quietly. 'All the time since the war I've been keeping my little nose to the grindstone because – because I wanted to get married. Well, that's all over and done with now. What's the use of going on working like this – in London? So long as I can keep myself ... You called me a married man in embryo once. Well, a married man works like hell. But afterwards ...'

He was silent. Lanard continued his sentence.

'Afterwards one settles down and goes on working,' he said evenly. 'One piles up comfortable things. One makes money, and that acts as an insurance against – mistakes. And presently one forgets, and one marries again.'

Dennison broke in. 'I'm damned if that's your creed,' he said roughly.

The other considered. 'It's the only reasonable creed,' he said at last.

There was a silence. Lanard got up and went to the window and stood looking down into the lamp-lit street, in characteristic attitude.

'It's not my business to butt in,' he said presently, without taking his eyes from the street. 'That's why one does it, I suppose. It's always seemed to me that it's never fair to take a girl at her word – at first. It's so different for them. And they expect to be given a second chance – traditionally.'

'I know,' said Dennison. 'They book their ticket at Cook's, return it after a couple of days, and a week later go and badger the life out of the clerks because they can't have it back again.'

Lanard turned to him, his brow wrinkled in perplexity. 'Which means?' he said.

'A journey to China, I should think,' said Dennison, a little wearily. 'The clerks haven't got any self-respect to lose, I suppose. But in this case, when the ticket was returned it was final.'

He turned to Lanard. 'You're barking up the wrong tree,' he said again. 'If I had the money I could get married tomorrow. I think I could probably count on being married next year if I wanted to be. I could probably afford it by then.'

He paused. 'The point is that I was turned down because I was going to China, and for no other reason at all. Well, you see – I was going to China for her, and if she couldn't come to China for me . . . It was a sort of test case, you see. She cared – quite a lot. But not enough to come to China. That absolutely put the lid on it.'

Lanard turned from the window. 'I see,' he said slowly.

'That being the case,' said Dennison, 'it wasn't any use going on. Marriage has to be everything or nothing, you know.' He paused. 'Sixpence for fourpence halfpenny,' he said very quietly. 'It was a bad bargain.'

He laughed suddenly, and there was a note in his laughter that Lanard did not care to hear. 'I was done, all the same,' he said, 'because by the time I found it out, I'd spent the six-pence.'

It was inevitable that the Press should discover the experiment. They had kept the secret well, but as soon as the *Iberian* arrived in the Solent with a peculiar superstructure on her forecastle, ill-informed comment and speculation began.

'The only thing that one can say,' remarked Sir David, 'is that we have been very fortunate that it did not begin before.'

He stood in the chart-room of the *Iberian* with Morris and Dennison as the vessel proceeded down the Solent towards Spithead. It was early in the morning; the air was fresh and salt; the sun streamed in through the ports and fell in sliding patches upon the papers littered on the chart-room table. On deck was the catapult with the track laid down and extending over the hold to the forecastle, and on the catapult was the flying-boat with Rawdon and the chief mechanic making a final inspection. There were to be two trial launchings that day; the first with no load at all, the second fully loaded.

Sir David turned again to the pile of newspapers. No statement had been issued to the Press in regard to the flight, with the result that the graver journals barely referred to the matter, while the more democratic sheets seethed with inaccurate information about the 'birdmen and their giant plane'.

'Fair makes me retch,' said Morris crudely. He was fortunate in that the identity of the crew had not yet leaked out.

The two technical papers dealt editorially with the matter. One regretted the paucity of information and was strictly non-committal. The other assumed a bolder attitude and gave a remarkably accurate forecast of the flight in the first paragraph. In the remaining three columns the discourse touched rapidly upon the deplorable condition of maritime aviation and settled down with gusto to a tirade against the Navy, illustrated by anecdotes that should have been unprintable, finally declaring that dear old Clausewitz was right after all, and that all things worked together for good.

Finally, on the day that they sailed for America, *The*

Times, in a leading article, dropped a heavy benediction upon the flight.

The *Iberian* pushed her way out between the twin forts and headed for the Warner and the Nab Tower. Presently Sir David and Dennison left the chart-room and went up on to the bridge; Morris was left alone. On the first trial he was to fly the machine off the deck alone, after which he was to fly back and put down off Flanagan's yard. There the machine would be lifted on to a lighter, so that by the time the *Iberian* returned, she could be hoisted on board again, for a second flight.

They passed the Warner. Morris moved across the cabin to the port and stood looking down upon the machine, ready upon its catapult. Above the pulsing of the engines and the wash of the sea, he could hear the pumps clucking and sighing as they charged the reservoirs for the pneumatic ram that would catapult him off the deck into the air . . .

A mechanic climbed up on to the planes of the machine and commenced to turn a crank upon the engine; the propeller began to revolve, infinitely slow. It seemed incredible that she should start. Suddenly he heard a half-hearted spit; the propeller leaped forward and became half invisible, and a steady rumble told him that the engine was running. They were nearly up to the Nab.

Morris turned from the window and took his helmet and gloves from the table. He opened the door of the little house and stood for a moment in the doorway, looking back over the water to the Island. It was a warm, sunny day; the clouds were white and the sea was very blue. It was a day on which one could do anything.

He stood in the doorway and stretched himself. From below came the steady rumble of the engine. 'She runs very sweetly,' he thought. 'She's better on the benzole mixture than the other.'

As they passed the Nab, Morris was in his seat and running his engine up to its full power. Satisfied, he throttled down again. Rawdon stepped to the side of the machine and looked up at Morris in the pilot's seat above him.

'You all right?' he shouted.

The helmeted figure nodded cheerfully. 'Quite all right.'

Rawdon stepped back and stood with the engineer of the catapult by the gear that would release the machine. On the bridge, Captain Willett broke off his conversation with the baronet.

'All ready,' he said. 'All right – take the wheel, Mr Mate.' He moved down to the voice-tube of the engine-room and spoke quietly down it. 'All ready now. Yes. Whack her up. Yes. All right.'

The mate relieved a seaman at the wheel.

The *Iberian* turned into the wind, and immediately the difference became evident.

'This ought to help her off,' said Dennison.

The captain was still at the voice-pipe. He straightened up, leaned over the dodger, and waved to Rawdon. Rawdon signalled to Morris, who nodded in return; the note of the engine swelled to a roar, tremulously deafening. Morris raised his hand.

'Right!' shouted Rawdon to the engineer.

The machine leaped forward and shot away down the track. The ram came to the end of its travel with a dull thud and the machine ran rapidly down the deck. Some distance from the bows light appeared beneath the wheels; she touched again, then lifted clear. On the bridge the mate spun the wheel hard over; the vessel yawed wildly. But there was no danger of running down the machine. She lifted clear, put her nose up, and went up on a slant, levelled, and circled the *Iberian*. They could see Morris wave his hand; then he took a course for the Island and dwindled into the distance.

The vessel returned to the Solent.

The machine was waiting in Cowes Roads upon a lighter when they got back; Flanagan had done his work well and quickly. A derrick was swung out and the machine was hoisted bodily aboard and placed on the catapult again before lunch, a little miracle of organized handling by slipshod-looking gentlemen in mufti. Then came the wearisome business of filling three-quarters of a ton of petrol into her tanks by two-gallon cans. The vessel lay at anchor; Morris and Dennison sat in deckchairs in the sun below the bridge, half asleep. The second trial was to take place after tea if the machine were ready in time; this time Dennison would go with Morris.

The petrol-cans jangled monotonously throughout the afternoon. Dennison turned in his chair and glanced attentively at the sky to windward. 'Wind's dying,' he said. 'We shall have a flat calm after tea.'

Both were well aware of the significance of this. A calm would make it more difficult for the machine to leave the deck – and this trial was to be fully loaded.

Morris closed his eyes. 'There will be plenty of wind,' he said. 'Vertical . . .'

Dennison chuckled and relapsed again into his chair. Presently, roused by an indisputable snore, Morris raised his head and glanced at his companion. Dennison was asleep. For a moment Morris sat looking at him curiously, then he relaxed again into his chair.

The petrol was filled into the machine and five hundred pounds of ballast in sandbags was placed in her little hold, to represent the bags of mail. The *Iberian* weighed, and they had tea going down the Solent. At Spithead, Morris went on deck and found the mate. He drew him aside.

'Look here,' he said. 'You'll be steering her, won't you?' He paused. 'Well, it's going to be a touchy business in this calm. I may have to jump her off before she's flying. If I do that, we shall probably flop down into the water. Look. I'm going to edge to starboard as soon as I'm in the air.'

'I'll give her a cast to port,' said the officer.

'That's it. But for God's sake, don't let her run off till I'm clear of the deck or you'll put us in the ditch. Keep her straight till I'm clear. And one other thing. Boats, and all that sort of business. Have them ready.'

'That's arranged,' said the mate. 'Those two rafts astern. See? We cut them loose as we pass you.'

'Right you are,' said Morris. He returned to the chart-room as they passed the Warner.

At the Nab they took their places, Dennison beside Morris

in the little cockpit of the flying-boat. Before them stretched the track, level to within a short distance of the bows and then sloping away downwards to assist the machine to leave the deck. It seemed very short.

The engine was run up, throttled again, and they settled themselves into their places. Dennison had flown in the machine several times before, and he was well accustomed to his position. He strapped himself in, settled his shoulders comfortably against the back of his seat, and waited, watching his companion.

Morris ran the engine up to full power and raised his hand. For a moment nothing happened; then suddenly the machine moved forward and began to hurtle down the track. The acceleration was terrific. It was painful; the seat pressed intolerably upon the back. Dennison's legs were suddenly drawn under his seat by an invisible agency; he gripped the side of the cockpit and fought to draw his breath. He glanced at Morris beside him, calm and motionless.

There was a thud as the ram came home, and they began to run along the track. Morris pressed the wheel forward and the tail of the machine rose so high from the deck that from the cockpit it seemed that she must catch her long bow on the track and turn a somersault. So she ran along. Dennison watched the track, eager and curious. There was none of that buoyant feeling that he knew must come before she could fly. She was fifty feet from the end – thirty feet. It was coming; she bounced more lightly. Ten feet.

Morris pulled the wheel back sharply with both hands; the rail dropped suddenly and they were in the air. Instantly he pressed the nose of the machine down and dived for the water a couple of hundred yards ahead, yawing a little to starboard. Dennison, watching the manoeuvre with detached interest, saw from the corner of his eye the hand of the air speed indicator creeping up and knew that the danger was over. Ten feet from the surface Morris checked the dive and flew along close above the water for a mile or so, then gently pulled the nose up. The machine responded sluggishly and climbed from the water; in a minute they had climbed perhaps a hundred feet.

On the bridge there was a general relaxation. As in all such affairs, the tension had been most severe among the spectators. The machine had run to the very end of the track and had then leaped ten or twelve feet into the air. As the *Iberian* yawed to port, the machine had dropped slowly towards the water; then the fall had been checked and she had flown along in the manner of a cormorant for nearly a minute, barely clear of the water, rising not at all. Finally had come the gradual climb that showed that all was well.

The first mate wiped his brow and relinquished the wheel to a seaman. 'I wouldn't go in that thing for a thousand pounds,' he said fervently.

Morris flew the machine back along the Solent to Cowes and put down into the Roads. The machine sank down to the water at, perhaps, seventy miles an hour. She flattened out close above the surface and touched suddenly with a crash, a little shower of spray, and a great foaming of water beneath her bows. Morris raised his goggles and wiped the spray from his face, then turned her and taxied her into Flanagan's slipway, where mechanics in waders were waiting to guide the machine as he taxied her up the slip upon her wheels.

Morris and Dennison returned to the *Clematis* and lived in her for the next two or three days. During that time the flying-boat was taken to pieces and crated, and placed in the hold of the *Iberian* with the greater part of the catapult gear. It would be re-erected in New York, where the machine was to be rigged and placed ready upon the catapult. There it would remain till the vessel was approximately nine hundred and fifty miles from Cornwall. This was timed to be early in the morning of 2 June. A staff of mechanics would sail in the *Iberian*.

The *Iberian* finished her arrangements and moved to Southampton to ship a cargo. Originally laid down as a passenger boat, the war had caught her in an early stage of construction. For a time, work on her had been suspended; then, as the need for fast cargo vessels became more evident, the design was modified to the exclusion of the great part of the passenger accommodation. By reason of the change, the vessel was cranky and ungainly, but she was fast, and for this purpose she answered admirably. In her the promoters of the venture had found the necessary speed with the privacy that they desired.

She was to take three days loading. Morris and Dennison returned to London and separated, to meet again at lunch with Rawdon and Sir David Fisher the day before the vessel sailed.

There was no business to be done. Everything had been settled; the arrangements for the landing at Padstow were complete. There remained only to make a good lunch and to drink to the success of the flight.

'Oh, rot that,' said Morris. 'We can drink a better one than that.' He raised his glass. 'The success of the venture. Good dividends!'

Soon afterwards the party broke up. 'We meet again at Padstow,' said Sir David quietly. 'The very best of luck.'

Dennison walked a little way along the street with Morris. 'I don't suppose it's any good asking you to dine with me this evening?' he said.

'Not the least,' said Morris dryly.

Dennison smiled, a little pensively. 'All right,' he said. 'Meet you on the ten-fifty at Waterloo, then?'

'Right you are,' said Morris. He hailed a taxi. 'Keep me a corner if you're there first. Cheer-oh.'

He drove to Paddington and took a local train to his home in the suburbs. He lived in a house just outside the aerodrome, a little, high-gabled, 'New Art' house that he had built himself the year before. He had placed it well, overlooking the aerodrome, and had given himself a large piece of pasture for a garden. During the winter he had been very busy transforming a portion of this into a tennis-court.

He had tea with his wife overlooking the garden. It was beginning to have the appearance of a garden at last; he surveyed it with some pleasure. His wife was a great gardener. When they had built the house they had decided that they would have a 'proper' garden, and had straightaway planned a garden of flowering trees and hollyhocks and cypresses and crazy pavement and a sundial. It was taking shape; it ran from the house to the hedge bordering the aerodrome, perhaps an acre in all. While he had been away, Helen had planted the bald patches in the lawns with grass seed.

He turned to his wife. She was several years younger than he, hardly more than a girl. 'I say,' he said, and munched steadily for a moment or two. 'We ought to have a double cherry somewhere. We had one at school – it was just outside my bedroom window. Great.'

'M'yes,' said the girl doubtfully. 'I don't know whether it would do in this soil.'

'It would have a damn good try,' said Morris firmly. 'We'll look it up in the book of the words after dinner and see what it says.'

He went upstairs, changed into old clothes, and spent the evening laying down great russet slabs of crazy-paving along one of his paths, while his wife scratched the turf and scattered grass seed. He worked well, and had finished several yards when his wife came out and stopped him.

'Time you went and had your bath,' she said.

He straightened up and gazed at her affectionately, dusted his hands together, and trod heavily upon the last stone.

' "The benison of hot water," ' he said reflectively. Then ingenuously, 'Have we got a nice dinner?'

The girl laughed cheerfully, though she had little heart for it. 'I'm not going to tell you what you've got,' she said. 'You'll enjoy your bath all the more. The pleasures of anticipation.'

'I shall probably be able to smell it when I go indoors, anyway,' said Morris. He did not move, but stood meditatively wiping his hands upon the seat of his trousers, surveying the unfinished portion of the path.

'It does seem a pity to leave it,' he said. 'I never seem to get any time at home nowadays.'

The girl gave a little gasp. 'I'll – I'll get Adams to finish it while you're away,' she said.

Morris turned and took her arm, his grubby hand upon her white sleeve. 'Don't do that,' he said. 'I want to do them myself.'

'All right,' said Helen. She drew him a little closer to her, and moved towards the house.

Morris lingered for a moment, and looked over his shoulder at the unfinished paths. 'There's a lot to do yet,' he said. 'Still, we're getting on. And I shall only be away just over three weeks this time.'

He turned to the house and walked up the garden arm in arm with his wife. 'Then we shall have all the summer to get it into order,' he said. 'Only about three and a half weeks. That's hardly any time.'

But the girl did not answer, and they walked on up to the house in silence. They went indoors and closed the garden door behind them. Presently light shone out from behind thin curtains in the leaded, casement windows; cheerful lights, such lights as are to be seen in the dusk from any prosperous little suburban home where the middle-class business-man takes his ease of an evening in the bosom of his family.

The sky turned slowly to a deeper blue than ever the Council of the garden suburb had dared to paint the dial of a clock.

Dennison sat in the smoking-room of his club before the fire, a novel on his knee, a pipe in his mouth, and an empty coffee-cup by his side. Outside there was a touch of frost in the air; he found the fire comforting. Though he had dined alone, he had put on a dinner-jacket; he did not quite know why. It was half-past nine. He had made a good dinner, and he was very comfortable.

He could not read his novel. He had sat in the smoking-room since dinner, smoking his pipe, watching the flickering of the fire, and wondering dispassionately whether he would ever sit there again. He had done sufficient flying during the past month to be able to picture the flight in his mind beforehand. He knew what the Atlantic looked like. He had had some experience of it in the *Irene*. He knew what the flight would be like. They would be catapulted from the ship in a similar manner to the trial flight, would climb slowly from the water upon a compass course. Then would come hour after hour of monotonous travel across the waste, deafened and stupid with noise, and listening all the time with morbid anxiety for a splutter in the roaring of the engine. For ten hours they would sit like that if they were lucky – ten hours of watching the long Atlantic swell ahead of them, mesmerized by noise, numb and deaf. At the end of that time land would appear as a line upon the horizon; he would have to cast off his fatigue, find out what land it was, and guide Morris to Padstow.

That was the programme.

Presently he got up and left the club. He turned down a side street into Pall Mall and walked along to the St James's end. Outside the gate of Marlborough House there was a guardsman on sentry, stiff and erect; in the square the lamps were bright. It was very quiet. A taxi passed with a whirr and vanished into the Mall; the towers of the Palace were very straight and stiff.

One could not be afraid.

He turned up St James's towards Piccadilly. Near King Street he was accosted by a very old man; a man with long white hair flowing on to his shoulders from under a battered, old-fashioned hat. From the folds of his cape he drew a sheaf of envelopes.

'I beg your pardon, sir,' he said in a gentle refined voice. 'But do you by any chance patronize the Turf?'

Dennison paused.

'I can give you a remarkably good selection for Ascot,' said the old man. 'I can assure you that you may place every confidence in them.'

'I'm sorry,' said Dennison, 'but I'm not a racing man.'

'The Oaks?' hazarded the ancient. 'I could put you in the way of a very considerable turnover upon the Oaks.'

'I'm very sorry,' said Dennison, 'but I don't bet at all.'

For a moment the old man gazed at him searchingly, incredulously. 'Ah yes,' he said at last. 'I see. You never touch it. You never touch it at all. Well, perhaps that is the better way after all.' He moved aside. 'Good night, sir. I'm sorry to have troubled you.'

'One moment,' said Dennison. 'I never bet – I don't know enough about it to back my fancy. But – I am leaving England

200

tomorrow. A long journey, and perhaps a dangerous one. I should be very glad if you would drink with me this evening.'

The old man took the coins. 'That is extremely good of you,' he said. 'May I ask if you are going far?'

'To America,' said Dennison.

'Ah yes,' said the tipster. 'I once visited America, but I did not care for the country. I wish you a prosperous journey, sir, and a happy return.'

He held out an envelope. 'You will take this suggestion for the Oaks?' he said. 'I think it is a good one.'

7

It seemed that Antony was ill. That was not an infrequent event and Sheila would probably have heard nothing about it until it was all over but for the loquacity of her cook. As it was, the news was exact and recent, coming direct to Cook from the mother of the housemaid at the Vicarage. Mr Antony was laid up again and was in bed at Oxford with a cold in his chest. His mother was very upset about it, and suspected that it was caused by his landlady neglecting to air the sheets.

At the time the news did not appeal very much to Sheila. Antony was always getting ill, and Sheila had enough anxiety of her own to occupy her mind at this time. Since Dennison had left her she had had no word of him; that was nearly two months before. She knew that she must wait upon events; in all her trouble she was quite sure that he had given up Hong Kong. But – if only she could hear something of him. As the weeks went by she grew more anxious and more miserable; small inanimate objects seemed to combine together to irritate her, a conspiracy of pinpricks. The centre of this conspiracy was in her bedroom where things got in the way so that she trod on them and hurt herself. In some mysterious way her bed grew harder and coarser, so that she lay awake at night listening to things rustling and creaking about the room that had never rustled or creaked before. She realized that the trouble lay with her, and commenced to take a tonic.

But she had little thought for Antony and his ailments.

Gradually, however, the news of Antony's illness began to appeal to her. It was bad luck on him, just as the weather was getting nice, to be laid by the heels by a cold that would not go away. She knew how much he had been looking forward to the summer term, and now he was missing it all. In her loneliness, she recalled what good company he had been for the week after she had sent Dennison away; she began to think more of him. Antony was ill in Oxford, only eighteen miles away. She could quite easily drive over and see him.

'I'm sure I wish you would,' said his mother. 'He gets so tired of bed, and his friends come and sit on his bed all day so that the room is always full of tobacco smoke. I don't think it's right of them to smoke in a sick-room, do you? And they bring him such horrible things to read . . .'

So she had lunch and took the big car and drove herself over to Oxford. She knew the town fairly well and had sometimes visited her brother when he had been up after the war. Immediately she reached Carfax she noticed a great change in the type of undergraduate. The bronzed and cheerful men that she had been accustomed to were gone and were replaced by pink-cheeked youths, callow and arrogant upon the pavements. Oxford was herself again.

Sheila drove on down the High, turned into Longwall Street, and drew up at Antony's digs. She rang the bell and asked if she could see him.

A stout lady in a print apron beamed at her in the doorway and ushered her up three flights of perfectly dark stairs to the room where Antony lay in bed. As Sheila entered she cast a quick glance round and was in time to catch the merriment dying from the faces of his visitors at her arrival.

Antony was sitting up in bed in a cardigan, a muffler round his neck. His hair was tousled and there was a feverish look about him. 'I say,' he said. 'How perfectly splendid of you to come. Please sit down – oh, it doesn't matter about my clothes a bit. Or you can sit on the bed. Mrs Williams!'

In some mysterious manner his friends had faded from the room. 'Mrs Williams!' said Antony.

The landlady stood in the doorway, her arms akimbo, a placid smile upon her countenance. 'Yes, sir,' she said comfortably.

'Mrs Williams, I want you to give us tea in about half an hour.' He turned to Sheila anxiously. 'You'll be able to stay, won't you?' His brows knitted together. 'Please. I shall want the China tea in my silver teapot, and the silver milk-jug and sugar-basin – the crystal sugar, you know. And buttered tea-cakes, and could you send out and get a nice chocolate cake with the fluffy sort of chocolate on the top. And thin bread and butter, and a little of the medlar jelly.'

'All right, sir,' said the woman cheerfully. 'You shall 'ave them.'

Antony lay back on his pillows with a little sigh and turned to Sheila. 'It's so nice of you to have come,' he said. 'How did you get here? By car? Do you know, I was hoping that perhaps you might – I've been wanting to see you.'

'It's simply silly of you to get like this in the summer term,' said the girl. 'How did you manage to do it?'

Antony smiled reflectively. 'I think I'll tell you,' he said. 'It was such fun – worth every bit of it. I told my mother that it was the sheets not being aired, and that was rather unfair to Mrs Williams because she really is most careful about the sheets, and of course I shouldn't have stayed here so long if she did that sort of thing. But it really was the "Hysteron Proteron" – that's a club, you know; the last first and the first last. It was such fun. We had a whole day of it.

'First of all we got up and dressed for dinner. And one man had a drink of warm mustard and water because he said he always did that before going to bed when he was drunk and he was sure that he was going to get drunk at dinner. But I think that was carrying it too far, don't you? And then we met and sat round the fire drinking coffee, and then we had the port. And then, at about half-past ten in the morning, we went in to

203

dinner and went all through it from the dessert to the soup. And then we had a cocktail and then we changed and had a bath. And at about one o'clock, we had tea, and at about five we had lunch, and about nine o'clock we had breakfast – bacon and eggs and kidneys. And then the others went and had the before-breakfast bathe in Parsons' Pleasure. Only, of course, I couldn't do that, but I went with them and watched them. And there was such a heavy dew – the grass was wet with it, only I didn't notice it till I got home, and then I found that the legs of my trousers were quite wet. And next day I had this cold.'

'Anyway,' said Sheila, 'you'll never forget that the first should be last and the last should be first.'

'No – it's an awfully good lesson in humility, isn't it? That's what we all felt – it was such a good thing to do . . . and incidentally it was rather amusing.'

They chatted happily till tea-time about books and pictures. Antony's epic poem had made some progress and he was much exercised in his mind as to what was to become of it. Sheila gathered that it was quite unpublishable, too long for Oxford Poetry, and he could not bear the idea of putting it away in a drawer with a view to publication in future years among his Collected Works. The talk revived Sheila; she felt more herself than she had done for weeks. Antony, however, had been quick to notice the difference in her and to mark the gradual brightening in her manner. Presently came tea, and after tea the broader outlook engendered by repletion.

Antony snuggled down a little beneath his bedclothes. He had been worrying over Sheila. He had hoped that she would come to see him; now that she was here he was prepared to employ every means in his power to reach a solution of the problem that had been puzzling him. He was very fond of Sheila, and it distressed him to see her unhappy.

He threw an arm up round his head and ran his fingers through his tousled hair. 'What's Dennison doing?' he inquired.

The girl avoided his gaze. 'I don't know,' she said indifferently. 'We haven't seen anything of him.' She picked up a book from the table and fingered the binding. 'I do like these editions. They get them up so well.'

'Do you know,' said Antony, 'I think you made a frightful mistake in sending him away. I do hope,' he added, 'that you aren't going to go away, but you may if you want to. But it would be nicer of you to stay and amuse me, and it amuses me to talk to you about Dennison. And it's very good for me, too. I've been thinking such a lot about you. I do wish you'd married him.'

Sheila was dumbfounded. For a moment all that she could think of was — 'This serves me right for coming. I've brought this on myself.' His last words threw her into a panic and brought back the worst of her fears redoubled. How much did Antony know and why — oh, why had he put it so definitely in the past tense? She remained silent.

'You know,' said Antony, 'when I was a boy I used to think I was in love with you myself. I found out later that I wasn't, of course. I don't think I'm capable of ever loving anyone better than myself, and you simply weren't in it beside me, you see, and so I knew that I couldn't be in love with you. And ever since I found that out I wanted to see you marry someone you really cared about, and who cared for you. And then it didn't come off.'

Sheila found her voice. 'I suppose you thought I was going to marry Peter,' she said. 'Well, how do you know I'm not?'

Antony gazed at her round-eyed. 'But you sent him away!' he said.

'He'd have been perfectly miserable in China,' said the girl.

For a moment Antony's brain worked rapidly, then he sat up in bed. 'You sent him away because of that?' he said. 'But didn't you tell him?'

The girl turned away her head. 'Not about that,' she said at last. 'I — I just told him that I couldn't go to China. It was better that way.'

'I see,' said Antony slowly. 'But what's going to happen now?'

Sheila raised her head and smiled. 'I think he'll poke about and get a job in England that we can marry on,' she said. 'And then he'll come back.'

Antony lay back in bed and gazed out of his window. Outside there were chimney-pots, russet and black, and sparrows, and a great expanse of blue sky and white cloud. The girl, expecting some commendation, waited, and as she waited the smile died from her lips. Antony thought she had done wrong.

'He'll never come back,' said Antony.

He turned to her before she could reply. 'It's only the small men who come back,' he said, 'the men of no courage or the men of no principle. A man who acts on principles will never come back, because that would be giving in. Didn't you know that? Lots of men would far rather go unmarried than marry a girl who keeps them dangling on a string and expects them to come back. They stand by the first answer.'

The girl gazed at him steadily. 'Do you mean I've lost him?' she said.

Antony leaned forward and took one of her hands in his. 'I'm frightfully glad you came today,' he said. 'I don't think you've lost him at all. But you hurt him frightfully, you know. It was the wrong way to take him altogether. You see, he was giving up everything that he cared for to go to China for you . . . and you told him that you couldn't give up even the little things. Didn't you think it would pay to be honest with him?'

He paused and continued, 'Do you remember the morning he left, when he and I got up early to photograph the birds? You remember that etching I made of you? He asked if he might have it once before, and I had it all ready for him then, done up in paper. And he wouldn't take it.

'And then of course, I knew that he wasn't coming back. He's not the sort, you know.'

He lay back on his pillows. A copy of a gaudy French comic paper slipped from under the bedclothes and fluttered to the floor. Sheila realized that probably it had been secreted on her arrival. Mechanically she picked it up and placed it on the table.

After a time she got up. 'Do you know what I'm going to do?' she said. 'I'm going to walk up to the Turl and get you a bowl of hyacinths, in peat, you know. It's silly of you not to have any flowers. What colours would you like?'

Antony considered. 'White and blue, please, in a blue bowl,' he said. 'And think it over.'

The girl stood looking down on him, chewing her glove. 'You're rather a dear,' she said at last. 'I think I shall have to write to Peter, shan't I?'

'I should think it's the best thing you can do,' said Antony cheerfully. 'You ought to have done it weeks ago.'

It was a very long letter. Sheila wrote it in her bedroom one evening; it took a long time to write partly on account of its length and partly on account of the view over the woods from her window. It was evening, and whether the sunset influenced her letter or her letter drew her attention to the sunset is a point that probably will never be cleared up. For the rest of her life she remembered every detail of that evening; years afterwards she could sit down in the sunset and recall the phrases that she had written to her lover.

It was a very bulky letter, but she squeezed it into an envelope, walked down to the post, and posted it to Dennison in London.

It is curious how seldom one gets the answer to a letter of importance. One calculates the posts and one determines the hour of the arrival of the reply; it should come by the second post next Wednesday. On Wednesday morning, lying awake in bed, one admits a doubt, born perhaps of previous experience. Perhaps Wednesday was a little too soon to expect an answer. The answer to such a letter would take a little time to prepare; one could not really expect it on Wednesday and, whatever happens, one will not be disappointed if it doesn't come. Wednesday passes, and Thursday.

And perhaps the answer never comes at all.

Sheila was dismayed. She had been prepared for a rebuff, unlikely though she had thought it. But that Dennison should not have answered her letter at all was incomprehensible. It was not his way.

In her letter she had suggested that they should meet in

town to discuss their affairs. Now she sent him a postcard, stating very briefly where she would be lunching when she went to town on the following Saturday. To that there was no reply.

She lingered over her lunch till three o'clock, then took a taxi for Chelsea. Already she suspected that he must be away, yet she must put the matter to the test, whatever the cost. She could not return home with nothing accomplished, nothing discovered to bring her peace of mind.

Dennison lived in the middle of a long row of drab grey houses. Sheila paid off her taxi, marched up the steps, and rang the bell.

The maid came to the door. 'Can I see Mr Dennison?'

The maid hesitated. 'He's gone away, miss,' she said.

So that was it.

'I see,' said Sheila. 'Do you know when he'll be back?'

'I don't know, miss,' said the girl. 'He's gone flying – on the sea, you know. With them in the papers.' Then, with evident relief,–'Mr Lanard is upstairs if you would like to see him. He knows all about it.'

Sheila produced a card. 'Will you ask Mr Lanard if he can give me Mr Dennison's address?'

The maid took the card and went upstairs. Presently she returned. 'Will you come up?'

Sheila followed her upstairs and into the sitting-room. Gazing past the maid and past Lanard she saw her letter and her postcard on the mantelpiece.

Then her attention was directed to Lanard. He stood on the hearth-rug with her card in his hand, tall, dark, and very neat. He was not a handsome man at the best of times, and he greeted her with a particularly unpleasant smile. The girl's first impression was that this was the coldest and rudest man that she had ever had to deal with. His smile in itself was an insult, as though he had spat at her.

'Good afternoon, Miss Wallace,' said Lanard. He spoke with little cordiality, and he said no more. He knew perfectly well with whom he had to deal. He had read Sheila's postcard to Dennison. Dennison was in New York at the moment; Lan-

208

ard had determined to wait in that afternoon in case the girl turned up. He had been desperately worried over the flight. His was the temperament that broods and magnifies every danger in the imagination; he had been miserable since his friend had left. He blamed the girl who had started his friend on the run; he blamed himself that he had not gone with Dennison on the *Irene*. There were times when a man needed looking after. That had been one of them.

Well, here was the girl. This was the girl who would be glad enough to marry Dennison if he remained in England, but who could not face the prospect of going out to China with her husband. And yet, one who could not let him go, but must tag on to him as long as he remained in reach to prevent him settling down to forget that he had loved. As she came into the room the fire blazed up in Lanard.

'I'm so sorry to bother you,' said Sheila, '– but I wonder if you could give me Mr Dennison's address? Is he away for long?'

'He's gone to America,' said Lanard crisply. 'He's in New York.'

The girl faltered. 'In – in New York?' she said. 'Why – when did he go over there? Is he going to be away for long?'

'He'll be back in about a fortnight's time.'

The girl was evidently puzzled. 'Do you know what he went over there for? I mean, I saw him quite recently and there was no mention of it then.'

'I don't suppose so,' said Lanard. He paused and eyed her gravely, then continued picking his words with cruel care.

'He has had a good deal of trouble recently. After it was all over he went away for a bit, and got mixed up in this attempt to fly the Atlantic. In an aeroplane. You have heard about it? Dennison is the navigator. I believe the pilot is a friend of yours. Mr Morris.'

The girl gazed at him steadily. 'I knew nothing of this,' she said.

Lanard smiled again and raised his eyebrows. 'No?' he said. 'Your brother knows the details. I believe he dined with Morris the other day. Perhaps it would be better if you were to ask him to tell you about it. He can probably tell you more than I.'

The girl flushed angrily. 'When is the flight to take place?' she demanded.

'On June the second.'

'Can you give me Mr Dennison's address in New York?' She took a paper and pencil from her bag.

Lanard stiffened visibly. 'I wonder if I may ask – why?'

'Certainly,' answered the girl coldly. 'I am sending him a cable of good wishes for the flight.'

For a moment there was a battle of glances. 'No,' said Lanard. 'I'm afraid I can't give you the address.'

'Why not?' demanded the girl.

Lanard did not answer at once, but put his hands into his pockets, crossed to the window, and stood for a moment looking down into the street. When he spoke again it was in a gentler tone.

'Don't you think it would be better to let him alone for the present?' he said. 'This flight is a serious matter – a dangerous matter. It's very dangerous. People who do that sort of thing have to work very carefully on the preparations, you know. Nothing must be forgotten, nothing must be left to chance. They have to give the very best work there is in them to the preparations. If they don't, they get killed. The flight itself is nothing in importance to the work done beforehand. You see that? If you cable to him now, you'll put him off his stroke and spoil his work entirely. You'll upset him.'

He turned suddenly from the window. 'And damn it!' he said savagely, 'what right have you got to put him off like that? It was you that sent him into this infernal thing. Now the best thing you can do is to keep out of it. Let him alone. What do you want? You'll never get him back. You wouldn't go to China with him – but he'd have gone farther than that with you. He knows you now. He didn't before. You'll never get him back. Can't you make up your mind to let him alone?'

The fit passed, and he stood eyeing her moodily. She did not attempt to speak, but sat down on the edge of a chair and sat leaning forward, her elbows on her knees, playing with her gloves. For a full minute, it seemed to him, they remained like that without a word. Presently she raised her head and smiled at him, a little wistfully.

'We'll discount the heroics,' she said. 'I had heard nothing at all about all this. Thank you for telling me. I won't cable to him. I'll have back my letter and my postcard, please. Thank you.'

She rose, and stood fingering the bulging letter. 'As for China,' she said. 'I see you know all about it. I think you've got hold of the wrong end of the stick. Do you think it would have been good for Peter to have gone to China?'

'No,' said Lanard slowly, 'I don't.'

'Nor do I,' said the girl. She turned to go. 'Think it over, Mr Lanard.' She smiled. 'I think we shall be good friends one day,' she said. 'Good-bye.'

Lanard was left alone. Moodily he stood in the window and watched her out of sight down the street, conscious that he had made a most colossal fool of himself. Whether it was the excitement of the interview, or whether unconsciously he had taken a chill, he became aware of the approach of one of his chronic gastric attacks, a very prince of stomach-aches. He spent the evening huddled in his dressing-gown over a fire that smoked but would not burn, a glass of tepid water at his side, one of the most anxious and most miserable men in London.

Sheila left the house and walked away down the street, dazed and numb. In a sense she was relieved in that she knew everything now. That is, she knew the broad outlines of the matter. The details she must find out. She was hot with anger against her brother. He had known of this all the time, and yet he had not told her.

She turned into the King's Road, bought a budget of newspapers at a tobacconist, and sat down in a teashop to read them. During this interim period the subject had been largely dropped; she found little in the daily papers. One of the weekly journals printed a map of the North Atlantic, showing the approximate point of commencement of the flight. Sheila gazed at it for a while in a growing horror; it was right out in the middle, nearly half-way across.

In another paper she found a small paragraph to state that the *Iberian* had arrived in New York. Morris and Dennison were mentioned by name.

So it was true.

It was a painful week-end for Jimmie Wallace. It culminated in a journey, for instead of going up to town on Monday morning, he took the car and drove in a slightly different direction. He did not start till after lunch, so that it was nearly teatime when he came driving down the lane to the aerodrome.

He passed the entrance to the works, drove on for half a mile, and stopped outside the little new house that stood by itself among the rudiments of a garden.

The maid opened the door. 'Can I see Mrs Morris?' he inquired.

He was shown into the drawing-room. Outside in the garden he could see Helen Morris and another girl grubbing about in a border, and Morris's terrier puppy in vain pursuit of a bee. He glanced aimlessly about the room. Morris had never been a man for any display of his work and there was nothing in the house to show his profession, no ostentation of propellers or model aeroplanes. The room was very comfortable, with an open brick hearth surrounded by deep, chintz-covered chairs. To Wallace the whole room spoke of the man that he had known at Oxford. The little things were eloquent; the pipe upon the mantelpiece, the toasting-fork in the fender, the long untidy bookcases filled with the russet and black of old calf.

His examination of Morris's *ménage* was interrupted by the entrance of his wife.

She came into the room like a breeze. 'Mr Wallace,' she said. 'I'm so glad to see you. Can you stay to tea? Stephen's away – but of course you know that. I was forgetting.'

'I'd love to have some tea,' said Wallace. 'Afterwards I must get back – I motored up from Berkshire and I must get back in time for dinner.'

Helen Morris wrinkled her brows a little. 'That's miles and

miles,' she said in wonder. 'Would you like tea now – or wait till it comes? We can have it now – almost at once.'

Wallace smiled. 'I'd rather wait till it comes,' he said.

He took off his coat and sat down on the arm of a chair. 'First of all, I want to get my business off my chest if I may. I'm awfully glad to find you here. I was afraid you might have gone away for a change while Stephen is on this stunt.'

'No,' said the girl. 'Stephen wanted me to go home, but I wanted to get on with the garden, so I got Eileen Thatcher to come and stay with me. You remember Eileen? She was at Somerville when we were up. And I didn't want to go home.'

Wallace nodded. He knew something of the opposition that the girl had had to face at home over her marriage. She had been one of the Rileys of Gloucestershire and of all her relations the only one to take kindly to Morris had been her father, now a great age. She was an only child; one day they would be well off. Wallace, sharing rooms with Morris at Oxford after the war, had watched them from the start.

He perched himself on the arm of his chair and plunged into his subject. 'I've come to you because I want you to do something for me.' He paused, worried by the difficulty of broaching his subject to the girl. At last he said, 'Did you ever meet this man Dennison?'

The girl shook her head. 'No. Stephen wanted him to come here, but they were so busy before they left and he had too much to do.'

She glanced quickly at the perplexed young man. 'It's about Sheila, isn't it?' she said.

'That's it,' said Wallace with evident relief. 'She's been having rather a bad time lately.'

Helen Morris nodded. 'Stephen told me there was something in the wind between those two,' she said. 'He never heard any details, because the man wouldn't speak a word about any of you. And Stephen didn't mention it, of course. You told him about it, didn't you?'

Wallace, intent on piecing together his story, disregarded the question. 'Well,' he said, 'it was like this. She first met him about four years ago when he was in hospital, or rather con-

213

valescing with an aunt of mine. Then he went away and only turned up again at Easter – this Easter. Mind you, he was quids in all the time I think, only they didn't write or anything.'

Some strain of imagination latent in the girl enabled her to piece together this narrative and made the dry bones live. 'I see,' she said gravely.

'Well, then he got a job in Hong Kong or somewhere that was good enough to marry on – better than most. So back he came at Easter and put it to her as a workable proposition. Well, Sheila got an idea into her head that it wouldn't be a good thing for him to go to China. You see, it was pretty evident that he was only going out there because he wanted to get married. She thought that if they waited a year or two longer and he poked about a bit, he could get a job that they could marry on in England. So she turned him down, nominally because of China. It was taking a pretty big chance, of course. She thought that doing it that way would give him an incentive to find something else that he'd be happier in himself, and that then he'd come back again.'

'She didn't tell him?'

'No. She thought it would be better that way. As it turned out, she was a damn sight too clever.'

The girl gazed out of the open window into the sunlit garden. 'Of course, every man is a perfect infant,' she said, 'but they aren't such infants as all that. It was brave of her.'

'Anyway,' said Wallace, 'this lad took his pill and I was sorry to see him go. He's a good sort. Then – so far as I can make out – he went off in his yacht for a bit and got run down by your husband and co. That seems to have happened immediately after he left us.'

He paused for a moment. 'Now Sheila's found out all about it,' he said, 'and there's a most fearful scene of woe.'

Helen nodded comprehendingly.

'It's really rather rotten,' said Wallace gravely. 'She never thought he'd go off the deep end like this – I don't suppose she thought about it at all. And now she thinks she's sent him off on a thing that's dangerous. She thinks that his taking part in

214

this expedition is all her fault. She thinks he's going to be killed.'

The girl did not move.

Wallace rose to his feet and looked her squarely in the face. 'I came over to ask if you'd come and see her,' he said, 'and stay with her a day or two. I know it's a damn funny thing to ask. Perhaps it's a rotten thing to ask you – I don't know about that. But you're the only person who can tell her all about the flight and what the danger really is. That's what she wants to know, though she doesn't say so. She'll believe you. You know, and I know, that there's not much risk about it. They prepare so carefully. I've told her all that, but she doesn't believe me – she thinks I'm just saying it on purpose for her.'

'Stephen always says,' the girl said absently, 'that if anyone was to get hurt it would wreck the scheme at the outset – destroy the confidence of the public. It would ruin it financially. And they can't afford to let that happen.'

She turned to Wallace. 'Of course I'll come,' she said. 'I'm frightfully sorry Sheila's taking it so much to heart. I think I can tell her as much as anyone can. I'm awfully glad I can help.'

There was a silence. The girl moved slowly to the mantelpiece. 'He left his pipe behind,' she said in a troubled tone. 'Wasn't it silly of him? He'll be miserable without it. I do hope he got one in Southampton.'

Wallace could find nothing to say.

The girl left him and walked down the garden to where her friend was still weeding the border, to where the puppy was still snapping at the bees.

'Eileen!' she said. 'Come here. I've got a funny story to tell you. I've got to go away tomorrow.' She laughed queerly. 'I've got to go and convince a girl that there's really no danger in flying half-way across the Atlantic.'

She explained the circumstances.

Her friend plucked a grass and chewed the end of it. 'Best thing in the world for you,' she said.

So Rawdon's arrangements underwent a modification.

He sat in his shabby little office on the aerodrome, laboriously construing an article in a German technical paper with the aid of a dictionary. It was half an hour after lunch on a hot afternoon. He was unbearably sleepy; he could hardly keep his eyes open; the print grew misty before his eyes. He sat relaxed in his deck-chair, his brows knitted in a frown, the paper on his knee. One would have said that here was an amateur golfer reckoning his handicap in the club-house of an impecunious golf club, instead of a celebrated engineer at work.

A knock at the door made him raise his head. 'Come in,' he called, in a voice curiously soft and deep.

His commissionaire opened the door. She was a pretty child about fifteen years of age, with short fair hair, dressed in a blue gym tunic. She gazed kindly at the red-haired man in the chair.

'Please, sir,' she said, 'Mrs Morris would like to speak to you.'

Rawdon laid down his paper. 'Tell her to come in,' he said. He gazed at her severely. 'Then you'd better go and find your hair ribbon.'

The child put her hand to her head and smiled shyly, then disappeared. Rawdon heaved his great bulk out of the chair. A moment later Helen Morris entered the room.

Rawdon greeted her and gave her his deck-chair. Then he sat himself on his desk and swung his legs like a schoolboy.

'Well,' he said, 'I've got rooms at both hotels. The arrangements are that we meet at Truro on the evening of the first. Then we get up very early next morning and drive to Poldhu and wait there for the wireless from the *Iberian*. That should come in about eight in the morning – as soon as they get away. Then we drive to Padstow and get there in time for lunch. I've got rooms at the hotel there for us all – for you, Sir David, and myself – and also for Dennison and your husband. They should be arriving about six in the evening, if they get away up to time.'

Helen nodded. 'I understand,' she said. 'We meet at Truro, then.'

'That's it,' said Rawdon. 'I'm driving down in my car –

probably I'll take two days over it. But I'll meet you at Truro. Sir David will be coming down by train. Have you ever met him?'

'No,' said Helen. 'But what I came to ask you was this. Do you mind if I bring another girl with me?'

Rawdon hesitated. 'We don't want to get any more people there than we can possibly help, you know,' he said gently.

'I know,' said the girl. 'This is a friend of mine – and of Dennison. I couldn't leave her behind.'

Briefly she explained as much of the circumstances as she thought it necessary for the designer to know.

'Anyway,' she said finally, 'I can't possibly go traipsing about the country with you and Sir David without a companion.'

Rawdon smiled, but still hesitated. From the start he had been opposed to taking Helen Morris to Padstow, though it had been impossible to refuse. He owed that to Morris. But he had never lost a certain feeling of uneasiness. He was a level-headed man and had to look at every aspect of the situation. Suppose the thousandth chance turned up to defeat all their care and labour, and the machine were lost. Padstow would be no place for the wife of the pilot.

And now there would be two of them . . .

He turned to her. 'I don't suppose Sir David will mind,' he said, 'so long as she keeps her mouth shut. You'll impress that on her? It'll be nice for you to have a companion. I'm afraid you'd be very bored otherwise.'

He slipped from the table. 'So that's all right,' he said softly. 'We shall like to have her very much. I'll write and get an extra room at the hotel.'

8

Rawdon came out of the little wireless house and walked down the path to the car.

'Nothing in yet,' he said.

They had left Truro early in the morning for Poldhu. Rawdon drove with Sir David beside him, Helen and Sheila in the rear seat.

It was a delicious morning, calm, sunny, and fresh. Rawdon laughed, settled himself into his seat, and swung the car along the deserted roads at a good pace. As they drove through the lanes, Sir David leaned back chatting cheerfully with Sheila, in contrast to his habitual reserve. It was exhilarating. Upon all of them lay the feeling that that day history would be made; that that day there would be a tiny advance in the utilization of science, in the civilization of the world. And they were the only people in England who knew about it. At that moment in the towns and cities the people were going to work as they had done every morning of their working lives. To them this day would be like any other day. But to the little party motoring through Cornwall, this day would be different, a day to which they would look back with wonder as one upon which they had helped in doing something new.

Sir David got out of the car, fumbled for his watch, and closed it again with a sharp click.

'Twenty minutes to nine,' he said briefly. 'They're late off the mark, I'm afraid.'

They chatted for a little round the car, then turned and fell to pacing up and down the road, Rawdon and Sir David a little way ahead of the others.

'We are fortunate in the weather,' said Sir David. 'A very high barometer.'

Rawdon did not answer. Sir David glanced at him; he was evidently uneasy and paced up and down in silence for a little. At last, 'We ought to be hearing something by now,' he said.

'They must have got away by this time.'

Sir David glanced again at his watch. 'They may not be in position,' he said. 'If the vessel were too far out they'd have to wait, of course – even if it meant finishing the flight in the dark.'

Rawdon bit his lip. 'I know,' he said. 'We ought to have given them night-flying equipment. It comes out so frightfully heavy. The dynamo, and the batteries ... For that we could give them extra fuel for half an hour.'

At a quarter past nine Helen Morris came strolling towards them. 'No news?' she inquired.

'Not yet,' said Rawdon, in his soft, gentle little voice. 'It means that the *Iberian* hasn't got within flying distance up to time. We're going to give them an hour more, then we'll try and get a message through to them and find out what's happening.'

He laughed, and stretched his immense frame. 'I didn't have half enough breakfast,' he said cheerfully.

They turned and walked up and down the road again. Presently Rawdon stopped and glanced towards Helen and Sheila. They were not looking at them.

'Look at that,' he said to the baronet.

He pointed to a cottage about a mile away to the north of them. From the one stone chimney a thin wreath of blue smoke rose almost vertically into the air and drifted seawards.

Sir David regarded it for a while in silence. 'Coming out easterly – nor'-easterly,' he said at last. 'I was afraid it might with this high glass.'

He turned to Rawdon. 'Probably entirely local,' he said. 'It comes round that hill.'

The designer did not speak, and they resumed their pacing up and down the road. Presently Sir David stopped.

'How would it be to try and get through to them now?' he said. The wind had risen to a light air, and fanned his cheek as he spoke. 'They ought to know about this east in the wind. We didn't count much on that.'

'It was a hundred to one against it at this time of year,' said Rawdon fretfully.

They turned towards the wireless-house. As they approached, a man in shirt-sleeves appeared at the door and waved a paper at them. Rawdon looked at the baronet for a moment without speaking.

'That's bad luck,' he said quietly, and went to fetch the message. It ran:

9.57. Goods safely despatched as arranged Scheme one 963 miles. Willett.

Helen looked over Rawdon's arm at the paper. 'What does Scheme one mean?' she asked.

'Scheme one means coming to Padstow,' said Sir David. 'Scheme two was for use if it was very bad weather and meant making for Baltimore Harbour – west of Ireland, you know.'

'I see,' said Helen.

Rawdon turned cheerfully to Sheila. 'That's all right,' he said. 'That's just over nine and a half hours' flight. They'll arrive about half-past seven in the evening, in time for a late dinner.' He turned to the car. 'Talking of food,' he said, 'what about another breakfast? We've got all day to get to Padstow.' He turned. 'Where's Sir David?'

'He went into the wireless-hut,' said Helen.

Rawdon left the girls to pack themselves into the car and swung jauntily down the path and into the office. He found Sir David at a table, pencilling figures on a scrap of paper.

Rawdon's jaunty bearing dropped from him like a garment. 'They're cutting it mighty fine,' he said grimly.

Sir David tapped his pencil on the table and gazed at the other for a moment in silence. 'Evidently they were late in getting to the spot,' he said. 'It was to be a maximum of nine hundred and fifty miles.'

Rawdon nodded. 'Nine hundred and sixty-three miles,' he said. 'That's just over nine and a half hours' flight, say nine hours and forty minutes – in a calm. And petrol for ten and a quarter hours. They didn't count on having a head wind,' he added grimly.

Sir David glanced out of the door at the open moor. 'It's probably entirely local,' he said again.

They returned to the car and drove back to Truro. At the hotel where they had passed the night they had a second breakfast.

'I say,' said Sheila. 'Let's get some lunch put up and have it on the way. We shan't want much after a breakfast like this.' So they set off for Padstow, driving in the sunshine through the heart of Cornwall.

Sir David sat in the front seat by Rawdon, calm and impassive. They did not speak at all. Behind them Helen and Sheila were cheerful enough; the keen wind and the sunshine had lifted their troubles from them and they were enjoying the drive.

At about half-past one they stopped for lunch on the summit of the moor, not very far from the point where the road branches away down-hill to Padstow. On the moor the wind blew strong and free. Rawdon and Sir David left the girls with a perfunctory remark or two, and walked up on to a knoll while they laid out the lunch.

For a long while neither of them spoke.

At last, 'Fifteen miles an hour at least,' said Rawdon. 'Probably nearer twenty.'

'Will they know they have a wind against them?'

Rawdon considered. 'The smoke of a steamer might tell them,' he said. 'Nothing else.'

There was a pause, and presently Rawdon spoke again. 'One couldn't have foreseen a wind like this at this time of year,' he said. 'The weather report said south-westerly. It's practically dead east.'

He turned to the other. 'We may as well face the facts. If this wind holds all day, they can't do it. They haven't got the petrol.'

Down the road the girls sat on the heather beside the car, the lunch spread on a patch of grass before them. Helen Morris gazed at the two men on the knoll a little anxiously.

'What's the matter with them?' she said to Sheila. 'Why don't they come?'

They looked uneasily at the men. Presently they stirred, and rose to their feet. 'What are they talking about up there?' said Sheila. 'There's something up.'

'I know.'

The wife of the pilot went to the other side of the road and stood erect upon a little heap of stones looking intently round at the sunlit moor, at the yellow gorse, and at the sea, mistily blue away upon the horizon. Sheila stood watching her, reminded in a queer way of a child that ventures timidly into a darkened room.

Helen turned slowly towards the knoll; the breeze caught her hair and blew a wisp of it across her face.

'Oh!' she cried. For a moment she stood quite still, then turned and walked across the road to Sheila.

'My dear,' she said quietly. 'I know what it is. It's the wind. It's blowing against them – and it's very strong.'

That afternoon dragged wearily away. They made a hurried lunch and drove down to the little seaport town. At the hotel Rawdon was very good to them, and showed them to their rooms overlooking the estuary. Sir David, on the other hand, had retired absolutely into himself and had become again the man of affairs. He left them and retired to the manager's office and the telephone. Rawdon joined him as soon as he could decently leave the two girls.

Helen and Sheila wandered out into the little town and along the quays, miserably endeavouring to hearten each other. Down the river the wind blew strongly, raising little rollers upon the surface.

At the end of the jetty Sheila turned to Helen.

'I've never been here before,' she said, 'but Peter knows it well. He's often been in here in his boat.' She paused. 'I suppose he rows up to these steps in his dinghy,' she said, 'and ties her up to that ring. And then he walks up there and does his shopping. Bully beef, and tinned milk and things . . .'

Helen passed a hand through her arm, but could find nothing to say.

The other did not move. 'It all seems so unreal,' she said.

'I've never seen a flying-boat close to and I – I don't know what it's like . . .'

Presently they returned to the hotel. At tea Sir David was more communicative. He had managed to get a telephone call through to the Admiralty where he had spoken to a cousin of his. A destroyer would be held ready to proceed to sea at Plymouth. No authority for her to sail could be issued till the machine was two hours overdue. Sir David was to put through another telephone call at ten o'clock, if necessary.

At the end of the day they got into the car again and drove out to the headland at the mouth of the river, Stepper Point. It was half-past seven when they arrived, the time fixed for the arrival of the machine. They left the car in a lane and walked over a field to a stretch of open gorse-covered land where they could see the whole expanse of the western horizon. The wind was dying with the evening.

Sheila and Helen sat down together on a mossy slab of gran-ite overlooking the sea; Rawdon and Sir David stood behind a little way off.

'I'm afraid there's not a chance of it,' said Rawdon quietly to the baronet.

'It was better to bring them out,' said the other. 'And we can do nothing till ten.'

Slowly the sun drew nearer the horizon; in the deepening sky appeared the silvery disc of the full moon. The day had been very hot; on the headland the falling breeze grew cool and refreshing. At last Sir David closed his watch with a sharp click. Rawdon raised his eyebrows.

'Twenty past eight,' said the baronet. By calculation the petrol would be exhausted by a quarter past.

'It would be possible to run for a little bit longer,' said Rawdon. 'By cruising at a slower speed they might get as much as half an hour more.'

The sun sank lower and lower. The two girls sat together motionless, now and again speaking a word or two in a whisper. At last the lower limb of the sun dipped into the sea. Rawdon looked at his watch; it was nearly nine o'clock.

He glanced towards Helen and Sheila.

'Damn it,' he said. 'We oughtn't to have brought them.'

The baronet shifted a little, and raised the collar of his ulster. He was stiff with standing, and suddenly to Rawdon he seemed to have grown old.

'We must get them back to the hotel,' he said. 'Will you take Mrs Morris? You know her better than I.'

He moved forward to where the two girls were still watching the afterglow of the sunset. 'Come,' he said, and there was nothing of the man of business about him now. Only an old man was speaking to the two girls; a man tall, white-haired, and a little old-fashioned in his manner.

'Come,' he said. 'We must get back to the hotel. They must be down by now. I think by the time we get back to the hotel we shall find a message from them from Ireland.'

He turned to Sheila and offered her his arm. 'Will you come with me?' he said.

The girl took his arm and they went stumbling over the heather towards the car.

'All evening,' she said, 'I've been watching the gulls. They do it so easily – so effortlessly. All along the cliff.' She turned to the old man. 'It's worth it, isn't it?' she said pathetically.

'My dear,' said the baronet, 'you should ask them.'

And that was all that anybody said until they reached the hotel.

Rawdon dropped them at the porch and took the car round to the garage. Sir David ushered Helen and Sheila into the hall. He dropped his hat on to a peg and turned to face them.

'You must go upstairs and go to bed,' he said incisively. 'I promise you that I will come and tell you the moment we get any news.' They stood before him like two children, mesmerized by their own trouble, by his sharply-defined features, by the clear enunciation of his words. 'You understand? You are to go straight upstairs and get your things off and go properly to bed. And go to sleep. Good night.'

Without a word they turned and went upstairs.

To everyone in pain there comes a breaking point, the point where fortitude breaks down. As often as not the crisis is precipitated by some discomfort of the most trifling description, the last straw in very fact. To Sheila as she lay in bed came the last straw. For three hours she had lain tossing from side to side, feverish and hot. Now as a crown to her misery came an irrational booming in her ears, a droning that she knew she could not stifle from her head.

And then, suddenly, she knew that Dennison was dead. She had reached the breaking point.

For a minute she lay stupefied, then came diversion. Through the thin partition between her room and Helen's, she heard the bed creak suddenly, heard a footstep on the floor, and heard a window flung up. Then there was silence for a little; the girl opened her eyes and lay listening.

Somewhere down the passage another window opened, a door slammed, and then there was Rawdon bellowing in the passage outside her room to Sir David in the manager's office.

'Fisher! I say, Fisher! All right. They're coming in now.'

Sheila leaped from her bed and opened the door. 'Where are they?' she asked.

Rawdon turned to her with a broad grin. 'Listen,' he said.

Faintly they heard the booming rising and falling gently on the night air, and a little louder.

'That's them coming in,' he said in his soft little voice. 'Go and put something on – you'll catch cold.' He tapped at Helen's door; they went in and stood together at the window. Helen was leaning on the window-sill.

Outside the moon was bright, the air very still. Beneath their window lay the river, black and mysterious, running out of sight into the darkness. From the night came the roar, louder now, droning and pulsating. Suddenly it ceased.

'Shut off,' said Rawdon quietly. 'They're putting down into the harbour.'

For an interminable time there was no sound. It must have been three minutes or more before there was a sudden sharp burst of engine, clearer now, and much closer. Then, after a long pause, came a gentle rumble rising and falling, now and again shutting off altogether. Rawdon relaxed his attitude and stood erect.

'All over now,' he said. 'They're on the water – taxiing into the beach, I should think.'

He bent again to listen. Far away down the estuary sounded the rumble, subdued and steady. It broke into a roar, died, and roared again. Then came a curious, slow coughing noise, a choking murmur and then silence, perfect, absolute.

Helen turned to Rawdon. 'What did they put the engine on like that for?' she asked.

'Climbing up the beach. Now watch – they'll send up a flare in a minute to show us where they are.'

For a quarter of an hour they stood by the window, staring into the darkness, watching for the signal. At last Rawdon stood up and looked at his watch.

'Half-past one,' he said. 'They must have run out of Very lights.' He turned to Helen. 'I'm going down to see if I can raise a motor-boat,' he said. 'I don't know that we shall be able to do much before dawn.'

9

Dennison sat beside Morris, cold and stiff. He had long ceased trying to peer ahead into the darkness and, but for an occasional glance over the side at the coast they were following, concentrated his attention on holding the electric torch steady on the compass. The torch was the only provision for night flying that they had made; it had been put in as an afterthought. Already the light was very low, but it would last them out.

He leaned over Morris to scrutinize the dim coast. They were flying on a compass course at about three thousand feet, the coast just visible on their beam and below. As Dennison leaned near Morris he could hear him singing something above the roaring of the engine, and smiled a little. Morris had a habit of singing old-fashioned Puritan hymns to pass the time; occasionally he would beat time with the unoccupied hand upon his knee.

> 'He who would valiant be
> 'Gainst all disaster,
> Let him in constancy
> Follow the Master.
> There's no discouragement
> Shall make—'

Dennison touched him on the arm and pointed seawards to a light. He raised himself in his seat and placed his mouth close to the other's helmet.

'Lundy,' he shouted. 'North End. We ought to pick up Hartland in a minute.'

Morris nodded without making the effort to reply, stooped, took Dennison's hand and directed the torch to the watch and to the petrol gauge. Then he replaced the hand in its former position with the light on the compass and nodded cheerfully.

In a minute they picked up Hartland Light. Morris stirred in his seat, throttled the engine a little, and put the machine on a slow downward slant. Dennison caught his eye and nodded. This was the last lighthouse on the coast before the entrance to the river; both were afraid of overshooting Padstow and flying on in search of it, uncertain of their bearings.

Morris brought her down to a thousand feet and flew close along the coast, scrutinizing every bay. At this height the visibility was better; they could see every beach and headland and even the cottages on the cliffs, bright in the moonlight. After a quarter of an hour Dennison touched the pilot's arm and spoke again.

'This is Pentire Head,' he shouted. 'It's a mile on the other side of this – one mile.'

Morris nodded and held up one finger in comprehension. They passed the head; before them lay a gap in the coast. It was Padstow Harbour.

Morris beat his hand cheerfully upon his thigh.

Dennison raised himself in his seat again, and pointed. 'Put down well inside the low point,' he said, 'because of the bar.'

Morris settled himself into his seat, nodded again, and pulled back the throttle. The roar of the engine died from behind them; silence leaped up from the darkness and hit them shrewdly. Dennison put his head over the side and peered downwards. Already they were nearly over the mouth of the harbour; they sank rapidly towards the level, faintly corrugated water.

Lower and lower they sank. Silently they flitted between the points and into the mouth of the river. Morris sat tense and motionless, straining his eyes forward in an attempt to read the dim surface of the water. Gently he flattened the glide and settled to the surface. Suddenly, at the last moment, he thrust the throttle hard open. The engine burst into life with a roar; Morris swung the machine through a small angle, shut off the engine, and sank down on to the water.

The machine took the water with a crash and a heavy lurch to starboard. Morris was flung from his seat on to Dennison; a cloud of spray came over them, the water foamed along the gunwale. One wing-tip dipped perilously into the water; Morris, half out of his seat, thrust violently upon his controls. The machine steadied on to an even keel and lost way upon the surface.

'Damn it,' said Morris. 'I must have put her down cross wind after all. Feel if she's making any water.'

Dennison stopped and felt beneath his feet, and listened.

'All right,' he said.

They looked towards the shore. 'There's a beach that we can put her up on over there,' said Dennison. 'There – just beside that hill. The town's the other side – over there somewhere. We can't get near it. It's all rocky over there.'

'Get the wheels down,' said Morris. Dennison began to wind the wheels into the landing position; Morris opened up his engine and turned towards the beach.

The machine, running at ten knots, took the beach with a lurch and a jar, rearing her long bow up the sand. Morris gave her a burst of engine; she wallowed forward and crawled out of the water upon her wheels and up to the beach. Another burst, and she was ploughing through powdery sand above high water level. The sand, caught up by the propeller, beat stingingly against their faces.

Morris leaned clumsily forward to the instrument-board and switched off the engine. The rumble died to an irregular, intermittent coughing; the engine choked and came to rest. From all sides the silence closed in upon them strangely, so that their tiniest movements made a rustling that their stunned ears were able to detect and wonder at.

For a long time they sat motionless in the machine. At last Morris put up a hand and tugged feebly at the straps of his helmet. Dennison followed his example, unfastened the chin-strap with fumbling hands, and pulled the helmet from his head.

Morris sighed deeply, tried to raise himself from his seat, and sank back with a spasm of cramp. 'Poop off a Very light,' he said.

Dennison felt for the pistol in the rack beside his seat. Pistol and rack were gone. 'I smashed against it when we landed,' he said. 'I expect it's gone down into the bilge.'

With an effort he heaved himself from his seat, drew his legs over the gunwale, and dropped down on to the sand. Morris followed him; they stumbled painfully a little way along the beach, working their cramped muscles. Presently Dennison climbed back into the machine and searched vainly for the pistol; it had slipped somewhere into the recesses of the hull beyond his reach.

'Leave the bloody thing,' said Morris from the beach. 'It will be light in a few hours. I'm going to lie down up in those sandhills. Chuck down the seat cushions and my helmet.'

Dennison dropped down from the cockpit and they went ploughing through the heavy sand to the dunes at the top of the beach, clumsy in their fleece-lined suits.

They found a hollow and threw themselves down. Morris scraped a hole for his hip, drew up the deep fur collar about his ears, and shifted the leather cushion beneath his head.

'Thank God that bloody job's over,' he said sourly, and fell immediately into a heavy, restless sleep.

Slowly the dawn came. The east grew grey, then rose colour as the light spread over the estuary. In the sand-hills one or two birds began to stir and twitter in the spear-like grasses; on the edge of the grassland appeared the dim forms of the rabbits in little clusters. A shaft of sunlight struck the summit of Stepper Point; the sleepers stirred and blinked uneasily at the light.

Dennison roused, raised himself on one elbow, and watched Morris go stumbling down to the water's edge. As he walked he loosened the heavy collar from his neck and pulled the suit open a little. He reached a little pool of sea water in the sand, knelt down beside it, and began to bathe his face.

Dennison sat up and looked about him, moistening his dry lips. His mouth was dry and gritty with the sand, and his head, enveloped in fur, was hot and stuffy. He pulled the helmet off and threw it on the sand, stooped down, and began to unfasten the flying-suit from his ankles and wrists. Presently he wriggled out of it and felt better.

He looked about him. On the beach lay the flying-boat lying over on one wing-tip with a rakish air of dissipation, one wheel buried in the sand. Behind her, on the far side of the estuary, lay the town, brown and gabled and without a sign of life. A brown-sailed lugger was creeping into the river from the sea, hugging the opposite shore.

Dennison looked for Morris. He was on the machine, standing up on the lower plane, doing something to the engine with a spanner. Dennison watched him curiously. Presently he produced from his pocket the little cup from the top of the empty Thermos-flask.

He was drawing a little water from the radiator for a drink.

Dennison, his mouth parched and dry, got to his feet and went down to the machine, drawn as by a magnet. The water from the engine tasted very cool and sweet.

'It's been well boiled, anyway,' said Morris.

Dennison went down and completed his toilet in the sea. Returning, he found Morris looking intently over at the town.

'I suppose we stay here till somebody happens to wonder

what we are and comes to have a look,' said Dennison.

'If they don't come soon,' said Morris, 'I'm going to totter away inland and look for breakfast. I saw a farm just up there, about half a mile away.' He strained his eyes at the town. 'As a matter of fact, there's a boat coming out to us now.'

On the still morning air they caught the beat of an engine; a small brown motor-boat crept out of the harbour and headed straight for them.

There were five people in the boat, one evidently the fisherman owner.

'Rawdon and Sir David,' said Morris, 'and my wife. I don't know who that is with her. There's a buckshee girl there. Look.' He turned to Dennison, and saw that he was looking. He laughed, and turned away. 'All right,' he said. 'You can have that one.'

Dennison did not answer. The boat drew nearer; he turned to Morris.

'That's Miss Wallace,' he said. 'Jimmie Wallace's sister. I suppose your wife brought her for company.'

'Maybe,' said Morris. The boat grounded on the beach a hundred yards away; they walked down to meet it.

The greetings over, Morris turned to the baronet.

'We've made a mess of this, I'm afraid,' he said.

Sir David glanced at the machine and back to Morris. 'In what way?' he inquired.

'We haven't brought the dummy mail,' said Morris. 'We had five hundred pounds of firebars nicely done up in sacks and sealed. I got the wind up at the last moment and tipped them out and put in petrol instead – thirty cans. We used that to get here. We haven't brought anything at all – barring empty cans.'

There was a deep sigh of comprehension from the party.

'I'm damn sorry about it,' said Morris. 'It happened like this. We'd arranged to get away about six in the morning, GMT. Well, at six we were seventy miles too far out. That put us in a fix, you see. I didn't dare to push off at that distance; it would have been running it too fine. I decided to

231

wait till ten – and even that gave us more distance than we wanted. I couldn't leave it any later than that because I didn't want to fly at night – no landing-lights or anything, you know.

'So I decided to tip out the cargo. It didn't much matter what we brought so long as it weighed five hundred pounds, you see – and I thought it might as well be petrol. I don't mind telling you, I had the wind up – we were running it a bit fine. Anyhow, I loaded her up with thirty cans and we pushed off at about ten. She got off quite well. Much better than when we tried her at full load before. Funny. We had a light breeze from the south-west which must have helped a bit, of course.

'Well, we went trundling on our way. We saw one liner outward bound about half an hour after starting, and after that we never saw a soul. It was damn lonely. I managed to persuade her up to five thousand feet in an hour or so, and we kept at that, cruising at about ninety-eight. It was a beautiful day – a regular joy-ride. I had to undo my Sidcot, I got so hot.

'At noon Dennison got a shot at the sun and worked it. We'd been flying just over two hours, and it showed that we'd made good a hundred and eighty-seven miles. It was a bit on the low side, but I didn't worry much – particularly as Dennison said he couldn't guarantee it to within eight miles.'

Rawdon turned to Dennison. 'You used an ordinary sextant?'

Dennison nodded. 'We had a pretty good horizon most of the day,' he said.

'Well,' said Morris, 'we trundled on a bit and at two o'clock he got another shot. This showed we'd made good a hundred and sixty-two miles in the last two hours – or only three-forty-nine since we started.'

He paused a little.

'It made me laugh like hell,' he said grimly. 'Damn funny and all that. It was pretty obvious we were up against a wind of sorts. Dennison said that if we went down close to the water he'd try and spot what it was. Well, we went down and flew along about twenty feet up. There was a rotten-looking swell running, and with our speed and the swell and the wind across the swell – I was damned if I could tell which way the wind was. Dennison was pretty clear about it, though. He knows more about that sort of thing than I. He said it was south-east and about fifteen miles an hour. I asked him how he knew it, and he said because he saw a puffin.'

'Perfectly correct,' said Dennison. 'There was a little flock of them all steaming head to wind. I didn't know they went so far out.'

'Fifteen miles an hour and south-east,' said Morris. 'That checked fairly well with our progress – it would have been stronger up above, you see. So we went up a bit and thought it over.'

He leaned against the wing of the machine. 'Well,' he said, 'it was pretty evident that if we went on we should be down before we got here. It didn't really matter, of course – we'd got the petrol to finish the trip. But that swell had put the wind up me. I thought that if we put down in that to fill our tanks … well, it wasn't good enough, you know. For one thing, I don't think she'd have got off the water again in the swell that was running then. I'm not sure – I don't think so. No, it was pretty evident that we must get into smooth water to refill. And that meant Ireland.

'So at about a quarter to three we set a fresh course and made for Baltimore. The engine ran beautifully all the time – like a sewing-machine. Dennison got another shot at the sun to check our position, and we trundled on till we made out Ireland about seven o'clock.

'Well, we didn't go to Baltimore. You see, all we meant to do was to find a patch of smooth water where we could put down, fill our tanks, and get away again. We only meant to stay half an hour, and then get on and finish the flight in daylight. It struck me that if we went near civilization, there'd be police and Customs and harbourmasters – people in motor-boats crashing alongside and sticking boat-hooks through the wings – you know. We'd never have got away before next morning. Dennison knew the coast, and he took us to an island, not very far from Baltimore, where there was a little landlocked pool of a harbour with a sandy beach. It was an ideal place for the purpose, and nobody about to worry us.'

'Sherkin Island,' said Dennison. 'The harbour was Kinish.'

They found smooth water under the lee of Sherkin and put down just outside the entrance to the little landlocked harbour. On the water Morris turned the machine and taxied into the pool through the rocky entrance.

Inside there were firm, sandy beaches running gently down into the water. They got the wheels down and taxied up on to the beach, turned so as to face the water, and taxied down a little way so that the rising tide would lift the machine should she sink too far into the sand. Then they stopped the engine.

With the first move that they made from their seats came the realization of their fatigue. They had been flying for nine hours; every muscle ached and quivered uncontrollably. They were stupid with noise, and shouted at each other in hoarse voices. It was impossible to continue the flight at once.

'It means flying at night if we don't,' said Morris huskily. 'There'll be a good moon.'

They decided to rest for an hour. Wearily they clambered out of the machine and walked a little way up the sand to the top of the beach. There Dennison began to shed his clothes.

'What does A do?' he said, weakly facetious. 'Answer adjudged correct; A has a cold bath.'

Morris stared at him blankly for a minute, then laughed and followed his example. They wriggled out of their fleecy suits and out of their clothes, and hobbled down the beach to the water. A short bathe and they were dressing again, cool and fresh and only very tired.

They took their full hour of rest. Taking the remainder of their food, they climbed up on to a knoll that dominated the harbour and sat down to eat their meal. Near by they found a spring from which they drank their fill in company with two sheep, the only living creatures that they saw upon the island.

Then for the precious minutes that remained they sat and watched the sun drop down towards the sea.

It was a sunset such as only the west of Ireland can afford. Away to the north lay Mizzen Head, shrouded in a thin, opalescent haze; to the east the bay swept round towards them dotted with promontories and islands, clear in the sunset light. To Morris, stretched comfortably upon the soft turf, life was suddenly very sweet. His eye fell upon the flying-boat below them on the sand, and suddenly he wondered why they should go on at all. Here they were in the British Isles, having brought their cargo in up to time. To go on meant that they would expend the petrol that was their cargo. Surely, to have got the cargo so far was as good as to go on to Padstow without it? He thought of his little house in the suburbs, and the unfinished paths in his garden, and his wife, and his puppy.

He had never flown a flying-boat at night before, far less landed one in the darkness with no flares. They would touch the water at not less than fifty miles an hour.

Then came to his mind a quaint pride in their achievement. True, they would have expended four-fifths of their cargo. They would still have one-fifth to take to Padstow – the empty petrol-cans. If they were to stop now, Sir David would count the flight as a failure; it was little use commercially to land a cargo two hundred miles from the spot intended. To give up now would be – failure.

He glanced at his watch. Their time was up.

'Let's get down to the machine,' he said.

'Well,' said Morris. 'By the time we'd got the petrol into the tanks it was a quarter to nine. The sun was getting pretty low, but I didn't care much about that – the moon was up already. And then came the real difficulty – starting her up again. I don't know now what it was; it may have been that we got her too rich – I don't know. We were both pretty tired to begin with, and we took turns at swinging on that bloody crank till we were pretty nearly sick, while the other sat and twiddled the starting mag. And all the time it was getting darker.

'We got her going at last. It was half-past nine by the time she fired, and then we had to get our things on and get settled down. It was practically dark when we taxied out of Kinish and took off.'

He paused, weary of his tale. 'Well, that's about all there is to it. We put down here about one-fifteen. I didn't risk the crossing direct to Cornwall, though it would have been much shorter, of course. The only light we'd got was that rotten little torch, and if that had packed up when we were half-way across so that we couldn't see the compass ... It wasn't good enough. We came home with one foot on dry land. We went along the south of Ireland and crossed by the Fishguard Route, and then along the south of Wales nearly up to Cardiff, till we could see the other side. We went pretty far up, you see. Then we came down the north coast of Devon. We found this easily enough – it's a good mark on the coast. I put her down rather badly, as a matter of fact – we nearly as possible went over – cross wind, you know. You'd have banked on it blowing up and down the river, wouldn't you? Well, it wasn't. And then when we came to look for it we found we'd lost the perishing Very pistol ...'

He answered one or two questions, then turned to Sir David with a sudden spasm of nervous energy. 'Look here,' he said, 'It's just damn silly trying to do this flight direct. I didn't see that before, but I do now. Look. Wash out Padstow and make the terminus Milford Haven. Then the machine can make for the west of Ireland and come along the south coast, easy as shelling peas. Then you can have an emergency refuelling station at Baltimore, in case you get a head wind. You won't need it one flight in ten – but if it's there you can take more chances.'

They broke into a discussion on the commercial aspects of the scheme.

Tiring of the discussion of ways and means, Dennison turned away and began to walk up the beach to the sand-hills to collect his kit. He had not spoken to Sheila. Once he had glanced at the girl, but she had avoided his eyes. After that he had concentrated on the story of the flight that Morris told.

At the top of the beach he glanced backward. She had left the others and was coming up the beach towards him. Blindly he stooped and fumbled with his flying-suit upon the sand. Then, as the girl drew near, he turned to face her.

'Good morning,' he said gently.

The girl faced him steadily, bareheaded against a deep blue sea breaking on the yellow sands. 'I oughtn't to have come, of course,' she said. 'But I got worried, and I wanted to come and say I was sorry. And then Helen said she'd bring me down here, and I came.'

'I see,' said Dennison. He glanced at her, and laughed suddenly. 'Half a minute,' he said.

The girl stood gazing at him anxiously.

He raised his head. 'Before you say any more,' he said, 'I want you to think of one thing. It's never very wise to make a decision in a hurry, or under exceptional circumstances – if you can put it off. This flight has put us all out of step a bit. Suppose we put off discussing it – till next week?'

The girl smiled. 'But I only heard of this flight a week ago. And before then I had written to you to – to say that I'd changed my mind, and ... I'd come to Hong Kong with you, if you'd have me.'

And after that there was no more to be said.

'As a matter of fact,' said Dennison a little later, 'the Hong Kong scheme is off.'

The girl drew herself up and looked at him in wonder. 'But, Peter,' she said, 'is there anything else? What are we going to do?'

'I couldn't very well go to Hong Kong,' said Dennison. 'I've got to sail *Chrysanthe*, Sir David's new yacht, at Cowes. I shall have to do that every season, I expect, so of course, I couldn't go abroad.' He spoke seriously, but there was a gleam of humour in his eyes.

'But Peter, dear,' said the girl. 'You can't let that decide – everything ...'

'Sir David quite saw that, of course,' said Dennison. 'As a matter of fact, the same objection holds for any job. I shall have to have a couple of months off in the yachting season, you see. It meant a special arrangement. I'm being absorbed into the legal department of the Fisher Line. It's rather a good job, I think – I'm to be second-in-command to the old chap who does all their legal business for them now. And it's the work I'm keen on.'

Down by the flying-boat the discussion drew to a close. Morris stood leaning against the lower wing, one arm round his wife's shoulders, talking earnestly to Rawdon and Sir David Fisher. Behind them the fisherman was swabbing out his motor-boat, oblivious of his part in history.

Morris made his last point and stood erect by the machine. 'Anyway,' he said. 'Let's have some breakfast and talk about it afterwards.'

His wife caught his eye. 'Give them a little longer,' she said softly.

All four turned and gazed at the two figures sitting together in the sand-hills at the head of the beach.

Rawdon laughed shortly and turned away. 'God bless my soul!' he said tersely. '*They* don't want any breakfast.'

Wilbur Smith

THE SUNBIRD   50p

'A screaming nightmare of blood and flame and smoke, a horror of shining black faces and sweat-polished bodies . . .'

Another magnificently entertaining and imaginatively portrayed novel of high adventure by the author of WHEN THE LION FEEDS.

From the drama and excitement of modern Africa – big game hunts, terrorists, intrigue and merciless bushmen – the chief characters are projected into the battles, romance and tragedy of their Carthaginian past.

'A bonanza of excitement' – NEW YORK TIMES

Also available in PAN:

WHEN THE LION FEEDS   40p
THE SOUND OF THUNDER   40p
SHOUT AT THE DEVIL   40p
GOLD MINE   35p
(shortly to be filmed starring Roger Moore)
THE DIAMOND HUNTERS   35p
THE DARK OF THE SUN   35p
(already filmed as THE MERCENARIES)

'A natural storyteller' – SCOTSMAN

James Leasor

FOLLOW THE DRUM   50p

'A whirlwind of passion, hate, fear and courage'
                    SUNDAY TIMES

India, 1857 – when the lives of millions
changed forever . . .

A sweeping panorama of terror, excitement
and bloody incident mirrors the lives of very
human men and women, both real and imagi-
nary, overtaken by the cataclysm of heroism
and tragedy that was the Mutiny.

Trapped in those dangerous days are the hot-
blooded daughter of a regular officer and an
idealistic nineteen-year-old who began that
summer as a boy and ended it a man . . .

'No author in years has produced a novel deal-
ing with the period that is any way compar-
able with this tremendous story. FOLLOW THE
DRUM is a minor masterpiece.'
                    BOOKS AND BOOKMEN

These and other PAN Books are obtainable
from all booksellers and newsagents. If you
have any difficulty please send purchase price
plus 7p postage to PO Box 11, Falmouth,
Cornwall.
While every effort is made to keep prices low,
it is sometimes necessary to increase prices at
short notice. PAN Books reserve the right to
show new retail price on covers which may
differ from those previously advertised in the
text or elsewhere.